THE PASHTO SCHOOL

THE FIXERS SERIES

A FAMILY'S LOSS, A NATION'S OUTRAGE, ONE MAN'S MISSION

THE PASHTO SCHOOL

THE FIXERS SERIES

A FAMILY'S LOSS, A NATION'S OUTRAGE, ONE MAN'S MISSION

A NOVEL

MURRAY ESKENAZI

QUANTUM SHIFT
PUBLISHING

Port St. Lucie, Florida

The Fixers Series

Editing, cover, and interior design by Quantum Shift Media

ISBN Print 978-0-999306-74-1
ISBN eBook 978-0-999306-75-8

Library of Congress Control Number: pending

Printed in the United States of America

Second Edition

QUANTUM SHIFT
PUBLISHING

Port St. Lucie, Florida

To Doris and my friends.
Their support and encouragement
are the impetus that keeps me going.

ACKNOWLEDGEMENTS

Doris was my wife and the lady I worked for. I may think I work to make Murray happy, but I am deluding myself. I really work to satisfy Doris. Doris forced me to finish this book, and I have her to thank for it. She kept reminding me, "Did you write anything today?" Doris is the final arbiter of what is acceptable. It isn't easy being Doris because she has to live with me—and everyone knows I am eccentric, strange, and just plain weird. But I am me, and she seems to be satisfied, so why should I rock the boat?

Capt. David N. Orrik, USN (Ret.), a Navy UDT member, my oldest friend from high school and Columbia, a unique presence in my life, is the person I trusted to read the first draft of this story. His criticism has made this a better story and saved me from embarrassing errors.

Dory Brodherson is my biggest fan. She thinks I am smarter than the average bear. Thank you, Dory, for critiquing my effort.

I owe a special thank you to Robert Salem. Bob does everything from a thoughtful perspective, and his criticism was a welcome addition to clarity and consistency in this story.

No acknowledgement would be complete without thanking Keren Kilgore, my editor. She knows more about book publishing and editing than I will ever experience. Thank you, Keren.

There are more stories lurking somewhere within my head. They may someday emerge. Watch out, world!

CONTENTS

MAP OF PAKISTAN

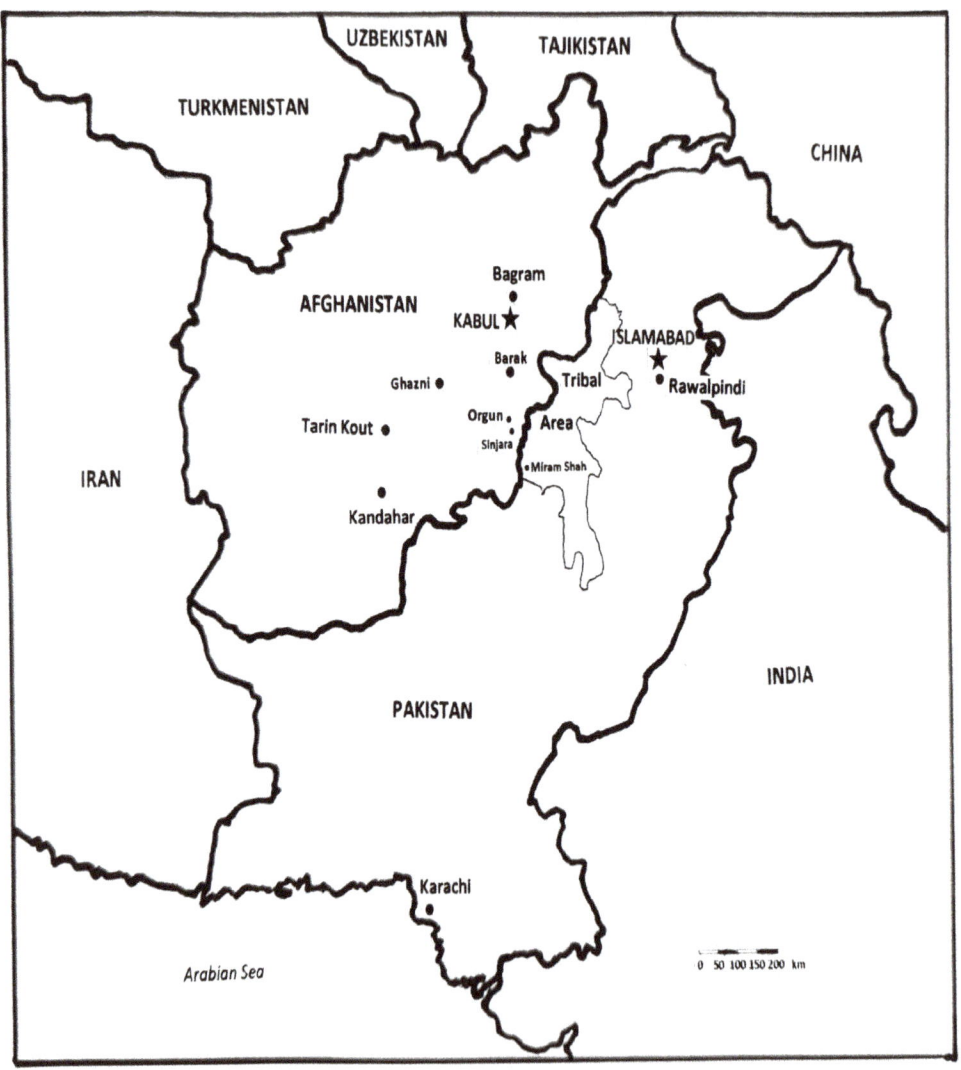

1

JACK MILLER

Tarin Kout, Afghanistan
Friday, March 6, three years earlier

Jack Miller, USMC, worked his way through the heart of Tarin Kout surrounded by devastation. Here and there, a building had a defiant corner wall standing or a stone chimney flipping the finger at the sky. Windows gaped like hollow eyes, glass blown away. The wreckage seeped with the stink of death—basements were filled with crushed body parts and thousands of rats feasting on the bonanza. Shelter was a fantasy. Everything, the earth, the stones, the rubble—was the color of sand.

The Taliban and the Afghan security forces had been fighting for two weeks for possession of Tarin Kout. The Afghan forces were gaining territory one day, and the Taliban were taking back the gains the next day. Lives were being blown away just so the other side could not claim ownership of the rubble piles. The whole effort was pointless.

Jack was moving stealthily from one sand-colored pile of stones to another. The area he was in was temporarily controlled by the Taliban. Jack was hunting for Omar Siddiqi, a Taliban leader from the Haqqani Network. Omar was famous for not letting any prisoners live more than an hour, and that last hour was spent screaming in excruciating pain. Omar had the further distinction of wearing a short, ratty scarf of Islamic green color, always tied around his neck.

Jack would know him when he saw him.

Jack hunkered down in the rubble behind a low remnant of wall, scanning the area through his binoculars, hoping to locate his target. He could feel the uneven surfaces through his BDUs. The thought repeating itself in his head was, *Show yourself, you sneaky bastard—I only want to kill you.*

Marine Major Jack Miller, on detached duty to the CIA, was one of the deadliest snipers in Afghanistan. If Jack wanted you dead, there was a 98% chance you would die. At 5'11" and 190 pounds of hardened muscle, he blended into the crowd with an almost forgettable plainness—brown hair, brown eyes, a shadow of black stubble. That anonymity was his greatest camouflage. Beneath it lay a mind as lethal as his rifle: an IQ north of 175, an electronics engineering degree from Cornell, fluency in Arabic, Pashto, and more. Jack practiced no religion. His life experiences convinced him that religion was one of mankind's worst inventions. The promise of life after death is one of the greatest cons ever perpetrated on gullible humans.

A sniper is normally accompanied by his spotter. But Jack's man caught a piece of shrapnel from an exploding mortar shell. His left foot got chewed up badly. Jack sent him back to the aid station and elected to carry on alone. Omar Siddiqi is a low-life killer and torturer. Jack really wanted his hide.

Jack was scanning a pile of rubble about 100 yards away when he caught a movement behind the pile. He focused his binoculars on the pile but saw nothing moving. Aha, there it was again. He brought his M40A5 sniper rifle to his shoulder and focused through the telescopic lens. His finger lay lightly beside the trigger guard, waiting. There was movement again, and he saw the head of a thin girl moving a stone to see what was under it. In a moment, the head of another girl, dressed in an abaya with no face veil, a few years older, also appeared.

Jack lowered his rifle and switched back to the binoculars.

As he watched the two girls, it became obvious to Jack that they were searching in the rubble for something. It was also obvious that they were in a very dangerous location that could receive incoming fire from any direction.

Jack decided he could not let the two girls continue as they were. He began working his way from rubble pile to rubble pile until he was behind a low wall near the girls' pile of crushed stones and bricks. He spoke to them softly in Pashto, "You girls had better stay down low. It is very dangerous here."

Neither of the girls reacted with alarm. The older one, in a soft voice, said, "The Taliban aren't shooting at us, and the government troops are hoping the Taliban will kill us. No one has shot at us all day. Besides, both sides have terrible aim. They shoot and never hit anything unless they get lucky."

Jack was amazed at the cool answer he had received from the girl. "Can I come over to your pile?" he asked in a whisper.

"Are you going to shoot us?" the younger one asked.

"No. I don't like shooting civilians, especially young girls."

"All right," said the older girl.

Jack scuttled over to the pile of bricks and stones the girls were behind. "Why are you digging through the stones?"

"This place was once a bakery before it got blown up. We thought there might be some old bread buried here that we could eat," explained the older girl.

Both girls were covered with scabby scratches wherever their skin was exposed. They were both undernourished and thin. Their clothes were essentially rags. Even though their faces were drawn and smudged with dirt, they were both pretty. Both had eyes that were luminous blue. The hair of the younger one was matted and stringy; the hair of the older girl was covered, but Jack was pretty sure it was the same. At one look, you could tell they were sisters.

The older girl looked closely at Jack, "Are you an American?"

"Yes. My name is Jack. What is yours?"

"I am called Inaya (In-aye-ya). My little sister is Naila (Nah-ee-la).

"How old are you?"

"I think I am 12. I know Naila is three years younger than me. Do you have anything to eat?"

"I have some combat rations. You can eat those if you want."

"Will you really share your food with us?"

Jack dug through his rucksack and took out his combat rations. He had a meatloaf with gravy packet and a chicken packet. MREs, he thought: *Meals-ready-to-eat or meals-rejected-by-Ethiopians?* It just depends on how hungry you are.

Jack handed one package to each of the girls. Inaya helped Naila open her package before opening her own package. "Eat a little and save the rest for later," she instructed.

"Where is your family?" asked Jack. Distant gunshots sounded, and Jack instinctively ducked a little lower even though the shots were far off.

"Mama got killed by the Taliban last year. Just before the fighting started here, Papa took our three brothers and went to Pakistan," Inaya said.

"You are telling me that your Papa left you here alone and went to Pakistan with your brothers? He didn't take you, too?"

"We are just girls," she said. That seemed to be more than enough explanation.

"What are you going to do now?"

"We'll be fine as long as we are together," Inaya whispered. "I'll take care of Naila."

Jack was so moved by her confidence and independence that he decided the girls should not be left to fend for themselves in a combat zone. Both girls were obviously very intelligent. "Have you ever been to school?" he asked Inaya.

"We are just girls. We don't go to school," she replied.

"I know a school nearby where you will be safe, where you will have enough to eat, and where you will learn to read. I would like to take you there."

"Is it a real school with real teachers?" asked Naila, the younger sister.

"It is a real school. It is run by kind people. There is even a doctor there in case anyone gets sick or gets hurt. He could help heal all the scratches you both have. I have seen the school, and it is only for girls like you two. Will you let me take you there?" Jack was thinking about Omar Siddiqi—the bastard will just have to wait. I'll get him soon enough. Getting these two off the battlefield is more important right now.

Inaya, the older girl, was reluctant to trust Jack. "I am not sure we should leave here. If Papa comes back, how will he find us?"

"Papa will find a new wife in Pakistan. He might not come back here. I will tell the government soldiers that you two are going to the school, and they will write your names in a book. If Papa asks about you, they will tell him where you have gone."

Naila said, "Let's go to the school, Inaya. I want to learn to read."

"You won't hurt us?" asked Inaya.

"I won't hurt you," Jack promised. "But I think we should all get out of here before someone starts shooting in our direction. They might get lucky and hit us."

Eventually, Jack won the girls over, and for three weeks, he became their protector; they bonded into a semblance of a family. Jack knew he could not possibly keep the girls with him in a war zone, nor could he continuously care for them since the possibility of his own death was all too real. Jack had heard of the Pashto School and that it was run by an American couple. He took them to the school and kept in touch with the girls and with Clara Wilson, who ran the school. He even made regular contributions to the school despite the strain that put on his limited income. He and the girls would exchange letters about every two to three months. He became their "Uncle Jack" and they became his only descendants, his two Afghan nieces. Jack even wrote them into his will, providing money for them to study at American universities if they ever became qualified for admission.

2

INAYA & NAILA

The Pashto School
Sinjara, Afghanistan
Monday, July 9, three years later

Girls in the Middle East reach physical maturity at an earlier age than in the industrialized Western nations. Some begin menstruating as early as 9 years of age. At the first sign of blood spots, the girl goes under the abaya, the full-body covering indicative of reproductive maturity. By the age of 11, almost all girls wear the abaya. Breast development is associated with the hormonal activity triggered by menstruation. Depending on local tribal customs, head and facial coverings are important elements of maturity. Once a girl has begun menstruating, even though she is still a child, in Islamic society, she is considered to be a woman of marriageable age. Many a child bride has been given or sold in marriage to a man 20 or 30 years older than she is.

In Islamic society, a woman who is menstruating is considered unclean and has to be isolated from the males of the family. At the Pashto School, no such rules are imposed upon the girls, and they are taught Western-style personal hygiene.

Within the Pashto School, an almost 100% female culture, girls are allowed to be girls without the strictures imposed by Islam. There are no abayas. All students wear the school uniform of a blue jumper, a white blouse, blue sneakers, and, if they desire, a light blue headscarf. No one wears the veil across her face.

Jack had safely delivered Inaya and Naila to the Pashto School more than three years ago. It was a suitable place for them, and they thrived in the school environment. Inaya, now somewhere between 14 and 15 years of age, had grown into a lovely young woman. She was doing so well academically that she was tutoring some of the younger girls. She had a gift for explaining ideas and concepts, and she had decided that she wanted to be a teacher when she grew up. Inaya was a good person with good instincts. She was a natural leader, and the girls of all ages followed her ideas willingly.

For her part, Naila was just happy that she had learned to read. She spent most of her free time in the library reading whatever books were available and dreaming about the places she would visit someday when she was old enough to leave the Pashto School. Maybe she and Inaya would be able to travel the world together.

On this late afternoon, several Pashto schoolgirls sat in a circle outside, in the shade of a building. The temperature was over 100°F. No one was complaining because this was a typical July temperature. Inaya was helping them learn to read. "Benazira, read the third and fourth sentences for me, please," said Inaya.

Benazira stood up from the circle, "Gulnar went to the well to fetch water. Many women and girls were gathered around the well."

"Very good, Benezira. Now, Murchakai, continue the story where Benazira stopped."

Murchakai got slowly to her feet. She was 9 years old. Her left leg had been badly damaged in a terrorist bombing that had killed both her parents. Despite her sad history, she had a happy disposition. "At the well, the women were talking about the poppy harvest. They prayed to Allah that it would be a good harvest. There would be food to eat when the poppy seeds were sold."

"You did well, Murchakai." Addressing the group, she asked, "What do you think about selling the poppy seeds? Is it good or is it bad to harvest the poppies?"

Shahay raised her hand, and Inaya nodded toward her. "I think it is bad to raise the poppies and sell the paste. It makes people sick all over the world."

Roshina waved her hand. Inaya recognized her. Roshina sat where she was and said, "My family were poppy farmers when they were alive. The poppies are the main thing that will grow here, and if we don't sell them, the people of Afghanistan will all starve."

Benazira offered a thought, "No one eats poppies. Couldn't the farmers raise other crops that we could eat instead of poppies?"

Shahay offered, "We raise wheat to make bread, and we grow vegetables. Why couldn't we grow wheat and vegetables to sell? Why do we only sell the poppy seeds?"

"That is where we get the most money from," said Roshina. "When the poppy harvest is good, then we do not go hungry in the winter. We had a good harvest last year. There was extra money, and before he got blown up, my father bought an AK-47 so he could protect our family."

The girls spent the next ten minutes discussing the pros and cons of raising poppies. Finally, Inaya stopped the discussion. "I wanted you all to see that what you read caused you all to think about the words on the page. They are not just words. The words bring meaning to thoughts. We must reflect on what we read so that we can become better individuals. One day, Afghanistan is going to need educated people to make our country a better place for all of us to live. We will have children of our own, and it would be better if they grew up in a peaceful country rather than one that is always at war. Think about the poppies. Think about the farmers. And also, think about the men who trade in the poppy paste. What kind of world have they made for us? Is that the kind of world you want to live in?

"Soon it will be time for the evening meal. Let us all go get cleaned up. And don't forget to say your prayers." Inaya dismissed the group and went toward her dormitory. *They are good girls,* she thought. She was satisfied that she had made her girls think, in addition to helping to teach them to read."

3

HENRY & CLARA

Henry Wilson, M.D. & Clara Wilson, Ed. D.
The Pashto School
Sinjara, Afghanistan
Monday, July 9

Henry "Rope" Wilson, M.D., arose early every morning. Rope was 68 years old, born and raised in Arizona, as skinny as a rope, hence his nickname, which he had carried since he was 5 years old. Because his name was Henry, he was also sometimes referred to as "a Hank of Rope."

The local people of Sinjara had adopted "Dr. Rope" because he treated their illnesses and injuries, and even more so because he treated them with respect. Dr. Rope had a head of gray hair, brown eyes, a neatly trimmed gray beard, and a kindly disposition that matched his friendly face. In a place where few people smiled, Dr. Rope always smiled.

At 6'-3" and 172 lbs., there was not a spare ounce of flesh on his body. A surgeon by training, he was used to being in the O.R. at 5 a.m. for a regular day of work. Now he was in Afghanistan with his wife, Clara, a retired high school principal, tending to the needs of 230 teenage girls in a residential school founded and run by his wife. Most of the students were orphans. Those who weren't orphans were abandoned refugees from war-torn locales. Eight girls were local residents of Sinjara. Dr. Rope ministered to their bodies; Clara Wilson ministered to their minds.

Dr. Rope also ministered to any local Afghans who came to his daily outdoor clinic. The most common trauma injuries he saw were bullet wounds, followed by land mine cases, and then the losers of knife fights. He liked to joke that he stitched more wounds in a day than a baseball factory did in a week. Normal civilian illnesses, pregnancies, inoculations, childhood illnesses, and parasitic diseases made up the bulk of the rest. Because of local Islamic customs, he could not treat men and women at the same time. The women, girls, and young children had the morning hours from 6 to 11 a.m., while the men and older boys had the afternoon hours from 12:30 to 4 p.m. The days were long, and there was never enough of what he needed in the way of medicines, supplies, or time. Creative adaptation became one of Rope Wilson's greatest medical skills.

Clara Wilson was almost a year older than Henry. They had been best friends since they met in a second-year English class at the University of Arizona. She once had dark brown hair, now turned gray, and her pretty face was lined by the cares of her girls at the Pashto School and by the incessant Afghan winds. Her deep brown eyes had developed a permanent squint because of the sun and wind. She stood 5'-5", 125 dynamic pounds, held together by a steel will and an incisive tongue. When she was younger, she regularly ran marathons and half-marathons. If you look in the dictionary for the definition of determination, there is Clara's picture next to the word.

One morning, while reading about orphans in the *Arizona Republic* newspaper as collateral victims of the Afghan war, Clara had a defining moment. She was already restless from just sitting idle in retirement for almost six months. Clara was not one to hold still once she decided upon a course of action.

"Rope, I think we should open a school for orphaned girls in Afghanistan. They really need a place of refuge where they can be safe and get an education."

"Clara, are you nuts? That is the most hare-brained idea you have ever had in a lifetime of weird ideas. First, Afghanistan is a war zone filled with religious fanatics. Second, Americans are their enemy of choice. Third, the place is uncivilized. Fourth, there wouldn't be a supportive community. Fifth, we lack the language skills to communicate effectively with anyone, let alone run a school. Lastly, it is so dangerous that we'd be risking our lives daily. The answer is No. Flat-out, absolutely NO! We aren't opening a school in Afghanistan!"

"Well, no one is caring for the orphans, especially the girls. We have no children, no grandchildren, no heirs. We were going to leave everything to the university. They will never miss our few dollars. Instead, let's sell the house and use the money where it will do some real good. We can make a difference in a lot of lives if we open a school."

"You think we will get a building for a school for free? The expenses will eat through our money in no time."

"We paid off the mortgage on this house many years ago. With inflation and the tight housing market, I figure we could clear $400,000 after taxes on the house. We have our savings, my pension, your IRA, and our Social Security payments. There might be a chance we could even get some government money, too. We ought to be able to do this." Clara showed Henry the pad where she had been totaling their assets.

"Right. And we can also get killed. Two non-Muslims in a Muslim country. Two more civilians as collateral damage. Even better for the body count, we would be American civilians. The answer is no! Flat-out, absolutely no!"

"Well, I feel it is something we should think about doing," answered Clara with finality.

The upshot of Henry's refusal was that they spent nine months learning Pashto from Rosetta Stone programs and with the help of some Pakistani friends. Pashto is one of the common languages of eastern Afghanistan; the other widely spoken language is Dari in Western Afghanistan, near Iran. Clara was going to open her school, regardless of whether Henry approved of the plan.

As of today, the Wilsons had already been in Afghanistan for almost 5-1/2 years. So much for a flat-out, absolute no. In his heart and his head, Henry knew, as soon as Clara had proposed the idea, that they would ultimately wind up running a school in Afghanistan.

*   *   *

Afghanistan is a harsh country with harsh customs and tough people. It was once a waypoint on the old Silk Road to China. The national government is very weak in the cities and virtually non-existent in rural areas. The country is dry, mountainous, and land-locked with Turkmenistan, Uzbekistan, and Tajikistan to the north (all three were once part of Soviet Russia), Pakistan curves around from the east to the south, and Iran to the west. A tiny tip of land in the east touches China.

The Afghan borders are arbitrary lines that were drawn by the victorious European powers after World War I. Afghans have minimal national identity. Tribal and ethnic loyalties are very strong and extend across artificial borders and regions. None of these neighboring countries wants to be friends with Afghanistan. In return, the Afghans trust no one and only want to be left alone in their own tribal space.

Most of the Afghan population is Sunni Muslim, with a small Shi'a minority in the west, near Iran. The main agricultural crop is opium poppies, and opium paste is the main cash export. If you control Afghanistan, you control the supply of opium and all its derivative drugs as well.

For thousands of years, invaders have tried to conquer Afghanistan. Like Mount Everest, Afghanistan is there, and to some invaders, that is reason enough to make the attempt. The most memorable invaders were the Persians, the Greeks under Alexander, the Arabs, the Mongols, the Tartars, the British, the Russians, and the Americans. There were also many others. If you think you have conquered Afghanistan, you are deluding yourself. In 3,000 years with so many invasions, no one has ever truly succeeded. The invaders are only temporary. Afghanistan remains permanently unconquerable and ungovernable.

Clara established her school in the small village of Sinjara, with a population of 850, in eastern Zabul Province. Sinjara lies between Kabul, the Afghan capital, 240 km to the northeast, and Kandahar, 200 km to the southwest, and only 80 km from the Pakistani border to the south. It is in the dry, desert-like southern mountains of Afghanistan. The village, no more than a bump in the road, is so small it does not even appear on most maps.

At first, the locals were sure the two Americans would soon leave. Eventually, mainly because they could speak Pashto, the Wilsons were tolerated. Both Clara and Henry worked hard to understand Afghan culture and to earn the trust of the local population. Eventually, they became a part of the Sinjara community.

The Pashto School began as two buildings located a short distance away from Sinjara. Over the past 5½ years, it has expanded to twelve buildings, including classrooms, dormitories, a commissary, and a medical facility, all surrounding a large, open central courtyard. A salvaged diesel-driven generator, U.S. military surplus, on a 4-wheel trailer, provides electricity when the government power lines fail to deliver the juice. The school is situated on a flat piece of scrubland that is too dry and rocky for farming. As a concession to the never-ending fighting, a 3-meter (10-feet) high surrounding concrete wall was recently added. The men of Sinjara donated their labor for the wall.

The students are mostly poor, mostly orphans, and had only the clothes they wore when they enrolled in the school. Clara decided that ragged clothing was inappropriate; the girls needed uniforms. She declared, "I won't have my girls wearing rags. Not if I can help it." So, the school provides navy blue jumpers over white blouses, navy blue sneakers, and light blue headscarves. Clara would have preferred no head covering at all, but many of the girls felt as if they were undressed and vulnerable with uncovered hair, so Clara gave in on the headscarves. But the headscarves are optional.

An unintended benefit of the school is that it purchases food from local farmers in the area and uniforms sewn by local women. Thus, the Pashto School gives a welcome boost to the economies of Sinjara and several nearby villages.

Many times, local farmers have thanked Dr. Rope for his medical skills by presenting him with a chicken or a goat. Henry calls them "eggs and milk on the hoof." Because of its goats, the Pashto School has a substantial milk, cheese, and yogurt production facility. The chickens provide eggs and poultry. The students tend to the flocks under the watchful direction of one of the staff.

Without family to protect them, the girls of the Pashto School would have become enslaved servants or exploited for prostitution—if they even lived long enough to reach adulthood.

The local Islamic extremists hate the Pashto School because it is run by Americans and because it is educating girls. Girls do not need their heads filled with useless book learning. They need to be taught how to please their husbands, cook, and bear children.

Two years ago, the provincial government, recognizing that the school would remain for a while, assigned six policemen to guard the school and built a small barracks outside the front gate to house them. After more than five years, Miss Clara, Dr. Rope, and the Pashto School have become part of the local landscape.

Miss Clara leads a staff of fourteen teachers, all Western-educated Afghan women. They teach basic Pashto reading, writing, and arithmetic skills to their students, most of whom have never attended school before. Additional subjects taught are world and Afghan history, household skills, commercial skills, personal hygiene, sex education, physical education, and karate for self-defense. Most students can speak a little English. An elite few are taught to read and write English as well. The teachers sleep in the dormitories with the students and have effectively become surrogate mothers to the girls. The heavy hand of Islamic customs always hovers in the background.

Clara has become an expert at scrounging school supplies wherever she can find them. Many are supplied by the military or the regional government, some supplies are sent from supporters in the U.S., and others are purchased using Clara and Henry's own money. The Gates Foundation helps with computers. Somehow, Clara always manages to muddle through.

"Rope," Clara called, "How can we get more full-size note pads for the girls? I need about 500 pads, 750 would be better."

"I think the American base at Bagram might give us what we need. Sergeant Bryant is the quartermaster and likes what we are doing here. The Aussies down in Kandahar are overdue for another touch from us, too. They might be good for a few pads. Would a mix of 8-1/2 x 11's and A4's be OK?"

"As long as it's paper. You call the Australian brigade. I'll get in touch with Bagram. Maybe they can spare some ballpoint pens, too."

Clara picked up the landline telephone on her desk. No dial tone—again. She then picked up her satphone and dialed the Bagram base. Afghansat is a dedicated communications satellite in a permanent synchronous orbit over Afghanistan. It usually works, and it made her connection this time. The switchboard at Bagram picked up. Clara said, "Sergeant Bryant in the Quartermaster Office, please."

After a few clicks and a brief delay, the phone was answered. "Quartermaster," announced the soldier who answered.

"Sergeant Bryant, please. Clara Wilson calling."

"I'll get him Miz Wilson. Hold on." Then Clara heard the soldier yell, "Hey, Sarge, telephone call for you."

A few moments later, Clara heard, "Sergeant Bryant. How may I help you?"

Hi, Sergeant. It's Clara Wilson at the Pashto School."

"Hey, Miss Clara. How are you guys doing?"

"We're doing good, Sarge. Things are quiet here, and the girls are doing well."

"What's on your wish list today? As long as it won't explode, I'm sure the lieutenant will sign off on it."

"Today, we could use 750 to 800 note pads. Lined, 8-1/2 x 11. And a few dozen ballpoint pens. Dr. Rope is almost out of field dressings and sutures as well. Could you spare some for us?"

"I'll run it by the lieutenant and get back to you in a few hours."

"Sounds good. And thanks again. You guys always come through for us."

"The work you do is without equal anywhere in this crappy country. You guys give us one less thing to worry about. It's we who owe you thanks. Have a good day, Miss Clara."

"Thanks. The same to you, too, sergeant."

Clara felt good after hanging up. Every once in a while, it's nice to hear someone say that you're doing a good job.

Dr. Rope poked his head inside Clara's door. "I just got off the phone. The Aussies are coming through for us again. They will drop off 300 pads in a few days.A truck will be passing through on its way to Kabul. They also found six chairs in an abandoned house that they think we could use. They'll drop those off, too."

"Sounds good. We can always use more chairs. New girls arrive every week. I also asked the sergeant for some field dressings and sutures. Let's see if they come through for us like they did last time."

"God bless the American G.I.," Rope said. "They'll give you the shirts off their backs if they think you need it. And it's for sure that we need whatever they are willing to share."

"Henry, you had better get moving. It is time for your afternoon clinic hours with the men. Go sew up another baseball."

"Yes, Missy Clara, I'm on my way," Henry said as he headed out the door to the clinic building."

4

JUBAL EL-MADOUSH

The Pashto School
Sinjara, Afghanistan
Tuesday, July 10

Walls and doors are built to be breached—but the Pashto School did its best to defy that truth. A ten-foot wall of reinforced concrete enclosed the compound, its center dominated by double steel doors painted the same pale blue as the students' headscarves. An armed policeman stood guard there at all times.

The doors were massive—each five feet wide, twelve feet high, and forged from half-inch steel plate supplied by the nearby American air base. Local Afghan craftsmen had built them with precision, their weight such that only a strong man could heave them open. Together, they created a ten-by-twelve-foot passage, large enough for a truck to roll through. For pedestrians, a smaller Judas gate had been cut into the right-hand door, also sheathed in steel.

Security was strict. Both main doors remained shut unless a vehicle was cleared by the guard inside the compound. Foot traffic passed only through the Judas gate. At night, heavy steel bars dropped into place across both entries, bolted into pivots, and brackets sunk into the wall. From seven in the evening until dawn, the school was locked down tight.

It was 11:45 p.m. A solitary fixture with a single light bulb over the doors provided the only illumination. A metal sign, screwed to the wall beside the right door, announced in Pashto, English, and French that you were at the Pashto School.

Jubal el-Madoush drove his pickup truck up to the guard's lean-to by the closed doors. He stopped at two orange traffic cones 20 feet in front of the gate, killed the engine, and got out of the truck. The policeman on guard duty stirred himself awake and walked over to Jubal. A Kalashnikov, its muzzle pointed at Jubal, dangled from a sling on his shoulder. His right hand was on the pistol grip, his forefinger was on the trigger.

"The gate cannot open until 6 a.m."

"Yes, I know that," answered Jubal. "I will wait. I want to be first in the morning. I have to do an electrical repair."

"Suit yourself. Leave the truck where it is. You will need permission in the morning to enter the school," said the policeman and retreated to his lean-to shelter.

Jubal let down the tailgate of the pickup and sat on the bed of the truck, his legs dangling off the back, smoke from his cigarette curling into the cold night air.

At midnight, another policeman emerged from the barracks and relieved the guard on duty. The new guard motioned toward Jubal and raised his eyebrows in a questioning who-is-he gesture.

"He's an electric repairman. He's waiting to be first in the morning," the first guard explained to his replacement.

The new guard looked at Jubal, shrugged, and then sat down in the lean-to. Within 30 minutes, he was snoring softly. Jubal slid quietly off the end of the pickup and got into the cab. He started the engine, intending to move the truck closer to the steel gates.

Immediately, the guard awakened from his slumber. "Don't move the truck," he called, "leave it right where it is."

"I wanted to turn on the heater to get a little warmth," answered Jubal. To himself, he cursed his bad luck that the guard was a light sleeper. Jubal let the engine idle for 5 minutes, then he turned off the ignition.

Fifteen minutes later, the guard was snoring again. Quietly, Jubal slipped out of the cab. He did not close the door completely, for that would have made a noise that would have woken the guard. He softly walked down the road. On his cell phone, he sent a one-word text message:

Ready

When he was about 200 meters from the truck, he reached into the breast pocket of his jacket and extracted a small black plastic case. Again, he waited.

Soon, a caravan of three more pickup trucks and two large vans arrived. The lead pickup stopped next to Jubal. The trucks were completely dark with no headlights or lights of any kind visible. A total of eighteen men, fully armed with rifles, pistols, and knives, were in the trucks.

The leader of the group, who called himself al'Asad Aljibal (the Lion of the Mountains), motioned for Jubal to get into the cab of the first truck. Al'Asad Aljibal was a large man, weighing approximately 200 pounds. At six feet, he was tall for an Afghan. With a heavy black beard and cruel, dark eyes, he glared at everyone and everything. His presence was always menacing. Aljibal was the successor to Omar Siddiqi, who had been killed by a sniper a few years ago. Aljibal seemed to be in a perpetual state of great anger. A scar in his left eyebrow extending up into his forehead made his face look even more ruthless. He was universally hated by those he attacked in the name of Allah and feared by the men he led. "Blow the bomb," he ordered.

"The truck is not in the best position. It isn't close enough to the gate," Jubal explained.

"Do it anyway," ordered Aljibal.

"As you say, Rayiys (Chief). But the truck is in the wrong position."

Jubal extended a short telescoping aerial on the box. He pressed a button on the small box and grinned as the pickup truck in front of the gate exploded in a giant roar. The snoring policeman guarding the gate was killed instantly. The front of the barracks building was blown in, killing one man inside and injuring the other four policemen.

The two steel doors in the wall were dented in slightly, and the light blue paint was scorched from the blast, but they had held shut. In a moment, with the debris from the pickup truck still falling, the five trucks moved forward to the gate in the wall. A loud alarm bell began clanging inside the school, and yelling and screaming erupted as the entire compound came to life.

Al'Asad Aljibal was very angry that the steel doors had not blown in. Jubal had screwed up by parking the truck too far from the doors. He should have killed the guard and moved the truck right up to the doors. Their attack would have to wait for another day.

A teacher inside the school had gotten to the top of the wall and was shooting three-round bursts of rifle fire at the last truck in the caravan.

Aljibal ordered, "Let us go before that bitch gets lucky and hits one of our men. We will come back another time."

The caravan of five trucks moved forward and was soon swallowed up by the darkness.

The sign bearing the school's name swung slowly by one corner screw that was still loosely attached to the wall. The lonely light fixture over the doors was a memory.

5

JACK & LAURA

Washington D.C.
Saturday, July 14

A week after their return to the U.S. from Saudi Arabia, Herbert Watson, III, Jack's CIA boss and handler, informed Laura Halevi and Jack Miller that they were summoned to the White House where President Samuel Decker intended to award each of them a medal for their rescue of Ambassador Stuart Keaton, Mrs. Adelle Keaton and their 14 year old daughter Suzanna Keaton from the clutches of al-Qaeda in the Arabian Peninsula and their fanatical leader Abdel Karim Washim al-Nasirah.

Jack Miller was a major in the Marines, on loan to the CIA. Miller was not Jack's real name. He had adopted the last name because it was one of the world's most common names and was found in many cultures. He had been Miller for so long that if you called him by his real name, he would not respond. Not using his real name protected his parents from any danger by association with him. In his last assignment in Saudi Arabia, he had been code-named *Pogo*, a name he found very much to his liking.

Laura Halevi, code-named *Koala*, was an Israeli Mossad officer. She had dark hair in soft curls, a beautiful face, and a strong, athletic body. She moved with natural gracefulness. She never used makeup, nor did she ever need it. She just had a healthy aura about her. Laura's eye color was dependent upon the ambient light. Sometimes her eyes were gray with blue tints, and other times they were blue with gray tints. Those eyes always drew the observer into their depths. Laura was a talented computer hacker, an expert and an instructor at Krav Maga (the Israeli deadly art of unarmed warfare), a natural warrior, and almost as good with weapons as Jack. She was cool under pressure. In short, she was beautiful and lethal, yet still a good person.

Jack and Laura's first meeting had been anything but ordinary—she came to Maryland to kill him. Her twin brother, Zvi, a Mossad agent deep undercover in Yemen, had posed as a Palestinian bomb-making instructor. Jack shattered that cover when he destroyed the training camp, killing the recruits, and, unknowingly, Zvi himself.

Both men had been chasing the same target: Abdel Karim Washim al-Nasirah, leader of al-Qaeda in the Arabian Peninsula. But Zvi's cover was so convincing that, in the chaos, Jack believed he was eliminating a Hamas bomb-maker. That single event tied Jack and Laura together in blood and vengeance from the start.

Laura, by dint of her hacking skills, managed to pierce the CIA's computer firewalls and establish the identity of the man who killed Zvi and locate his home address.

One night, Laura slipped into Jack's house with murder in her heart and revenge for her brother burning in her veins. Jack survived her attack—but instead of killing her, he offered her a choice: join him. Against all odds, she accepted.

From that night on, they were more than allies. Together they became a lethal partnership—two warriors whose combined skill was matched only by the intensity of their bond. Their closeness was total; since Laura's failed attempt, they had lived side by side, almost never apart, and neither seemed to want it any other way.

Love grew out of blood and danger, binding them as tightly as their mission. They fought, lived, and risked everything together. Jack and Laura were so attuned that they often moved as if they were one.

Stuart Keaton, the American ambassador to Saudi Arabia, was kidnapped by al-Nasirah along with his wife, Adelle, and their daughter, Suzanna. Because Keaton was a close friend of U.S. President Samuel Decker, al-Nasirah believed the Americans would pay a staggering ransom for their release.

Instead, Jack and Laura—operating under their CIA and Mossad codenames, Pogo and Koala—tracked al-Nasirah down and rescued the entire Keaton family. Officially, the credit went to Saudi Arabian Special Forces. The truth—that two operatives succeeded where an entire military had failed—was buried.

For that operation, one that would never appear in any public record, Jack and Laura were quietly honored by the U.S. government.

The awards ceremony took place in the Oval Office on July 14, with President Samuel Decker presiding. Stuart Keaton and Adelle Keaton were present, along with Herbert Watson, III, Arnold Greensman, the Director of the CIA, and Maurice Shalom, the Israeli Ambassador to the United States. Jack was wearing his best suit, a navy pinstripe, with a navy striped tie. Laura wore a gray pantsuit with a tailored jacket, an outfit she had had to buy especially for this ceremony since almost all the clothes she owned were back in Israel. Because of the secrecy involved, no photographs of the event were taken to record the ceremony.

President Decker began with words of welcome. "Thank you all for coming here today. It is my great honor to recognize a team that thinks effectively and creatively, and then acts decisively. A team that is clearly greater than the sum of its parts."

He motioned for Jack and Laura to step forward. "Pogo and Koala, you began your operation by defending against an attack where you were outnumbered sixteen to two. When that battle was over, the score stood at sixteen for the good guys and zero for the bad guys.

"Then, after the attack and kidnapping of Ambassador Keaton and his family, you both performed an amazing job of tracking al-Nasirah to his lair, and against significant numerical odds, you managed to rescue the Keatons from the clutches of al-Qaeda. And best of all, you prevented further harm to our amazing Suzy Keaton. Additionally, you retrieved very important intelligence in the form of al-Nasirah's computer and phone, as well as the phone of his chief lieutenant. An invaluable intelligence haul which is already paying dividends in our efforts to eradicate al-Qaeda. You also captured al-Nasirah alive, and although we have yet to extract information from him, we have confidence that he will soon become a valuable source of intelligence.

"What we do here today is small compensation for the debt that the world owes to you two. It is my privilege to award Pogo the Intelligence Star medal for valor during combat against the enemy. The Intelligence Star is the highest recognition that the CIA can award. Most Intelligence Star medals are awarded posthumously. Rarely does the recipient survive the events for which the award is given. We are all happy that you are here unharmed and in good health to receive this honor."

At a nod from the president, Arnold Greensman, the Director of the CIA, stepped forward and held out the medal in a wooden case lined in dark blue velvet. Also in the case was a military style campaign ribbon for wearing on a uniform. The president took the medal and pinned it to the left breast pocket of Jack's suit jacket. Then he shook Jack's hand. Sincere applause from the small assembled group greeted the presentation of the medal.

Turning his attention to Laura, the president said, "Koala, you and Pogo are a formidable team. I pity the bad guys that you two are assigned to bring to justice. You have earned the same award for valor as Pogo, but because you are not an employee of the Central Intelligence Agency, we cannot make the award you have so deservedly earned. Accordingly, I have exercised my discretion as President of the United States to award you the Presidential Medal of Freedom With Distinction. This is the highest honor that the United States can bestow upon a person who is not a citizen of the United States. Israel is fortunate to have you as one of their star agents. America is fortunate that we can all work as allies.

"Together, you have made the world a better place. Your skills, your valor, your dedication to freedom and democracy, and human dignity set a standard that is hard to equal. I am proud to present these awards and to extend my gratitude to both of you for a job well done. America and Israel are proud of you."

At a motion from President Decker, Herb Watson stepped forward with Laura's award in a polished wooden case lined in gray velvet. In the case were the Medal of Freedom on a blue neck ribbon, a pin-on version of the medal, and a military style campaign ribbon for wearing on a uniform. The president took the Medal of Freedom on its long blue ribbon and hung it around Laura's neck. He clipped the ribbon at the back of her neck, then he shook her hand. All those in attendance broke into a fresh round of applause.

Ambassador Keaton motioned with his hand, "Mr. President, may I say a few words?"

"Certainly, Stu. You have the floor."

"Pogo and Koala, I don't even know your real names, but I speak for myself and Adelle, for Suzanna, and for my son Andrew, who is serving in the Navy in the Persian Gulf and cannot be here today. What you have done is to give life back to the Keaton family. I shudder to think what harm the animals of al-Qaeda might have done to our family. The debt we owe you is a never-ending obligation from all of us to both of you. No matter where or when or why, if either of you should ever need anything that is within our ability to do for you, it shall be done, no questions asked. You risked your lives to save ours. It is inadequate, but the least we can do as a partial repayment to you. This promise has no limits, no caveats, no qualifiers. It is unconditional and for as long as we are alive. By the nature of the kind of people you are, I know that no request from either of you will ever bring dishonor to us or to America or Israel. Thank you from the bottom of our hearts."

Jack cleared his throat. It was clear that the emotions of the moment had gotten to him. Laura fidgeted uncomfortably. Neither of them was used to having praises heaped on their heads.

Finally, Jack said, "Thank you, Mr. President and Ambassador Keaton. When we saw al-Nasirah's video of the damage he did to Suzy, we both swore to ourselves that we would bring him down. That we actually succeeded in destroying their schemes and bringing al-Nasirah to justice is sufficient compensation. We do what we do because there are bad people who must be stopped from harming good people. As long as we can be certain that we are on the side of the good guys, we will continue to do our jobs. Thank you for the recognition you have given us. Both of us are honored and humbled to receive these awards."

More applause followed Jack's little speech.

Laura didn't say anything other than a quiet "Thank you, Mr. President."

Arnold Greensman then explained, "Pogo and Koala, because of the classified nature of your exploits, neither of you can publicly wear your medals or even acknowledge that you ever received them. I request that you return the medals to their wooden boxes."

One of the stranger elements of the awards ceremony is that no one actually said Jack or Laura's real names, even though their real names were engraved on the backs of the medals. They were referred to only as Pogo and Koala, the code names they used during their operation. The Keatons still did not know the names of the two people who had rescued them from their kidnappers.

President Decker motioned for Stuart and Adelle Keaton to have a private word with him. When he was done whispering, both Keatons nodded their heads in agreement. The president turned again to the small group gathered in the Oval Office. "I want you all to be the first to know that later today at a news conference, I intend to nominate Ambassador Keaton to be Assistant Secretary of State for Near Eastern Affairs. Both he and Adelle have accepted my offer. I will ask the Senate leadership to expedite his confirmation. The job is based here in Washington, but Stu will likely be doing a lot of traveling."

The announcement was greeted with sincere applause and congratulations to Stuart Keaton. Everyone left the Oval Office feeling upbeat and happy.

As they drove back to Silver Spring, Jack glanced at Laura. "You know what we need? A real vacation. Somewhere warm. I'm thinking St. Barths."

"St. Barths?" She asked, raising an eyebrow.

"French West Indies. Technically, St. Barthelémy, but nobody calls it that. It's the off-season now, so flights and hotels are cheaper. No winter crowds. Restaurants are wide open." He shot her a grin. "Jimmy Buffett even wrote *Cheeseburger in Paradise* about the place."

Laura laughed. "Sold. After Yemen and Saudi Arabia, paradise sounds perfect. We could use some pampering and a little rest. Those two countries were not exactly garden spots."

When they arrived home, they hugged and kissed and looked at their medals for a few minutes. "It's a pity that no one will ever know we got these," Laura said.

"I have a place to lock them away," Jack offered. "I installed a strongbox concealed in the concrete floor of the house where I keep certain weapons. They'll be safe there, and some days when we are feeling under-appreciated, we can take them out, look at them, and then make love for a few hours."

"Everything has to do with sex where you're concerned. If you feel under-appreciated while I am with you, then I am not doing my job right."

"Woman, you are the best friend a man could want. When you are with me, I always want all of you all the time. Do you realize that we have never been away from each other for more than a few hours at a time since you came to kill me?" Jack smiled and hugged Laura in a total full-body press. "Hmm. I love your bumps and hollows," he whispered.

"I notice that you are developing a bump of your own," Laura observed. I think we should do something about that before the situation gets out of control."

Later, Jack, tired but content, sat down at his computer and surfed through air carriers and hotels in St. Barths. With a few keystrokes and some phone calls, their plans were set. They would fly American Airlines to St. Maarten via Miami and take Winair to St. Barths. A room was booked for fifteen days at Le Lever de la Lune Hotel. They would pick up a rental car at the airport in St. Barths. All accomplished by the magic of credit cards and the internet.

6

THE PASHTO SCHOOL

Sinjara, Afghanistan
Saturday, July 21

Eleven days had passed since the attempted attack on the Pashto School. Life had returned to normal, and the heightened awareness regarding security matters had subsided. Clara was running the school; Dr. Rope was running his clinic.

A few days earlier, two of the older girls had reattached the sign with the school name to the wall. It was somewhat worse for wear due to dings from shrapnel and scorched paint on one side. It was also slightly crooked. Still, the sign and the school were both still there.

The school staff and the local residents were unsure about who had attacked them. The militia people, led by the headman of Sinjara, were inclined to believe it was ISIS's forces. The Wilsons were leaning toward the Taliban as the culprits.

The residents of Sinjara had grown proud that the school was in their town and were genuinely incensed that someone would think to attack 'their' school. Tensions were still high among the students. Several of the girls had been raped before and were fearful of a repeat attack, bringing more pain and shame. Their sense of security in being safe in the school had been sorely damaged.

Dr. Rope had a long phone conversation with the provincial governor, who promised to increase the guard force to twelve men in the near future. Lieutenant Colonel Higgins, the American commander in the area, apologized that he could not assign any men to watch over the school, but he did send a military radio so that the Pashto School could call for help if another attack occurred. Zahara, one of the teachers who spoke English well, was taught the rudiments of operating the radio, and its presence added an element of security to the school. Higgins was aware, but did not actually say, that the Americans were 32 km away from Sinjara. On war-damaged secondary roads, it would take 45 minutes to arrive. By helicopter, if any were available, it would take 12 minutes to scramble a team and then travel to the school. Still, the radio was much better than having to depend upon unreliable telephone service if the school needed to call for help.

On this day, Clara and Henry were conducting a security tour of the school. Each of them was alert to the new situation.

Henry observed, "The girls have painted the gate light blue again to hide the scorch marks from the blast. There is no way we'll be able to get the major dent from the explosion out of the door. But it still works and can do its job of sealing the opening, so I guess it will just have to remain dented."

Clara asked, "When you spoke to the provincial governor and he promised to double the number of police guarding the school, did he give you a time frame for their arrival?"

"No. I truly have no faith in his keeping that promise. I'm happy that he actually replaced the six police officers we had before. I am sure he intends to forget his promise of six extra men. He is well-intentioned, but he doesn't have enough manpower as it is."

"At least the new men don't have the complacent attitude that our original force had. They treat everyone who wants to enter the school as a potential terrorist."

Henry chuckled, "Since they are new, they don't know who a regular visitor is, or who is a local versus who is a stranger. Everyone gets scrutinized and run through the wringer. It can take 30 minutes for a regular delivery truck just to get through the gate. But it will ease up when they get to know who belongs and who doesn't."

"I hope so. I also hope they never get as complacent as the old guys were. That led to sloppy security."

"It's partly our fault," Henry observed. "We let it happen because we didn't demand stricter compliance with the security practices. We cannot let our guard down again."

"A determined attacker will always be able to inflict pain on regular people. A demented attacker will do worse damage because he doesn't care if he lives or dies. Either way, there is going to be pain. I don't want to live in an armored security shell. What we've got has served us well enough for over five years. We'll just have to hope it will serve us for the next five years."

"I think we should put our minds to improving the security of the school, or we will have more such attacks," Henry said. "The next time we may not be so lucky. On an absolute scale, security at the school is still very sketchy."

"Well," said Clara, "there is still the local militia. Almost every rural Afghan home has at least one firearm for each male in the house over the age of fifteen. Every man imagines himself to be a warrior. In the final analysis, if there is any genuine security for the Pashto School, it has to come from the residents of Sinjara protecting their school."

"You may be right, but it wouldn't hurt to think a little bit more about our own security here."

Henry and Clara continued their survey of the school, and when they were done, nothing much had changed.

The daily grind of life continued. Sinjara was quiet once again.

7

ARCHER M. HADLEY

United States Secretary of State
General Headquarters Pakistan Army
Rawalpindi, Pakistan
Tuesday, July 24 & Wednesday, July 25

An official visit to a nominal ally who is not an ally can be a tedious affair of negotiating with liars, hypocrites, thieves, and double-dealers. And that is just the dealings with officials representing the government.

The official United States plane carrying the Secretary of State, his official party, and the press corps was due to land in Rawalpindi in about an hour. Archer Hadley had just called his aides together for a short lecture about Pakistan. Only a handful of his people had ever been to Pakistan before. The press was not invited.

"Ladies and gentlemen," Hadley began, "please put away your cell phones for a few minutes, take out your ear buds, and pay attention. I'd like to bring you up to speed on the situation in Pakistan and why we are making this trip.

"Ernie, you have been to Pakistan several times before. I would like you to monitor communications while this is going on. Don't interrupt us unless the president calls or it is a national emergency. You already know what I have to say."

"Yes, Mr. Hadley. I'll get right on it." Ernie stood and walked forward to the plane's communications center.

Hadley continued, "Pakistan receives billions in military aid from the U.S. every year. Whenever Pakistan suffers a natural disaster, the U.S. is often the first to respond with humanitarian aid, including medical teams, search and rescue teams, and billions of dollars in food and supplies.

"The U.S. tries to be the buffer between Muslim Pakistan and Hindu India to keep these two nuclear-armed adversaries from blowing each other off the face of the Earth. In return for our politically motivated friendship, Pakistan has consistently provided America's enemies with safe havens, training camps, military aid, intelligence services, and medical care for their wounded fighters. Many of these services to America's enemies are paid for using U.S. foreign aid. Pakistan's gratitude to Uncle Sam is boundless.

"Every high diplomatic visit comes with a review of the assembled honor guard. These troop reviews are another pain in the butt. The troops spend all day getting spiffed up for the review. Then they stand in formation in the hot sun for two or more hours waiting for the visiting Mega Honcho (that's me) to show up for a two-minute walk by. The band plays martial music and national anthems. Just once, it would be nice if the band played Seventy-Six Trombones."

A few chuckles from the group followed the boss's little joke.

"Everyone salutes multiple times. Flags wave and honor guards march by. We place wreaths on symbolic memorials in a token show of respect and reverence. Rifles fire blanks in salutes of the honorable guest. Because of our exalted position, we will receive a nineteen-gun salute.

"Fifteen minutes total, and it is over. Every Pakistani flag officer present will probably receive an additional ribbon for the fruit salad on his uniform. What a waste of time and effort! I suppose the honor guard review serves as a pretext for the talks that are the main focus of the trip. Still, I feel sorry for the troops who stand in the sun for all those hours.

"After the opening troop review and the obligatory lunch or dinner, we finally get to why we have traveled halfway around the world. We will be talking about how much money or weapons the USA will give the government of Pakistan. America will attempt to secure some cooperation in return, usually in the form of access to bases, fly-over privileges, or intelligence sharing. With the Pakistanis, it is intelligence sharing and the ability to resupply our forces in Afghanistan through Pakistani airspace. The only fly in this ointment is that the intelligence isn't worth spit. It is always too little, too late, or just plain misleading."

Archer Hadley is not a physically imposing presence. But when he speaks, the entire world listens attentively. He does not waste words. He is right to the point—always. Hadley is in his late 50s, thin of face and body, with white hair just beginning to recede, rimless eyeglasses, and a courtly manner that covers a steely will. Harvard-educated, a brilliant lawyer, he does not suffer fools easily. Hadley gave up a lifetime seat on the Federal Appeals bench to accept President Decker's appointment as Secretary of State. One of the least loved aspects of his unenviable job is trying to keep the world's most unstable nations from declaring war on their neighbors. When he must deal with Iran, North Korea, China, or Russia, there is never the fiction of friendship involved. They are adversaries, plain and simple. However, with a nation like Pakistan, nothing is simple, and everything has the potential to be layered with more lies upon more lies. Fortunately, this visit would only be for four days. But, he reflected, we must dance our silly minuet and pretend that we value their friendship and cooperation, even though they aren't our friends and they cooperate with our enemies more than with us.

Hadley continued his impromptu lecture, "This particular trip is to meet with Field Marshal Hakim Mouhammed Bouradin and President Mahmoud Harraf. The president is not the head guy. The field marshal is the top dog in the pecking order. Whatever he agrees to, the president also agrees to. If the field marshal disagrees with something we want, he ducks it by saying, 'I must get the president's approval on that point.'

We both know the president really has nothing to say about anything except the color of the rug in his office.

"To deal with Pakistan, one should understand the organization of the various government offices and bureaus. The field marshal, in addition to commanding the army, the navy, and the air force, is also the head of the entire Pakistani intelligence community. It is in the control of the intelligence agencies where the real power resides.

"The most powerful intelligence agency is the Directorate for Inter-Services Intelligence (ISI). This group collaborates with both military and civilian officers on any matter related to foreign or domestic intelligence. The director-general of the agency is appointed by the president and is an army general chosen by the field marshal. Pakistanis are rightly scared to death if the ISI decides to arrest them. Think of an agency that is a combination of the FBI, CIA, and the Gestapo. That is the ISI."

One of Hadley's aides raised her hand. "Yes, Jimmy."

Martha James, a really smart 23-year-old with a bright future at the state, nicknamed Jimmy by the staff, asked, "I have heard about Directorate S. Could you tell us what we should be aware of regarding this group while we are in Pakistan?"

"Good question, Jimmy. Inside the ISI, there's an elite unit known as Directorate S. Officially, it doesn't exist—yet it's the most powerful arm of the service. They can reach anyone, anywhere, anytime—and people who cross them simply vanish. Directorate S once shielded Osama bin Laden, and today it still gives cover to ISIS and the Taliban. It bankrolls terror networks, spies on critics of authoritarian rule, makes democracy advocates disappear, silences journalists, murders judges who step out of line, and crushes dissent among politicians. For an office that doesn't exist, it is the most feared force in Pakistan.

"Additionally, each branch of the military, the Army, Navy, and Air Force, has its own intelligence arm. All three intelligence services are under the command of another army general appointed by the president but chosen by the field marshal.

"Espionage is the nominal responsibility of the Intelligence Bureau (IB). This is a civilian agency, but the military exercises heavy control over its operations. India, Afghanistan, and Iran are the primary focuses of this group. They also monitor Russia, Israel, the U.S., and NATO. China is a friend to Pakistan, but the Pakistanis do not trust it; however, they will accept China's gifts of money for major infrastructure projects. When you are paranoid, enemies are under every rock, and real enemies are waiting for you to make a mistake.

"Pakistan has roughly thirty-five different intelligence agencies, each charged with rooting out internal anti-government elements. Democracy advocates are viewed as the greatest internal threat, so these so-called subversives receive the most scrutiny. Externally, India remains the primary adversary, with the U.S. pressing both sides to preserve a fragile peace. Open expression is dangerous in Pakistan, where anyone can be treated as a spy or a traitor. And above all, one name inspires the deepest fear—Directorate S."

Hadley paused to take a drink from a bottle of water, then continued, "Now, everyone, if you need a restroom break, now would be a good time to do it. Then, please return to your seats. You can once again become your electronic alter egos by worshipping your cell phones. We should be landing at Nur Khan in about 40 minutes."

When the plane landed at the Nur Khan Air Force Base in Rawalpindi, the secretary was met on the tarmac by Field Marshal Bouradin and the honor guard. Nur Khan AFB is really a section of Benazir Bhutto International Airport, a civilian facility, and both military and civilian aircraft share the runways.

The honor guard and the wreath laying at a memorial to Pakistani airmen killed in combat during Pakistan's military actions against India and Israel went off without a hitch.

Then the State Department group was transported to the Islamabad Marriott Hotel in a caravan of vehicles arranged by the U.S. Embassy. They all needed to check in and reorient their internal biological clocks to the Pakistan time zone, 9 hours ahead of Washington. When it is noon in Washington, it is 9 p.m. on the same night in Islamabad. Jet lag can be a major impediment for negotiators if they ignore the insidious effects it has on their mental faculties and skills. No official business would be conducted until the next day.

*   *   *

The following day, Tuesday, July 24, at 11:00 a.m., Secretary Hadley and the field marshal met in an elaborately paneled conference room in the Pakistani General Headquarters Building in Rawalpindi. Oil portraits of previous Supreme Commanders of the Pakistani military, in all the splendor of their dress uniforms, stared down on the meeting's participants. Another wall was devoted to a gigantic TV screen showing a map of Pakistan and India, and all the known deployments of Indian military units and the Pakistani units that are prepared to oppose them at a moment's notice.

Field Marshal Hakim Mouhammed Bouradin cut a flamboyant figure—mustache trimmed to perfection, paratrooper boots gleaming like black glass, and a chest weighted with a riot of campaign ribbons. A blue and gold braided cord spilled down his shoulder, and under one arm rested the ultimate symbol of authority: his field marshal's baton. He had come with a wish list of military hardware, rattling off demands as though shopping from a catalog. Price was irrelevant; Pakistan would never pay a rupee. The billions would flow from this year's American aid package.

Across the table, Secretary Hadley listened, stone-faced, as Bouradin explained not only what weapons he wanted but also what conditions he would not tolerate. They sat alone, each with a single aide. No translators, no diplomats—just two men trapped in a negotiation neither cared to attend. The field marshal's Oxford-tinged English was as smooth as his polished boots, but beneath the civility ran a current of mistrust.

The top items on the field marshal's list were an advanced radar targeting system for the Pakistani Air Force, some F-35 fighters, and high-speed patrol boats for the Navy. "We need the radar targeting system for our Air Force. If you won't sell it to us, we will be forced to obtain the equipment from China. India has such capabilities, and we must match theirs or they will gain a tactical advantage over us. And don't tell us we cannot use such systems for offensive purposes.

"Further, last year you gave India thirty-eight high-speed patrol boats. We would like parity with them."

Hadley silently marveled at what he had just heard. Is there a Urdu word for *chutzpah*? "First of all, we will not sell you the radar systems. They are too highly classified and advanced for a military as full of Russian and Iranian moles as yours. If India has such a system, it is because they bought it. Second, you have less than 10% of the coastline that India has. If you want parity with India, we can sell you 3.8 high-speed patrol boats.

"You have more than enough defensive capability from previous years of aid. What the United States will not do is give you offensive superiority in any area of military endeavor. An equivalent of the radar system you want was developed by Israeli engineers and manufactured in Israel. India purchased its system from Israel. Surely your engineers can develop a similar system. Alternatively, you can buy the system you want from Israel."

"We will not do business with the Zionist entity. They have invaded and occupied Muslim lands. You know that we do not even recognize their government exists, no less suggest that Pakistan do business with outlaws."

"Well, the United States will not sell the system to Pakistan."

"Surely, said Bouradin, "you do not intend to insult the government of Pakistan with such a response. Are we not allies in the war against terror? How are we to counter our mutual enemies without proper military hardware? Let us speak frankly. The U.S. is being most uncooperative, Mr. Secretary. As a Muslim nation, we take enormous risks in being your friend in international affairs. Our military is a bulwark on the frontier, defending American interests here in the Middle East."

Hadley once again thought about *chutzpa*. "Since you are speaking frankly, then I will do the same. I noticed that Directorate S was very helpful in assisting Osama bin Laden in finding a nice place to live and then offered him continued protection. They assist ISIS, the Taliban, and the Haqqani Network. I expect you to rein in Directorate S's activities.

"And we deeply appreciated your friendship two weeks ago when you voted against our draft resolution at the U.N. regarding increased assistance for Iraqi and Afghan refugees, an effort that would not have cost Pakistan one rupee but would have provided humanitarian relief to suffering people.

"There is another urgent matter, since we are being frank with each other, that is critical to this visit. Last week, your friendly Navy seized an American civilian oceanographic research vessel in international waters in the Arabian Sea and accused it of spying for India. The rationale for the seizure was that one of the eminent research oceanographers on the staff, Dr. Mujibar Patel, is of Indian ethnicity but a United States citizen by birth. I expect that vessel and its crew—the entire crew—to be released before I leave Pakistan, or there will be no aid at all this year or next year or the year after that. If the crew and the vessel are not released, you can expect that the 5,800 Pakistani citizens studying at American universities will have their student visas revoked within seven days' time. Every one of them. And that is because we are friends and not adversaries. Were we adversaries, President Decker would have ordered two aircraft carrier battle groups to be off the coast of Pakistan at this moment. Then you would hear the sound of U.S. Navy jets breaking the sound barrier over Islamabad. So, my frank and friendly ally, do we know where we stand on these matters?"

"Humph," was all the field marshal could muster.

"In addition, Directorate S should curtail its aid to ISIS and the Taliban. Do you really think we are so stupid that we do not know what you are doing?"

"That is an unjust accusation. We do not support terrorist organizations."

"Your support is not going to little old ladies in a knitting circle. If you want our aid, you had better stop supporting the bad guys."

The field marshal rose, "Let us adjourn this meeting until tempers have cooled a bit. Shall we meet again tomorrow?"

"Release the imprisoned crew and the captured vessel, and we can talk tomorrow." Hadley also stood and strode to the door. His aide leaped to his feet and followed, hurriedly gathering up his papers. "Until tomorrow, when the crew is set free, and the vessel is allowed to continue its research."

"I do not know if the court can act by tomorrow."

"The crew is in a military prison, the ship is at a Pakistani naval facility," Hadley said. His anger was about to boil over. "You tell the judge that what I want is the same as what you want, and they will be set free within 30 minutes. I repeat: The complete crew. Further, if they have been physically abused by your people, that will cost you dearly in military aid. All you have to do is say it, and it will get done. If it is not done by tomorrow, then there is no point in our continued conversations. I hope we are clear in our understanding." With that, Hadley pushed open the door and walked out of the meeting room. His limo was waiting to take him back to the Islamabad Marriott.

After Secretary Hadley left, the field marshal summoned a general on his staff. "Call President Harraf's office. Instruct them to release the American research vessel and its entire crew by tonight. No apology is to be given. Order them to be out of Pakistani waters before 6 a.m. tomorrow, or we will arrest them again. I want no delays and no screw-ups. Get it done."

"Yes, sir. I will call immediately. Would it be acceptable if I sent Colonel Parvez to the prison to expedite the release?"

"That is good. Do it. I want to be rid of those people today."

"Yes, Field Marshal." The general saluted, did a British army about-face with stamping feet, and left the conference room.

Bouradin turned to the aide, a colonel who had been sitting quietly. "You are dismissed."

"Yes, sir," said the colonel. He stood, saluted, gathered his papers, and left the room.

The field marshal sat alone in the conference room quietly plotting how he would get even with Secretary of State Archer M. Hadley. No one is permitted to speak to Hakim Mouhammed Bouradin in the manner that Hadley just did. Such disrespect demands to be punished.

8

JACK AND LAURA

Grand Saline Beach
St. Barthelémy, French West Indies
Wednesday, July 25

Half a world away, Jack and Laura were sunning themselves on Grande Saline beach, a clothing-optional beach on the French West Indian island of St. Barths. Laura wore a pale green bikini thong bottom but no top. Having just the one piece of clothing was more sexy than if she had been totally nude.

Jack was letting it all hang out. Lots of sunscreen had to be applied to keep seldom-exposed skin from burning. The beach was truly secluded since it was summer and there were no vacationing crowds. Only one other couple was visible, and they were two human specks about 1,000 yards away at the far end of the beach.

Jack and Laura had been lying on large beach towels on the sand for about 40 minutes. Each had a second towel they were using as a pillow. The sun was baking their bones. They felt relaxed and happy to be in love with each other.

The sky was magnificent blue with a few puffy, white clouds that could have been painted by a great master. The only sound was the occasional splashing of pelicans as they dove into the sea to catch fish. A few shorebirds ran along the edge of the surf, digging in the sand for tiny clams. The surf was just a few inches high and very quiet. The gentle trade wind breezes stirred the palm trees at the back of the beach. Their cell phones were in their hotel room. They did not watch TV or read newspapers. Peace.

Laura ran some sand through her fingers. "What a difference between the sand on this beach and the sand in the Saudi desert. No one is shooting at us. I don't need that damn burqa. The Middle East may be my home, but this is like heaven."

"That is a correct and proper assessment. I totally agree. These make for complete perfection." Jack reached over and rubbed Laura's right breast and played with her nipple, making circles with his finger, until her nipple got hard in his hand. Then he reached for her left breast.

"You've caused enough of an uproar already. I think you should stop," Laura said with a smile.

"I have to make them even," Jack whispered hoarsely. "It won't do to have one nipple standing tall and the other idle and loafing away."

"My other nipple isn't loafing. You already made it hard. And from what I can see, your pogo stick is hard too. I think it's time for us to go for a swim and cool you off." Laura stood up and pulled Jack's hands until he was in a sitting position.

"If I go in the water with this guy in his present condition, I might get swept out to sea by the current."

"It's a risk you'll have to take. Let's go." Laura shucked off her bikini bottom and ran to the surf. Jack had no option but to follow her delectable backside.

The water was cool initially, but they quickly got used to it. Soon they were hugging in the gentle swells, chest-high in the water, trading little kisses and behaving like uninhibited children.

While they hugged, Laura wrapped her arms around Jack's neck, wrapped her legs around his waist, and pulled him tight against her. Jack made those little bumps and rubbing motions and noises that Laura knew from experience meant he was ready to make love. "Not now, not here," she said. "You will have to wait until we get back to the hotel."

"But it's Valentine's Day," Jack replied.

"Maybe on Mars. Earth's Valentine's Day comes in February. Either you missed the date, or you are a bit early. Either way, it isn't Valentine's Day."

"I'm also suffering from SBS. A very rare disease. I need immediate medical care."

"Oh yes, a rare disease, is it now? What does SBS stand for?"

"Semen Backup Syndrome. It's a Hawaiian disease caused by lack-a-nooky. The main symptom is little wriggly guys backed up past your eyeballs. They are constantly swimming across your vision so that you can hardly see anything, and you start hallucinating about Laura without her clothes on."

"Don't tell me your medical problems. This is not an urgent care clinic."

"What if I told you today is my birthday?"

"Just because you are wearing your birthday suit is not enough to convince me it is your birthday. I know when your birthday is, and it's not today. I am not making love on this beach as long as those other people are down there. But since I'm feeling sympathetic to your urgent medical condition, why don't we go back to our room right now? Maybe there will be a medical expert there who can offer emergency care."

"Sounds like a great plan. Let's go."

Twenty minutes later, they were back at their hotel, and soon, everyone was happy and satisfied. However, the bedspread was really wrinkled and full of sand transported by feet and bodies from the beach. The hotel chambermaid would have to deal with it.

9

SENATOR ANDREAS WITHERS

Foreign Relations Committee
United States Senate
Hearing Room SD-419
Washington, D.C.
Thursday, July 26

With two raps of his gavel, Senator Withers announced, "It is 9:30 a.m. I will call this committee to order. The Committee on Foreign Relations is hereby in session. A quorum of the committee membership is present. Actually, the entire committee is present. The only order of business today is to consider the nomination of Ambassador Stuart J. Keaton to be Assistant Secretary of State for Near Eastern Affairs. Ambassador Keaton appeared before this committee three years ago, and his confirmation as Ambassador to the Kingdom of Saudi Arabia was recommended to the Senate. Subsequently, the committee's recommendation was unanimously approved by the entire body.

"President Decker has requested an expedited confirmation hearing, which we will conduct today in this chamber. I request that the members limit their questioning to matters that have occurred since Ambassador Keaton last appeared before this committee."

"We are all familiar with the terrible ordeal the Keaton family experienced while prisoners of al-Qaeda and their successful rescue by the Special Forces of the Kingdom of Saudi Arabia. Ambassador Keaton's daughter, Susanna, suffered grievous personal injury at the hands of the kidnappers. We have all seen that video many times and were appalled by the barbarity of al-Nasirah's actions. Please spare Ambassador Keaton's feelings and refrain from asking questions about those events. Let us instead focus on what Ambassador Keaton can bring to the position for which he has been nominated by the president.

"Each member shall be allowed five minutes of questioning. If time allows, we will have an informal discussion with Ambassador Keaton afterwards. Will the clerk please swear in the witness?"

The committee clerk administered the oath to Ambassador Keaton. Anything Keaton might say going forward would be bound by the rules governing perjury.

The committee members sat on a curved, raised dais at the front of the room. Ambassador Keaton sat alone at a table on the floor of the hearing room, a microphone in front of him. Every participant had a nameplate on the table in front of them. Keaton was quite at ease before the committee. He knew many of the Senators personally and had been before this committee once before. The makeup of the committee had changed little in the intervening three years. Reporters and photographers were everywhere. Video cameras were in use by the various networks. A small crowd of people was jammed onto the public benches at the rear of the hearing room.

"To begin, I call upon Senator Alfredo Leon of the great state of Arizona. Senator Leon, you have five minutes."

Senator Leon nudged his glasses back up the bridge of his nose and shuffled the papers before him. "Thank you, Mr. Chairman. Ambassador Keaton, it's an honor to have you here. Our relationship with Saudi Arabia is stable—some might even call it excellent—and you deserve credit for that.

"Yet the Kingdom's record on human rights remains troubling. Strict adherence to Sharia law relegates women to second-class status. Minorities are denied permanent residency, and foreign workers are exploited to the point of near-slavery. Most concerning of all, religious intolerance is written into law—only Muslims may hold Saudi citizenship. Ambassador, can you tell us whether any progress has been made in addressing these conditions?"

Stu Keaton sat at the witness table in the well of the hearing room, a serious look on his face. "Thank you for your kind words, Senator Leon. For the foreseeable future, Saudi Arabia will continue on the same path it has followed since 1932, when King Abdullah assumed the throne. Women will still be required to wear the burqa. They will still be denied basic privileges that we in the West take for granted. Such as to earn wages for their labor; to walk about freely without a male member of the family to supervise what they do; to dress as they wish; to own property; or to travel outside of Saudi Arabia. Recently, women have been allowed to drive automobiles, but even that privilege must be exercised within the confines of Sharia law, with a male member of the family present in the car. Changing their culture will require a change of attitude at the top of their society. The current leadership is content with the state of affairs that they presently have established.

"Women, and the potential talent and productivity that they represent, will remain a repressed segment of Saudi society. That waste of potential talent will one day return to haunt their society. However, we must recognize that it is their country and their society, and they ultimately call the shots. We would be wrong to impose our values upon them, just as it would be wrong for them to impose their values upon the United States.

"Change will come to Islamic society. Women will one day achieve equality. It will just take much longer than it did in our Western cultures. As a nation, we continually strive to do better today and tomorrow than we did yesterday. It is this commitment to improving our own people's conditions that enables us to be a moral guiding light for others all over the world. Our greatest export is not what we produce in our factories and farms, but our concept of human dignity and basic human rights. As long as we adhere to these principles, oppressed people all over the world will be inspired to press for greater freedom and for real liberty." Keaton took a sip of water. It was obvious that he was done answering the question.

"Thank you, Ambassador Keaton. Mr. Chairman, I yield the floor." Senator Leon sat back and clicked off his microphone.

Chairman Withers said, "I offer the floor to the senator from the great state of Texas, Senator Martha Tyler. Senator Tyler, you have five minutes."

Senator Tyler, 68 years old, in her third term as a senator, was a blonde-haired woman with very few wrinkles, tanned and trim, and energetic, giving her an appearance 15 years younger than her actual age. Hers was one of the sharpest minds in the Senate. Yet the press always seemed more interested in what she was wearing and the accessories she chose than in what she said. Today, the press will report that she is wearing a no-nonsense gray pinstripe suit with a violet print silk scarf.

"Thank you, Mr. Chairman. Ambassador Keaton, I wish to further elaborate on the condition of women in the Middle East; I might even say the plight of women in Islamic countries. In too many nations, women are the workhorses of the family unit. They are denied education, property rights, birth control, may not drive, and cannot vote. In short, they are second-class members of their societies. What progress has been made in other countries of the Middle East besides Saudi Arabia regarding women's rights?"

Keaton smiled, "Senator, the picture is not totally bleak for women. In some countries, notably Lebanon, Jordan, Morocco, and to a lesser extent, Egypt, significant progress has been made toward women's equality. Educational opportunities are available. Travel is permitted. Women can vote and even stand for public office. It is accepted that women can work outside the home and have professional careers.

Enlightened leadership and political stability are key elements in progress. Unfortunately, Turkey appears to be sliding backward under its current leadership.

"In many Islamic countries, any injury, whether physical or social, demands personal revenge. This cultural trait leads to armed unrest and blood feuds. If the rule of law were more firmly established, offended parties would feel satisfied that the legal system would extract the revenge they feel they deserve.

"Any change, to be lasting, must come from within the nations themselves. We tried to impose democracy on Iraq. It has been a spectacularly expensive failure. Expensive in terms of money wasted, and even more costly in terms of human lives wasted.

"A key factor in fostering change in the Middle East is the availability of the internet, inexpensive computers, and cell phones. No longer do oppressed populations live in informational limbo. They are discovering what is happening in the rest of the world, and it whets their appetites for the political freedoms they see other people enjoying. People have become aware that with political freedom, it is possible to have material improvements in their lives.

"In summary, Islamic women have made great progress, but it is not universal. Time and patience will bring about the desired changes. I only hope we live long enough to see it happen." Keaton's last comment brought laughter from the press and the public benches.

Senator Withers rapped his gavel gently. "I must sadly cut you off, Senator Tyler, as your five minutes are up. Senator Withers allowed three more senators to ask Keaton questions, and then he said, "I will declare a 15-minute recess in these hearings so that Ambassador Keaton and the assembled body may all take a break. We will reconvene in 15 minutes." The chairman rapped his gavel once.

Immediately, the hearing room erupted in a hundred different conversations. Some people hurried to the restrooms. Reporters went into the hallway to call their editors. Senate pages hustled off on myriad errands. Within three minutes, the noise level had risen to a level worthy of inclusion in the Guinness Book of Records. Old Senate observers were not surprised in the least. This hearing was no different from hundreds of other hearings, except that Ambassador Keaton was being accorded maximum respect from the committee members. It all augured well for a speedy confirmation.

At the end of the 15-minute break, Chairman Withers rapped his gavel twice. It took another three minutes before everyone was seated and paying attention. "This committee is again in session. Ambassador Keaton, you are still under oath. I call upon Senator Mark Childers from New York. You have five minutes, senator."

"Thank you, Mr. Chairman. Ambassador Keaton, how do you view the power structure in the Middle East? And how do you view the Israeli-Palestinian conflict resolving itself?"

Keaton smiled, "Senator, that is one easy question and one that will require the combined wisdom of Solomon and Jesus to resolve. Let's address them in the order you asked them.

"My opinion of the power structure has Saudi Arabia leading the Sunni nations and Iran leading the Shi'a nations. Each player sends its surrogates to incite unrest in the other Islamic nations to increase their influence and power. Some of the more stable nations, such as Morocco and Jordan, have resisted these efforts and maintained their independence of thought and action. Other nations, particularly in Africa, as well as the Philippines, have fallen prey to Islamic insurrections and tribal warfare.

"The toll of these conflicts in human suffering is beyond belief. Most of these countries lack the traditions of respect for human rights that are common in Western nations. Abuses are the rule rather than the exception. Starvation, forced expulsions from homelands, torture, rape, and murder are all common occurrences, each area of conflict having its own particular emphasis on several abuses at the same time.

"Syria and Yemen are the killing grounds where the major world powers are jockeying for domination with no regard for the damage done to the civilian population. President Assad, with the support of

Russia and Iran, is interested only in remaining in power. Iran seeks to bolster a Shi'a nation. Russia is merely seeking influence and playing power games while testing its air force in combat. Mr. Putin wants Russia to be a world power again, as it was during the days of the old Soviet Union, and Syria is one of several venues where he has played his games. Opposing the Assad regime is a force of Kurds supported by much of the West and by Saudi Arabia.

"A third force is ISIS seeking to establish its Caliphate on Syrian and Iraqi lands. ISIS is being defeated on the battlefield, but its ideological base remains strong.

"The first step in Syria is to get all sides to stop fighting so that a political solution can be worked out. Until that happens, civilian deaths and senseless destruction will continue unabated.

"Your second question, Senator, is one that has defied resolution since 1945. The World War II victor nations decided that the Jewish population of Europe had suffered enough. Through the United Nations, they determined to create a Jewish homeland in Palestine, the ancient biblical home of the Jews since the exodus from slavery in Pharaoh's Egypt. This would effectively get all surviving Jews out of a hostile Europe. What appeared to be a win-win solution for the Jews and for Europe was not acceptable to the Arab world. Various Arab dictators saw an easy military victory over the essentially defenseless newborn State of Israel. As often happens in life, the underdogs won and kept winning time after time, year after year.

"The many times Israel was willing to trade land in exchange for peace were always rejected by its Arab neighbors. Israel has seen the futility of this approach. In effect, they have abandoned the Two-State Solution. They are building new settlements every month on land that the Palestinians once thought of as their country. The emotions stirred up by those elements that wish to destroy Israel make peace almost impossible to achieve.

"The Israelis are hard realists. They have no illusions about what the Arabs intend to do to them. The Arab opposition is clinging to the fantasy of the destruction of Israel. Certain Arab leaders use hatred of Israel and of the Jews and Christians and the West as their means of achieving political and personal power. Until these leaders can give up their fantasy of Israeli extinction and Islamic supremacy, face reality, and accept that Israel will be where it is for the foreseeable future, and until the Israelis are convinced that the Arab change of heart is sincere and enduring, there will not be peace in the region.

"Egypt and Jordan have done this. The three nations of Israel, Egypt, and Jordan cooperate in mutual ways that were once thought impossible. Unless the Palestinian leadership accepts the actual facts as they have existed on the ground since 1948, they will continue to live in political, economic, and human limbo. Peace in the area would remove the Palestinian leaders' reason for being. The conflict is the source of their power and importance. Therefore, they must keep the conflict alive.

"I might add that the Arab nations are not at all interested in absorbing the Palestinian refugees into their societies. If the Palestinian refugees were gone from Gaza, the West Bank, and Lebanon, then the major source of the friction between the Israelis and the Arab world would be lessened. The elements of Arab society that do not want the Palestinian refugee issues to be resolved are very strong and cynical in keeping this festering condition a continuous problem. Israel, much smaller in area, absorbs any Jewish refugees that seek asylum within its borders and society. Why can't the Arab world, infinitely larger and wealthier, do the same?

"No leader exists today who can bridge these differences between the Arab world and the Israelis. Nor does the will to achieve peace under present conditions exist. The United States has tried to be a sincere broker, attempting to find common ground for the two sides. We must continue our efforts to bring the two sides together. What would Solomon do? What would Jesus do? We already know what Mohammed would do. If anyone can figure out the answer to those two questions and then cause it to happen, the world might have a chance for peace in the Middle East."

When Keaton finished speaking, the people in the public benches broke into spontaneous applause. Even some of the senators and members of the press joined in as well.

The hearing continued until 12:45 with nine senators posing additional questions for Ambassador Keaton. The chairman asked the two senators who had not yet spoken, Senator Charles from Minnesota and Senator Hayes from Rhode Island if their concerns about this witness had been satisfied. If not, the committee would reconvene at 2:00 p.m. after lunch. Both senators said they were satisfied and would waive their privileges to question the witness.

At those answers, the chairman announced, "I will entertain a motion from the committee."

Senator Hayes said, "I move that the committee vote to approve the nomination of Stuart J. Keaton to be Assistant Secretary of State for Near Eastern Affairs."

"I second the motion," said Senator Childers from New York.

"All in favor of the motion signify by raising a hand," said Chairman Withers.

Every senator on the dais raised a hand.

"I see the vote for approval of the motion as being unanimous. Therefore, the committee shall send its recommendation to the full Senate for further action. This hearing is now adjourned." With a bang of the gavel, the hearing was over.

Everyone in the hearing room immediately started speaking to their neighbor. The noise level was again very high.

Stu Keaton wiped his brow with a tissue and grinned at his wife, Adelle who was sitting in the front row of the public benches. She returned a dazzling smile and gave her husband two thumbs up.

10

THE PASHTO SCHOOL

Sinjara, Afghanistan
Friday, July 27

Three years at the school had transformed the sisters. Inaya, now fifteen, brimmed with confidence, her quick wit and radiant smile making her a favorite among the younger children. Clara Wilson often pressed her into service as a teacher's aide, and Inaya thrived in the role, guiding small hands over chalkboards and whispering encouragement during lessons. She adored Miss Clara with a devotion that bordered on reverence—hero, mentor, and the model of what she herself longed to become: a teacher.

Naila, at twelve, was quieter, preferring the shadows of the classroom to her sister's spotlight, yet her brilliance was no less striking. Where Inaya's spark was bold and visible, Naila's glow was steady and deep, a quiet strength that Clara recognized and quietly nurtured.

Together the girls were no longer merely students; they were blossoming into young women with hope in their eyes and futures within reach.

By 10:15 a.m., the Pashto School was humming with life. Classrooms buzzed with recitations and the scratch of pencils on paper, while outside a cluster of girls kicked a scuffed soccer ball across the dusty field, their laughter rising above the thud of their feet. In the commissary, the first aromas of lunch began to drift into the air as pots clattered and water hissed to a boil. Dr. Rope moved steadily through his morning patients—mothers with weary eyes, children with coughs and fevers—listening, prescribing, reassuring. In her office, Miss Clara clutched the telephone, her voice warm and persuasive as she appealed to a charitable foundation in Chicago, fighting to secure the funds that kept this fragile dream alive.

At the steel gates, two policemen stood in their usual half-alert stance. Nothing seemed amiss. They swung the doors open to let a produce truck rumble out after its morning delivery. Another van waited to enter.

Neither officer noticed the traffic building on the road. A pickup with a large van behind it crept in from the north; from the south, two more pickups drew closer, with another van trailing in the distance.

The policemen moved toward the waiting delivery van—one on each side. Two pistol shots cracked in unison. Both men crumpled, hearts pierced.

The van roared forward through the open gates. Shouts erupted from the barracks as other policemen spilled out, only to be cut down by machine-gun fire from the approaching pickup. Within seconds, that truck barreled inside, followed by the van behind it. The southern convoy closed in; pickups and a van swung through the gates as if rehearsed.

One truck braked at the entrance. Four gunmen leaped from the bed, calmly finishing the downed policemen with shots to the head before slipping inside. The truck pulled through, and the jihadists barred the steel doors from within.

Chaos followed. Gunfire echoed across the compound. The girls on the soccer field screamed and scattered, a teacher frantically trying to herd them toward the buildings. She never made it—an automatic burst struck her down where she stood. Armed men poured from every vehicle, rifles raised, their takeover of the Pashto School swift and merciless.

Dr. Rope heard the gunfire, and he tried to get the mothers to hide with their children. "Go inside the clinic. There is a large closet at the back. Get inside with the children. Go now. Quickly."

One pickup skidded to a stop outside the clinic. Armed men spilled out, boots pounding on the stone steps. They burst through the wooden door, rifles leveled, and in seconds, Dr. Rope was surrounded.

Their leader's voice was cold, heavy with accusation. "Dr. Henry Wilson," he declared, "you have defiled Muslim women and girls. By order of the Islamic Caliphate, you are under arrest."

The words rang like a death sentence.

They tore through the office, ransacking shelves, sweeping medicines and bandages into plastic bags.

Then, they heard a thin wail. A baby, crying from the closet. The sound froze everyone in the room.

The door was yanked open, and terrified women and children stumbled out, herded at gunpoint.

Henry stepped forward, desperation breaking his voice. "These women are villagers. They are my patients—please, let them go. They have nothing to do with the school."

The leader's response was brutal. He struck Henry across the face, sending his glasses skittering across the floor.

"Silence, dog! We decide who goes free and who dies."

He ground his heel into the fallen glasses, crushing them to shards. "Bind his hands. Blindfold him."

The women and children were forced into line and marched at gunpoint toward the central courtyard. Behind them, the fighters scooped the last of the clinic's supplies into their bags, leaving the room stripped and violated.

Other fighters stormed the school office and seized Miss Clara. Her wrists were wrenched behind her, rope biting into her skin, and a blindfold plunged her world into darkness.

In the commissary kitchen, the cook and her two assistants—local Sinjara women—stood frozen in confusion. The gunmen cut them down where they stood. Bullets ripped through a massive soup pot, and scalding broth hissed from the holes, spilling over the lifeless bodies crumpled on the floor.

Zahara, the teacher who knew how to work the radio, sprinted toward the communications room. She never reached it. A single burst caught her mid-stride, and she collapsed in silence. No warning ever left the school for the American base.

With much shouting and pushing, the students, the Wilsons, the teachers, and Dr. Rope's morning patients were forced into the central courtyard, surrounded by twenty men armed with Kalashnikov AK-47 assault rifles. The attackers did not hesitate to shoot anyone who resisted.

Al'Asad Aljibal climbed onto the bed of a pickup, his rifle slung across his chest, and raised his voice over the terrified silence. "You are all our prisoners. We are the holy warriors of the Haqqani Network, servants of the Islamic Caliphate. The Holy Koran commands that women be subservient to men—created to serve, to bear children, to cook, and to lie with men when summoned.

"This school is finished. From this day forward, it no longer exists. Education is wasted on women. The Koran has spoken, and It is written in the Koran, and so it shall be"

Aljibal turned to one of his men and said, "Shoot the teachers and all of the staff. Load the oldest girls into the trucks. Take the doctor and the headmistress with us. They will be our prisoners."

The fighter replied to Aljibal, "Rayiys (chief), there are too many women here, many more than we need."

"Take as many as we can fit in the vans. We can sell the ones we do not need. Start loading the trucks now."

To the assembled crowd, Aljibal shouted, "You women now belong to us. We own you. We will shoot anyone who tries to escape, and we will leave your body for the jackals and vultures. We need wives and servants. The Prophet has decreed that as your fate."

"Each fighter can choose two wives and a servant from among the women. Of those that remain, we will select several to serve the camp. The rest shall be sold. So, make yourselves attractive to my men or you will end up as slaves in Yemen and Saudi Arabia."

Inaya, standing near the crowd of girls spoke up. "You cannot sell us. We are people, not sheep or goats to be sold in a market. It is not right to sell people."

Her words were met by murmurs of agreement from many of the other girls.

Aljibal jumped down from the pickup truck and strode over to Inaya. He towered over her, a menacing presence.

She did not flinch.

This angered him even more. "Allah has cursed you all by making you women. That you are our prisoners is the will of Allah. I can do anything I want with any one of you or all of you. Your words and attitude have earned you special treatment." He drew his Makarov pistol and pointed it at her. He fired point-blank into Inaya's face. The bullet exited the back of her skull. She fell backward onto the ground.

Aljibal, in a fit of fury, fired the remaining seven rounds in the magazine into Inaya's face as she lay on the ground, obliterating all her facial features and shattering her skull into bone chips. Brain matter was everywhere.

Shrieks of horror arose from the crowd of girls. Some broke into tears. Others just stared in shock at the cruelty of what they had just witnessed.

Inaya's younger sister, Naila, who was standing near Inaya, fell upon her sister's body, screaming her outrage and grief at Aljibal. "You have killed her for no reason. You are worse than an animal! I hate you."

Aljibal turned to his nearest mujahideen, "I don't like her screaming. Give me your rifle."

Aljibal fired a three-round burst into Naila's back. The bullets brought an end to Naila's grief. Aljibal handed the rifle back to his mujahideen. The two sisters lay on the ground, Naila's body partly atop Inaya's mutilated form. Aljibal turned and walked away.

Blindfolded with their hands tied behind their backs, Clara and Henry realized that something terrible had just happened and began to shout at the jihadists. Clara screamed, "Do not hurt my girls!"

Henry yelled, "What have you done? You are savages to hurt these girls! They have done nothing to harm you!"

The jihadist guarding Clara hit her with his fist. "Be quiet, no talking!" he yelled.

Henry heard Clara's cry of pain and began yelling at the guards. "You are not a man to hit a woman who is tied up. You are a snake and a coward."

Clara's guard said, "If you don't keep quiet, I will hit her again." Henry stopped yelling.

Aljibal climbed back onto the bed of the pickup, his gaze sweeping the courtyard.

"Does anyone else think they can tell us what we may or may not do?" he roared. "Now is the time to speak—and collect your bullets. If you are not goats, we will turn you into something worse than goat shit."

Silence answered him, broken only by the quiet sobs of a few girls.

"Excellent," he sneered. "When my men command you, you will obey. Immediately. Without question."

He turned to his fighters. "Load the women into the trucks."

The school erupted into chaos—shouts, rifle butts slamming against bodies, warning shots cracking in the air. The girls were herded like cattle, crammed into the backs of pickup trucks and vans. Doors slammed shut, steel clanging against steel, until nearly 140 terrified children were jammed inside. A fighter stood guard in each truck bed, weapon raised to ensure no one dared to flee.

Not everyone would be taken. Two jihadists dragged the surviving female teachers and staff against a wall. The rattle of AK-47s on full automatic tore through the courtyard. When the echoes faded, bodies lay sprawled where they had fallen—teachers, Dr. Rope's village patients, and the four women who had been unlucky enough to be present. Six small children clinging to their mothers were gunned down as well, their deaths dismissed with laughter, as though it were sport.

The caravan rumbled toward the gate. Men in the lead pickup unbarred the steel doors and swung them wide. In all, the assault had lasted just seventeen minutes.

Outside, Sinjara militiamen—drawn by the gunfire—had taken positions along the road, rifles ready. The village chief saw the faces of the girls pressed against the slats of the trucks and shouted for his men to hold fire. A single shot could kill a child.

The convoy veered northeast, engines roaring, leaving Sinjara behind as it pushed toward the mountains of Pakistan and the safety of the wild terrain.

11

AL'ASAD ALJIBAL

Camp of the Haqqani Network
The Mountains of Afghanistan
Friday, July 26

Not one of the forty-two ISIS fighters under al'Asad Aljibal's command were Afghans. All were foreigners originating from eleven different countries, and almost all were ethnic Arabs. One of his Algerian fighters jokingly referred to the Haqqani Network as the Arab Foreign Legion.

They mostly looked down upon the Afghans as unreliable drug-dealing peasants, not sufficiently dedicated to the triumph of Islam, and not worthy of inclusion as equals in the Islamic Caliphate. That the fighting and destruction occurred in Afghanistan and that Afghan civilians were often collateral damage was not their concern. Life or death was all the will of Allah.

Aljibal retreated with his captives to his camp in the Afghan mountains right next to the Pakistan border. The Afghanistan-Pakistan border was established in 1896 and is known as the Durand Line, named after an agreement between Sir Mortimer Durand, representing the British Indian Raj, and the then-Afghan Amir Abdur Rahman Khan. Today, both the Afghans and the Pakistanis feel as if they were cheated out of territory in the 1896 agreement. Yet the line remains.

Proximity to the border serves two excellent purposes for Aljibal's camp. First, in the event of an attack on their camp, they could retreat into the safe haven of Pakistan. Second, any military supplies that they might need were available from the Pakistani army or their ISI intelligence service, both of which were supportive of ISIS, the Haqqani Network, and the Taliban.

Henry and Clara Wilson, still blindfolded and with their hands tied behind their backs, were the first people unloaded from the trucks.

Aljibal ordered, "Take them to the clearing."

Jubal approached Aljibal. "Are we going to demand a ransom for the Wilsons?"

"No. The Americans will expect a ransom demand. They are wrong. I intend to put these two pieces of shit on trial. Then we will kill them."

While being led to the clearing, a large open area in the ISIS camp, Clara stumbled and fell on the uneven ground. "Christ! Get this blindfold off me so I can see where I'm going."

"No talking!" shouted the guard and punched Clara on the side of the face. She cried out in pain.

Henry heard the blow and Clara's cry of pain. "You cowards! You hit a woman who is blindfolded, with her hands tied behind her back."

Another guard slammed the butt of his rifle into Henry's stomach. Henry was knocked to the ground. He gagged and doubled over in pain, unable to breathe. "When we say no talking, we mean no talking. Now shut up or I will hit you again." For emphasis, he kicked Henry in the back.

Dr. Rope was sure the kick had cracked a rib because every breath was now very painful.

Finally, Clara and Henry were led into the clearing. The Wilsons were tied back-to-back to a heavy post set firmly into the dirt at one side of the clearing. A guard was posted, and they were again ordered, "No talking."

The girls were herded out of the trucks and driven to the center of the clearing. They huddled together, trembling, the memory of Inaya and Naila's fate raw in their minds. The murders of their teachers still echoed like gunfire in their ears.

The raiders fanned out, forming a ragged circle, rifles leveled.

Aljibal climbed onto the bed of a pickup and raised his voice above the silence. "We have taken you because it is Allah's will," he thundered. "We take what we need to restore the Islamic Caliphate. From this moment, you belong to us. Each of my men will claim two wives and a servant girl. You will obey. Any resistance will be answered with death. Remember what became of the two whores who defied me."

He swept a hand toward his men. "Choose. Do not fight among yourselves, this trash is not worth it. There are plenty."

A murmur of anticipation rippled through the gunmen. They moved in, grabbing girls by the arms, pulling them into groups of three. Some chose at random, scarcely looking at the terrified faces.

Even Aljibal seized three. One of them, Saroya, a shy fourteen-year-old, cowered as he loomed over her. Out of sheer cruelty, he drove his fist into her head and sent her sprawling into the dirt.

"You will do as I command," he spat at his captives. "Disobey, and you will suffer worse. Your duty is obedience. Now, follow me."

When the frenzy ended, about twenty girls were left standing alone in the clearing, unchosen. A heavy silence fell over them. Their dread was palpable. Whatever fate awaited them, it would not be mercy.

*   *   *

An hour later al'Asad Aljibal decided it was time to tell the world of his great conquest. First, he commanded Jubal on how to set up the scene and which people he wanted in which positions. Then he ordered, "Summon everyone to assemble in the clearing. Bring the prisoners. Get the video camera."

In a few minutes, a large crowd of people was in the center of the camp. All of the girls had found some piece of cloth with which to cover their faces. They still wore their school uniforms and light blue head scarves. No one had a burqa. Burqas with proper Islamic modesty would come later. Some of the girls had already been forced to have sex with their new masters. Those who resisted were beaten then raped. It was a crowd of defeated women and triumphant men.

Henry and Clara Wilson were brought to the front of the crowd and forced to kneel on the ground. Their hands were still bound behind their backs. They were still blindfolded. Additional ropes were now tied around their ankles, and then another rope was used to restrain their elbows tightly behind their bodies. Clara screamed from the pain of the elbow rope. Henry gritted his teeth and made no sound.

A masked mujahideen stood behind each of them, rifles pointed at their heads.

Aljibal stood on an upended wooden ammunition crate about two feet high to address the crowd. He wore camouflaged military fatigues. The lower half of his face was hidden behind a cloth across his nose and mouth. Only his eyes were visible and they radiated evil.

All the Haqqani fighters were similarly hidden behind cloths on the lower parts of their faces, or they were wearing balaclavas. Only their eyes were visible.

The battery-powered video camera slowly panned the assembled crowd, then the Wilsons, and then focused on Aljibal standing on his makeshift podium.

Speaking in a very loud voice, he proclaimed, "I am al'Asad Aljibal, the Lion of the Mountains. We are the holy warriors of the Haqqani Network of the Islamic Caliphate. Allah has directed us to re-establish his rule on Earth. We are invincible for Allah is with us. Such is the will of Allah, so it shall be.

"The Prophet, *Sal Allaahu Alaiyhi wa Sallam*, has written in the Holy Koran that women are to be under men, to bear them sons to be raised as holy warriors, that they shall do men's bidding and prepare their meals, that they shall lie with their men when the men feel the need of them. The sages have taught us that to educate women is to waste knowledge on ignorant beings who are incapable of learning. Better we should teach a camel to read than to waste such efforts on a woman.

Aljibal stood high on his ammunition crate, his voice cutting across the terrified crowd.

"Before us stand the women these two American dogs sought to corrupt at the Pashto School. We raided their school, and we have taken all the women we require.

"Clara Wilson—an American whore who dared to call herself a teacher—filled their minds with poison, teaching them to become Western whores like herself. Today she is no teacher. Today she is nothing. She is garbage—American garbage.

"Her husband, Henry Rope Wilson, pretended to be a healer, a friend to Muslims. In truth, he is a defiler of women and children, the very face of the American enemy. He too is in our hands, and he is lower even than the garbage that is his wife. He is slime.

"These women will now fulfill their destiny as commanded in the Holy Koran. They will serve our men, cook our meals, bear our sons, and honor Allah in the true way.

"As for Clara and Henry Wilson—they will stand before a court of holy men. If found innocent, they may live. If guilty, they will die."

A chorus of cries rose from the girls—"No! No!"—their terror piercing the air. They all knew the verdict was certain. The fighters answered with cheers, bullets cracking into the sky.

Aljibal lifted his arms. "Such is the fate of unbelievers who defile Islamic virgins. Islam judges. Islam punishes. The Caliphate will rise again. By Allah's grace we are invincible. Allahu akhbar! Allahu akhbar! Allahu akhbar!"

The chant rolled across the clearing, picked up by every mujahideen fighter. Rifles blazed skyward, black smoke drifting in the heat. Behind the camera, the videographer caught the last triumphant cries, then faded to black.

Al'Asad Aljibal jumped down from the crate. "Get that video to Al Jazeera right away. I want the world to know what we will do to the infidels when the Caliphate is triumphant."

The cameraman smiled and said, "It shall be done."

12

ARCHER M. HADLEY

United States Secretary of State
Islamabad Marriott Hotel
Islamabad, Pakistan
Friday, July 27

By 1:30 p.m., word of the massacre at the Pashto School had reached Islamabad. As the first details emerged, the scale of the tragedy left officials and journalists alike stunned into silence. Survivors—the few girls spared only because there hadn't been enough trucks—spoke in trembling voices of teachers executed against a wall, staff gunned down in their kitchens, and the brutal murders of Inaya and her sister Naila.

They told how Inaya had dared to protest, crying out against the enslavement of women. For that defiance, Aljibal's rage was unleashed upon her, his cruelty carved into her mutilated face.

Within hours, news outlets were carrying the story worldwide. The horror of the attack shocked the globe. Inaya's name spread quickly, hailed as both hero and martyr—a young girl who had stood unflinching in the face of tyranny, demanding freedom and human dignity, and paying the ultimate price.

There was great concern for the welfare of the kidnapped girls and for Clara and Henry Wilson. A ransom demand for the Wilsons was expected soon, a ransom that the United States could never pay.

Secretary Hadley was already extending confidential feelers to the Pakistanis and the Afghanis to pay any ransom that ISIS might demand.

Hours later, around 9 p.m., when Al Jazeera broadcast the video recording of the abuses of Clara and Henry Wilson, the shock only deepened.

The newspaper reporters traveling with the Secretary of State on his official visit to Pakistan wanted to know if Secretary Hadley would be making a statement. They received assurances that such a statement would be forthcoming once the shock of the news had been fully absorbed. The secretary was already on the telephone with President Decker, framing a response that would express their intention to extract punishment for the many murders that had been committed.

Almost two hours later, the press corps was notified that Secretary Hadley would make a statement the following morning in one of the smaller meeting rooms across from the main ballroom.

*   *   *

At 10 a.m., the following day, the assembled reporters and a TV crew from CNN were present in a small ballroom.

Secretary Hadley stepped up to the microphones on a lectern and paused.

An aide announced, "Ladies and gentlemen, the Secretary of State of the United States of America, Mr. Archer M. Hadley."

He waited for the scattered applause to subside. "We have received terrible news from neighboring Afghanistan. About 150 girls between the ages of 9 and 16 have been kidnapped from the Pashto School in Sinjara, Afghanistan. A video claiming that the Haqqani Network of ISIS is responsible for this atrocious crime was broadcast by Al Jazeera last night. Almost all these girls were orphans whose parents had perished in a cruel war that shows no signs of ending. These schoolgirls will be forced to marry ISIS fighters, and they will become enslaved labor and sex slaves to those cruel jihadists.

"Many of the school's women and girls have been murdered in cold blood. One brave young woman, named Inaya, protested the sale of people into slavery. She was brutally murdered, and her corpse was mutilated. Her sister Naila was also murdered in cold blood. Both were personally killed by Aljibal.

"The six Afghan policemen who were protecting the school have all been murdered.

"The school's two founders, Dr. Clara Wilson, a retired high school principal and a gifted educator, and her husband, Dr. Henry 'Rope' Wilson, a retired surgeon, have been taken prisoners and were shown being abused and brutalized by their captors in the video broadcast by Al Jazeera. They are an elderly couple who do very effective work running their school without any government funds or assistance at all.

"Also killed in the attack were many local women and six of their children, brutally murdered in cold blood.

"This vicious attack shall not go unpunished. We will find this mad dog, al'Asad Aljibal, and bring him to justice for his heinous criminal acts. I say to al'Assad: You will pay the price for your cruelty. The long arm of justice will reach you wherever you try to hide.

"Are there any questions?"

Hadley motioned to the nearest reporter. "Mr. Secretary, do we know where this Aljibal person is hiding?"

"Not yet. But we will find him. Our military people will not rest until he is either captured or killed. We will get him. His ability to move quickly is compromised by the number of people he now has. It is easy to hide forty jihadists, and a completely different task to hide 190 people. We are repositioning some of our satellites to search for him."

"Ted," Hadley motioned to another reporter in the second row.

"Are there any plans to rescue the kidnapped girls?" he inquired.

"We will do our best to try to save the girls unharmed. Unfortunately, they will suffer much abuse at the hands of their Haqqani captors. Rapes cannot be undone. The only thing we can do is to punish the perpetrators. Cruelty and trauma can be undone if we can rescue the girls in time and get them some treatment. Ideally, I would like to find these girls' homes in other Islamic countries where there is no war raging and where they can continue their development into productive members of society."

"Andrea," Hadley indicated a reporter frantically waving her hand.

"The reports from the scene of the school are that the raiders went northeast toward Pakistan. Do we intend to pursue them into Pakistan?"

"If they are in Pakistan, we will have to depend upon our ally to hunt them down."

One reporter in the pack said, "Yeah, the way they helped us get Osama bin Laden." The comment was met by bitter laughter.

An aide to Hadley stepped up to the microphones. "Ladies and gentlemen. We have run out of time. There will be time to file your stories before Secretary Hadley has to meet again with the representatives of the Pakistani government.

"Tomorrow, we depart for the airport at 6:30 p.m. Please meet in the lobby with your luggage at 6 o'clock to board the press bus. The bus will be leaving the hotel at 6:30 sharp. All luggage will be subject to a security search at the airport. Our plane will depart at 7:30 p.m., maybe sooner if we are all on board early. Make sure you are on the plane, or you will be walking home. Thank you all for your cooperation and understanding. That is all for now."

13

JUBAL EL-MADOUSH

Camp of al'Asad Aljibal
The Mountains of Afghanistan
Saturday, July 28

Jubal was checking his emails. It was a bit after 4 p.m. His first cousin, Amir el-Madoush, in Pakistan, had sent an email marked with a green dot. That meant the message was important but not critically urgent. Jubal opened the message from Amir. It read:

> Yankee Sec. State Hadley promises revenge against al'Asad.
>
> Look at CNN for the press briefing. Hadley still in Islamabad at the Marriott hotel.
>
> Leaving tomorrow, Sunday. Maybe we should send him a present before he leaves.

Jubal used his laptop to access CNN's news site and surfed until he found the press conference with Secretary of State Hadley. Hadley's speech was translated into Arabic subtitles as he spoke. He watched it twice. Then he took his laptop and went to find Aljibal.

"Rayiys (chief), Amir, my cousin, who is a big shot at Islamabad Airport, has alerted us to a statement by the American Secretary of State. I think you should watch it."

"Show me," said Aljibal. He also watched the press conference twice. Aljibal sat quietly for a few minutes. Jubal knew not to interrupt him at times like this.

Finally, Aljibal spoke, "Can we get to Islamabad before the pig leaves for America?"

"He is supposed to leave tomorrow evening. It is about 400 km to Islamabad. We would have to go through South Waziristan and drive all night. But we could do it. You have a plan?"

"He will be flying on a large jet with many people to attend to him. If we can get to the side of the runway with an RPG just as the plane is slowly taking off, maybe we can blow up the plane. It will be the only plane on the runway; all the other traffic will be held at the gates. We could blow the plane with a full load of fuel and kill a few dozen crusaders all at once. It would be worth the effort to kill the pig Hadley."

Jubal rubbed his hands together in excitement. "It is a good plan. The airport is closer to us in Rawalpindi, not really in Islamabad. We will need Amir's help with airport security, or they will not let us near the runways."

"I plan to shoot from outside the fence. Maybe we can find a spot where the sentries are sympathetic to jihad. After we shoot the plane, they can chase us, but let us escape. Contact Amir. Determine if we have any connections among the airport security personnel. If we do not, we will have to kill any security personnel who try to stop us."

Aljibal spouted instructions, "Let's get organized quickly. We will need a pickup with a six-man cab, two drivers, and two RPG tubes, along with twelve rockets, personnel to fire the rockets, blankets to conceal the rockets, and our rifles with ammunition. The RPG men can do the driving. We'll need food and water for three days."

Aljibal continued, "Don't tell Amir the plan. The fewer people who know, the safer we will be. Just get him to fix the security for us."

"It shall be done."

Jubal went into the camp. He knew exactly which men he needed. Jubal called out four names and gathered them together. He gave orders for what he wanted assembled and loaded in one pickup truck. He did not inform the men of their destination or the nature of their mission. They did not need to know.

While the men were busy following his directions, Jubal took out his laptop. A red dot email (urgent) to Amir was soon on its way:

Do we have any friends in airport security? Respond to my phone.

With or without the help of the security people, the attack on the Secretary of State was going to take place. Hadley could sleep in Hell with the other infidels. Hadley's prediction was wrong; no one was going to capture al'Assad Aljibal.

14

AL'ASAD ALJIBAL

On the road to Rawalpindi
Saturday, July 28 & Sunday, July 29

Anwar kept his eyes on the road, hands tight on the wheel. They had covered nearly 250 kilometers since leaving camp, bumping over ruts and potholes until, as they neared the capital, the pavement smoothed beneath the tires.

"We will reach the airport before dawn," al'Asad Aljibal muttered from the back seat. He leaned forward, his arm draped over the front seat, pointing out every hazard as though Anwar were blind. "Slow here. Watch that cart. Keep left—no, farther left."

Anwar clenched his jaw. The constant stream of orders grated on him, but he swallowed his irritation. Aljibal was the chief.

Every pedestrian, every road sign, every curve drew a warning from him. He was restless, shifting in his seat, his voice sharp with impatience. The men had never seen him like this before. For all his firebrand speeches, for all his certainty of Allah's favor, tonight Aljibal was jittery. Nervous. Almost afraid.

Jubal el-Madoush was also in the back seat next to Aljibal, dozing and gently snoring. The sour aroma of unwashed bodies filled the cab. The smell was something that was always with them, so none of the occupants was consciously aware of it.

Nadjim and Rafik, the other two mujahideen, were crowded into the front seat next to Anwar. Rafik was dozing against the passenger door. There was almost no conversation. Aljibal's tension was causing tension in Anwar and Nadjim, the two men who were awake. Rafik, Akram, and Jubal were sleeping; they were not affected by the boss's nerves.

The outside temperature was close to 2º C (36º F), typical of the hill country at night. During the day, it would soar close to 37º C (100º F).

Finally, Anwar suggested, "Rayiys, why don't you try to get some rest. We will need you at your best when we arrive at the airport. I promise to get us to Rawalpindi without popping the airbags."

Aljibal actually laughed. It was a short barking laugh. No one had ever heard him laugh before. Anwar and Nadjim were shocked. If only Rafik were awake to bear witness. None of the other mujahideen would believe them when they told of Aljibal actually laughing.

Anwar's comment broke the tension, and Aljibal sat back in the rear seat. "Maybe a little rest would be a good idea." He leaned back with his head on the headrest.

Nadjim glanced sideways at Anwar. Their eyes met and quietly acknowledged their mutual amazement. Neither man dared to say anything, Anwar returned his eyes to the road. They continued driving through the night in silence, two men awake, four men in shallow sleep, rockets and rifles in the bed of the truck, death in their thoughts, hate in their hearts.

15

LAURA

St. Barths, F.W.I.
Grande Saline Beach
Saturday, July 28

Icould get used to this kind of life. If I die and go to heaven, it will look like St. Barths. Jack and I have had a wonderfully relaxing time here. The food is delightful. The island is naturally beautiful and lush. The people are so friendly. The island pace of getting things done is so relaxed. And there is the perfect sun on the perfect sea. If Adam and Eve had been to St. Barths first, they never would have bothered with that damn snake and the apple. The only thing I would change would be the airport approach. Coming in over those hills and then the sudden drop to get to the end of the runway was a bit too much adrenaline rush for me.

Jack and I have made love so many times that it feels like a honeymoon. He is my man. I am his woman. We are so perfectly matched in so many ways. Yet we will surely face a shooting conflict with bad guys again one day. We will risk our lives, and it seems a shame that we might lose when we have so much to live for. But it is what we do, and if we did something else, we wouldn't be happy—we already know that life can be far more challenging and fulfilling than a

9 to 5 job—we would miss the dangers and the satisfactions of doing something bad to the bad guys of this world.

We are back on our beach. This time, we are the only people here. All our white skin has turned a delicious tan. The hotel packs us a daily lunch in a basket. We sit here on our towels, totally nude, enjoying some of the best food I have ever eaten. The small bottle of wine and the hot sun give us both a little buzz.

Jack said, "Let's go for a swim."

"Didn't your mother ever tell you to wait half an hour after eating before you go in the water?"

"Yes, she did. Mothers do that so they have another half hour of not watching to make sure their kids aren't drowning. It is part of a conspiracy that all mothers have joined."

"A conspiracy?"

"Yes. Along with such things as 'Don't run with scissors in your hand' or 'Chew your food slowly' or 'Don't play with your silverware at the table.' Stuff that begins with the line 'If I've told you once, I've told you a thousand times....'"

"That is common sense and good manners."

"Yeah. But all the mothers are in on it. That's what makes it a conspiracy."

"Next, you are going to tell me that the moon landing was a staged hoax."

"What? Do you think I'm a wingnut? I'm not a conspiracy whack-o. I just think that all mothers have voluntarily tuned into the 'Don't do that' frequency and are hearing voices in their heads to take the fun out of growing up in a risky world."

Laura laughed and said, "Okay, Nutjob. I'll go for a swim. But if I get cramps, drown, and die, it will be your fault."

"I think I can handle the guilt," Jack said as he stood up.

I just admire his body again and again. He is all muscles even though he looks so ordinary in his clothes. He reached out for my hand

and pulled me up. We wound up in a sandy, naked embrace, trading kisses and hugs. Finally, we headed for the sea.

The water was delightful. We both ran into the water and took running dives. We swam out until the water was deep enough that we could not stand. Then we went back to our hugging and rubbing. Jack had both hands on my ass and was pulling me in tight. We were kissing hard, and I could feel Jack hard against my belly. Then we both sank under the surface.

One of the drawbacks of being in excellent physical condition is that your body density is greater than that of water. You do not float. If you stop moving, you will sink.

We sank.

Then we let go of each other and came to the surface laughing.

We swam back to where we could both stand. Then we started hugging again. Hugging a naked person that you are madly in love with is a sure way of getting turned on. We were both turned on.

I said, "Let's go back to the towels. I have an idea."

We emerged from the water and walked back to our towels, holding hands.

"We are back at the towels. What is your idea?" Jack asked,

"You are going to lie on your back. I am going to get on top of you and ride you until we are both so exhausted that neither of us can walk."

I pushed Jack down on his back and sat straddling his stomach. Then I leaned forward and dangled my breasts in his face. "Start here by making nice to me and don't stop until you get to the end."

Neither of us stopped until we both got to the end together. Jack's back, my knees, and lower legs were coated with beach sand. We were almost too tired to stand. How I love that man!

16

JUBAL EL-MADOUSH

Islamabad International Airport
Rawalpindi, Pakistan
Sunday, July 29

Jubal el-Madoush phoned his cousin. Amir glanced at the caller ID—Jubal. He answered, and there were no pleasantries.

"We're here," Jubal said. "Do we have anyone in airport security we can trust?"

Amir answered, "There are several. Some are pre-boarding, conducting security checks on passengers before they enter the departure area. Some are ramp personnel. Others are mechanics or baggage handlers. Some are on perimeter security on the airport exterior."

"I need to contact the ones on the perimeter security detail. Do you have some names for me?"

"I cannot say names on the telephone. I will get someone to meet you at the fence of runway 10R. That is the runway farthest away from the terminal. Can you be there in 30 minutes? He will wait for you."

"Make it 45 minutes. We want to have a quick look at the layout before we make any plans."

"Fine, 45 minutes. He is an army officer and will be in a Land Rover 4x4."

Forty-five minutes later, the pickup truck drove slowly along the perimeter fence alongside the runway. About a kilometer away, a Land Rover with one military man was sitting next to the fence on the outside. The Rover was painted in desert tan camouflage. Almost every two minutes, a jetliner was landing or taking off. The Islamabad Airport was a busy place.

The airport has two parallel runways, oriented essentially east-west. Approaching from the east, the runways are designated 28L and 28R (280° heading on the aircraft's compass—the last '0' is dropped from the runway number). From the west, the runways are 10L and 10R (100° compass heading). The runway designations are painted in large numbers at the ends of each runway, making them easily identifiable from the air.

This morning the winds were coming from the east. All the air traffic was landing and taking off into the wind from west to east, so the 10L and 10R designations were being used by the air traffic controllers.

"I will do the talking," Aljibal commanded. "Don't say anything unless you think we are making a mistake that needs to be corrected or there is something that needs to be clarified. Cover your faces."

"As you wish, Rayiys." The men all nodded in agreement.

A minute later, they drew up next to the Land Rover. Aljibal greeted the army colonel in the Land Rover. "*As-salamu alaykum*" (Peace be with you).

"*As-salamu alaykum*", returned the colonel.

"The American Secretary of State's plane will be taking off soon. Can you arrange for it to take off from the runway nearest to the fence? And can you arrange for the sentries to be elsewhere when the plane is taking off?"

"That can be done. I do not want to know what you plan to do. But after you do it, my soldiers will have to chase you. My men will be in a Land Rover, similar to this one. They will fire many rounds at you, but all the bullets will be high and wide of you. If you return fire, do not harm them. Make sure you miss them."

"When they chase us, we will fire a rocket into the ground well in front of their Land Rover. They should not have any rockets, and our rocket should be an excuse for them to quit the pursuit."

"That is good. Just do not harm my men. The plane the Americans are using is white on top, blue on the bottom, and has United States of America painted above the windows. As a normal courtesy to an important government visitor, we would stop all other traffic while his plane was taking off. There will be no doubt as to which plane he is on. I do not want to know your plan, but may Allah guide your hands."

"Thank you, Colonel. We are all doing Allah's work today. *Subhan Allah* (Glory to God)!"

"*Allahu Akbar*, (God is great)" answered the colonel as he started his engine and drove away.

Anwar spoke. "Rayiys, we do not know what you want us to do when the Americans take off."

"When the plane reaches the end of the runway, it will pause before takeoff. That's when you stand in the bed of the pickup—high enough to see over the fence. Wait until it begins to roll. It will move slowly at first. On my command, fire at the fuselage just above the wing. The fuel tanks are there. If we strike true, the plane will erupt in flames, and every American aboard will die.

"As soon as I give the order to fire, Rafik will accelerate. Anwar, you drop down and reload the RPG—we'll need it when airport security responds. Remember, those sentries are sympathetic to us. Jubal, you will fire one rocket into the ground ahead of their truck. That is the signal for them to break off pursuit. They'll shoot, but not to kill. And we must not return fire. This is for show, nothing more.

"Now, let's prepare the rockets and wait for the moment to strike."

17

ARCHER M. HADLEY

United States Secretary of State
Islamabad Marriott Hotel
Islamabad, Pakistan
Sunday, July 29

Field Marshal Hakim Mouhammed Bouradin intentionally arrived ten minutes late for his 9:00 a.m. meeting with Secretary Hadley at a conference room in the Islamabad Marriott Hotel. He entered the room with his entourage of officers. "Good morning, Mr. Secretary. I have good news. President Harraf has ordered the release of the research vessel and the crew. I believe they have already left Pakistan."

Hadley was sitting at a wide conference table. On a post-it note, he wrote "confirm" and passed it to an aide. The aide immediately left the conference room. "That is good," said Hadley. "What would have been better is if they had never been seized at all. Now that we have that behind us, let us proceed."

"Your people must navigate more carefully in the future," offered the field marshal.

Hadley, who had thought the subject was behind him, was clearly annoyed. "Our satellite images definitely show the vessel was in international waters when your naval vessel intercepted it. There was no error of navigation on the part of the American vessel. Nor was there any error of perception on the part of the Pakistani naval vessel. We both know where the research ship was when your navy intercepted it. It was an unwarranted provocation on the high seas. If you wish to argue this further, we can be here all day. Are you ready to proceed with today's meeting, or would you like to rehash your provocation against free passage of vessels in international waters? If you insist upon defending an indefensible position, I have other things I can do with my time. Let me know what you prefer to do."

The field marshal was offended by Hadley's tone. He was not used to being addressed so bluntly. To be spoken to in such a manner in front of his own staff officers was a great loss of face. He was weighing his pride against the promise of a few billion dollars of free military hardware. He opted for the hardware. "Let us proceed to today's agenda," he said.

Hadley nodded his agreement. "The first item is that we are prepared to offer five coastal patrol vessels."

"Before I agree to that, what is the rest of the picture?"

"We will also offer you 16 A-10 Warthog aircraft with support equipment. These planes will offer you an advanced defensive capability plus advanced support for ground troops."

"We would rather have one squadron of the F-35 Lightning II's this year and another squadron next year," countered the field marshal.

"The F-35's are reserved for NATO partners. They are not on the table now or even in the near future. The A-10 Warthog is a proven aircraft that provides excellent defensive capabilities without disrupting the military balance between Pakistan and India. You already have 24 A-10 aircraft, and these planes will augment your close air support capability."

"I will need advice from President Harraf before I accept such an offer. It is clearly not in Pakistan's best interests." The field marshal intended to continue negotiations at a future date.

"Well, it is in the best interests of the United States to maintain the balance between you and your neighbors. If you want to deal with

China or Russia, they will sell you anything you want, but they will also demand payment in hard currency, dollars, euros, or Swiss francs. And you will have to put up with their troops and spies on your territory. If you decide to go that route, then this offer will also require payment in dollars. You can accept this as part of our foreign aid package and maintain the strategic military balance. Alternatively, you can deal with China and Russia to purchase whatever you want, but if you do, then our equipment will no longer be a gift. You can purchase our equipment with hard currency cash, with no terms or loans. It is your choice." Hadley was clearly done with the negotiations, even if the field marshal did not yet know it.

"You are departing for the United States this evening. I will communicate our answer after you have returned home."

"That is acceptable. There is no hurry," said Hadley.

"The government of Pakistan has prepared a luncheon for both our parties in the ballroom of this hotel. Will you be so kind as to be our guests?"

"Thank you. We will be happy to attend."

With that, the formal business of the day was completed. Everyone rose and walked to the lunch that awaited them.

The secretary turned to one of his aides and quietly directed, "Summarize what was said today and get a message off to state. Don't soft-pedal it with diplomatic niceness. Make it blunt like today's exchanges."

18

AL'ASSAD ALJIBAL

Islamabad International Airport
Rawalpindi, Pakistan
Sunday, July 29

Planning for the attack on Secretary of State Hadley's plane was complete. All was ready.

Aljibal spoke to his mujahideen. "When the plane is loaded and ready to roll to the runway, Jubal will receive a telephone call to alert us. When the message is received, the pickup truck will drive to the fence at the end of the runway to await the plane. The airport perimeter security detail will be absent during this time. The attack will take place, and the security detail will chase us with no intention of intercepting or catching us. All parties will be firing at each other for show. You are not to aim at the security detail. Shoot well above their heads. They will be shooting over our heads as well. We will fire one rocket into the ground ahead of their Land Rover. This will be a signal that they should not pursue us any further. We will then make our escape.

"Anwar will stand in the back with me. He will fire our only white phosphorous RPG at the plane. The white phosphorus will explode the plane's fuel tanks. Rafik will be driving the truck. When I give the command to fire, Anwar will fire the rocket, and then Rafik will drive the truck away in our escape. Akram will be in the cab with Rafik.

Jubal will be with me in the back of the pickup. If we are chased by perimeter security, Jubal will fire the rocket that convinces the security guards not to follow us. Jubal will only fire his RPG when I give the command. We will reload the RPG's immediately in case we need them again. Are there any questions?"

Nobody asked a question. The plan was simple and well understood by all the men. The only thing was to wait for the infidel Hadley to be within range of a jihadist rocket.

19

ARCHER M. HADLEY

United States Secretary of State
Islamabad Marriott Hotel
Islamabad, Pakistan
Sunday, July 29

At 6:30 p.m., Hadley entered the black limo sent over from the embassy. The car had bulletproof glass, armored doors, armor in the fenders, the roof, the engine compartment, and the undercarriage. In addition to run-flat tires, it also had several electronic systems that would never be found in a privately owned automobile.

As he settled in the rear seat with two aides, Marta 'Jimmy' James and George Sinclair facing him in jump seats, he declared, "This whole trip was a waste of precious time. The Pakistanis are not our friends, and no amount of free military hardware will ever make them want to cooperate with us. We could have done the whole thing with three telephone calls. A total waste of time."

"Well, at least there was some face-to-face animosity, so we know who the nasty guys are. And you got to call them out on Directorate S, too," commented Jimmy.

"Do you think because I told him we know what Directorate S is doing that they will stop doing it? I doubt that. They'll just do it in greater secrecy."

"Don't overlook the fact that you got them to release the oceanographic research boat and crew," observed Sinclair.

"We used the carrot of military aid as an incentive to get their freedom. If Bouradin had balked, I was fully prepared to use the stick of withholding any aid at all to bring him around. Fortunately, he saw what was to his advantage and he gave in to our demands. In truth, seizing the ship in the first place was an act of petty aggression to show us that they can assert their dominance over their coastal waters. They also wanted to show their continuing animosity toward all things Indian."

Hadley addressed the Marine officer sitting next to the driver, "Captain, let's get to the airport. I want to get out of Dodge as soon as possible."

"Yes, sir, Mr. Secretary. I was just waiting for the Pakistani motorcycle escort to form up properly. Should be another two to three minutes, and we can get rolling."

"Okay. We are in your capable hands."

Three minutes later, the captain radioed, "Let's roll." The motorcade, comprising three limousines, a bus for the press corps, four escort motorcycles leading the way, and four more motorcycles bringing up the rear, rolled out for Islamabad International Airport in Rawalpindi. Flashing lights and sirens announced to the public that someone important was commandeering the road.

The Secretary of State's party arrived at the airport, a joint facility of Nur Khan Air Force Base and Islamabad International Airport. The motorcade entered the airport through the Nur Khan AFB gates and rolled directly onto the tarmac in the military area, where the official American airplane was parked.

Despite the earlier announcement that there would be a security check of baggage prior to boarding, no such check was conducted. Pakistani air force ground personnel began unloading luggage from the bus onto a baggage conveyor that ran up to the plane's cargo hold.

The secretary and his official party boarded the plane via the front stairway; the press group boarded via the rear stairway. Twenty-five minutes later, the plane was ready for takeoff.

Air Force Lt. Col. Evan Singleton, the pilot, radioed the tower, "AF-5 ready to taxi. Request clearance to take off."

The tower responded, "Air Force 5, you will be using runway 10R. There will be a 10-minute delay while we clear the airspace for you. Taxi to holding area J16 and wait for clearance. When the traffic has been cleared, you will receive immediate clearance for departure on runway 10R."

Colonel Singleton repeated, "Waiting area J16, runway 10R. Roger tower."

On the plane's internal PA system, he announced, "This is Lt. Col. Singleton on the flight deck. We will be taxiing to a waiting area in preparation for takeoff in 10 minutes. Please make sure your seatbelts are fastened and that all loose items are safely stowed. Power off all electronic devices. Please put your phones in airplane mode until after we are airborne. Once we are airborne, you can power up your devices again. Sit back, relax, and enjoy the flight."

The engines revved momentarily until the 767 began to roll slowly from its parking spot toward area J16."

20

AL'ASAD ALJIBAL AND JUBAL EL-MADOUSH

Islamabad International Airport
Rawalpindi, Pakistan
Sunday, July 29

Jubal's phone buzzed.

"It is rolling," Amir said, then cut the line.

"The plane is loaded," Jubal announced. "Let's move."

The pickup eased down the dirt track beside runway 10R, its six occupants tense but trying not to draw attention. Rafik drove, with Akram beside him in the passenger seat. In the back, al'Asad Aljibal crouched near the cab, directing every move. Anwar, the RPG gunner, knelt beside him with the launcher braced on his shoulder. Nadjim huddled close, two armed rockets in his hands, ready to reload at a word. At the tailgate, Jubal el-Madoush waited with a second RPG, positioned to cover their retreat.

They reached the far end of the runway five minutes before the secretary's plane was due. Rafik swung the truck in a U-turn so it faced back the way they had come. The Haqqanis' single white phosphorous rocket was already seated in Anwar's tube, its purpose simple and devastating: ignite the fuel tanks.

The men crouched in silence, weapons ready, as the whine of jet engines grew closer.

The sounds of the airport dropped away to background noise as the traffic was diverted for Secretary Hadley's plane. Within a few minutes, the blue and white plane bearing the words United States of America on the fuselage arrived at the end of runway 10R. Slowly, it turned into the wind in preparation for takeoff. The engines revved to a roar while the pilot stood on the brakes. The plane could be seen vibrating from the power of the engines.

Aljibal ordered everyone to stand and for Anwar to take aim at the passenger's area just above the wing.

The plane started to roll.

Aljibal shouted "*Atlak alnaar* (shoot)!"

Through the open driver's window, Rafik heard the command. He slammed the accelerator and popped the clutch, jolting the truck forward.

Anwar pulled the trigger at that exact moment. The lurch spoiled his aim. The rocket streaked over the plane, arced upward, and slammed harmlessly into the terminal building nearly a kilometer away.

"Shoot again!" Aljibal roared.

Jubal swung around from the tailgate, steadied himself as best he could on the bouncing truck, and fired. His rocket also missed the plane. Instead, it struck the last of six baggage trailers being towed across the tarmac. The explosion shredded the cart, scattering clothing and suitcases in every direction. A goat in the second trailer smashed out of its flimsy cage and bolted wildly across the airfield. The driver of the electric tug leaped clear and sprinted for cover.

Sirens wailed. Alarm bells clanged. The airport locked down in seconds, bracing for a terrorist assault.

Rafik sped the pickup down the dirt track. In the back, Aljibal seethed, his fury focused squarely on Rafik. The truck had moved too soon. The attack had failed. Rafik would pay.

Nadjim gave Anwar and Jubal another rocket each, and they reloaded their launch tubes.

In the space of less than a minute, the pilot of the plane reached takeoff speed, rotated the yoke, and was airborne and out of range of the RPGs.

The crew and occupants of the plane were completely unaware that an attack had taken place behind them.

To observers, the attack appeared to be at the rear of the terminal buildings where the airliners were loading passengers. The security personnel at the perimeter did not chase the pickup truck; instead, they headed toward the terminal buildings.

Blouses and shirts billowed with the wind, skimming across the tarmac like restless tumbleweeds. Pages from a traveler's scattered papers twisted upward in wild, circling gusts. The luggage trailer roared in flames, the air thick with the acrid stench of melting plastic and burning cloth.

Fire crews held back, unwilling to risk themselves for a burning luggage cart while a terrorist attack might still be unfolding. The trailer burned for ten minutes before a fire truck finally advanced, dousing the flames with a stream of foam.

Aljibal's pickup truck left the area of the airport with no pursuers. A safe distance away, Rafik stopped the truck. Aljibal leaped out of the rear of the truck and ran to the driver's door. He jerked it open, grabbed the front of Rafik's robe, and hauled Rafik out of the cab. "You fool! You allowed the crusaders to escape! Why did you start the truck so soon?"

"I am s-sorry, Rayiys," stammered Rafik. "When I heard you order shoot, I thought I was supposed to start moving."

"You'll receive 100 lashes for your failure to follow my orders. You'll suffer for this."

Aljibal said to the other man in the cab, "Akram, you drive. This piece of shit is too stupid to drive a truck."

Turning to his men, he said, "Stow everything as it was. Remove the fuses from the rockets so they are safe to handle. Then get in the truck."

Jubal supervised the loading. When it was done, he said, "Rafik, you get in the bed of the pickup truck. You will ride back to camp on the outside. If you are lucky you will freeze to death before the Rayiys punishes you."

Jubal and al'Assad Aljibal sat in the front seat with Akram while he drove. Anwar and Nadjim were in the back seat. The disgraced Rafik was in the bed of the pickup. Aljibal was burning with fury. They were a subdued and deflated group. No one dared to say a word lest they incur his wrath.

21

LT. COL. EVAN SINGLETON, USAF

Aboard Flight Air Force 5
Punjab Province, Pakistan
Sunday, July 29

"Islamabad tower, this is Air Force 5 requesting permission to climb to 35,000 feet."

The tower responded, "Air Force 5. Do whatever you want. The airport is under terrorist attack. We are going to shelters."

"What part of the airport was attacked?" Col. Singleton asked. The response he got was dead air. No one was at the tower to answer him.

Col. Singleton pressed a button summoning a flight attendant to the cockpit. When he arrived, he said, "Sergeant, please request Mr. Hadley to come to the cockpit. Indicate that the request is important and confidential."

The sergeant went to Secretary Hadley's compartment and knocked politely. "Enter," said the secretary.

"Sir, Lieutenant Colonel Singleton requests your presence at the cockpit. The colonel says it is important and confidential."

Hadley stood up immediately and followed the sergeant forward to the cockpit. Once there, he asked, "What is happening colonel?"

Singleton said to the copilot, "You have the plane."

The copilot answered, "I have the plane."

Then, Singleton turned to face Secretary Hadley. "Mr. Secretary, as we were taking off, we heard an alarm siren at Islamabad Airport. The tower reports that there was a terrorist attack at the airport, and they have gone off the air. The tower personnel have abandoned their posts to take shelter. This does not appear to affect us in any way. I believe we should continue our flight as planned. I thought you should know about it."

Hadley replied, "You are the captain. Whatever you think is best is what we should do. Returning to Islamabad if the airport is under attack does not make sense. Continuing the flight as long as we are all OK seems like the best plan of action. In the interest of total transparency, I think you should make an announcement on the PA so that the press people know what we know."

Roger that, Mr. Secretary. It will be done when you return to the passenger cabin."

Archer Hadley said, "Thank you for keeping me informed, Colonel." He turned and left the flight deck and returned to his compartment.

A few moments later, Singleton was on the PA system. "Ladies and gentlemen, this is Lieutenant Colonel Singleton, your pilot. I have an announcement of interest to all of us. As we were departing the Islamabad Airport, there was an apparent terrorist attack on the airport itself. We have no details of what transpired on the ground other than that we heard the sirens alerting everyone to the emergency. I found out about the attack when I radioed the tower and requested permission to go to cruising altitude. I was then informed that the tower personnel were shutting down and leaving their posts. Unfortunately, I have no other details to report. Conjecture and speculation are not skills I possess, and therefore, please don't ask me for my opinion or what might be happening on the ground. I do not know. If I get any further news, I will report it to everyone. That is all for now. Thank you for your attention."

There was immediate excitement among the press members. They had been at the airport during a terrorist attack and had departed without getting the story. Their editors would be very disappointed.

About 20 minutes later, Singleton contacted the Islamabad tower again and reported the information he had received to his passengers. "This is Lieutenant Colonel Singleton. Ladies and gentlemen, I have been in radio contact with the Islamabad tower. I was informed that two rockets were fired. One rocket burst harmlessly against the rear concrete wall of the terminal, and one rocket destroyed a baggage trailer. That was the extent of the attack. No attackers have been captured. The identities of the attackers are unknown. No one has yet claimed credit for the attack. Normal airport operations had resumed with heightened security efforts on the ground and stepped up pre-flight screening. It appears that the attack was perpetrated by incompetent terrorists. May it always be so."

The reporters filled the long hours with speculation—wild theories about who the attackers were and what they had hoped to gain by striking an airport in Pakistan. Answers would have to wait. Maybe, once they touched down at Ramstein in Germany, the truth would begin to surface.

Meanwhile, the aircraft droned steadily westward. Ramstein would be a brief stop—refueling, a new crew—before carrying Secretary Hadley and his entourage across Norway, the empty stretch of the North Atlantic, over Greenland and Newfoundland, and at last toward American soil. Home was still half a world away.

22

PRESIDENT SAMUEL DECKER

The White House
Washington, D.C.
Tuesday, July 31

President Decker was halfway through his regular Tuesday press conference at the White House. He had already fielded questions regarding the upcoming presidential election, the budget, and relations with Congress, as well as tornado disaster relief in Oklahoma, Brexit's impact on American trade, and the ongoing fighting in Iraq, Syria, and Afghanistan. Then the president opened the press conference to questions from the reporters.

Half a dozen reporters posed questions, some of them were thinly veiled gotcha questions. Decker adroitly managed to avoid all the gotchas.

Then, the anchor from NBC News' Daily Drift Show was recognized by the President. "Mr. President, the Haqqani Network of ISIS has kidnapped 120 schoolgirls and two Americans, Dr. Clara Wilson and Dr. Henry Wilson, from the Pashto School. In the process of kidnapping these people, the ISIS raiding party murdered almost two dozen unarmed civilians. What efforts are being made to liberate the Wilsons and the schoolgirls from the clutches of ISIS?"

The President was expecting this question, and was surprised that it hadn't come sooner. "Our troops in the field are gathering the intelligence we need to allow our Special Forces personnel to track al'Assad Aljibal and to conduct whatever operations are necessary to free these orphans and the Wilsons. It won't happen overnight, but it will surely happen. We won't rest our efforts until these killers are either permanently put out of action or captured and brought to justice.

"Aljibal has been a thorn in the side of the Afghan government for the past few years. His latest raid is an attempt to poke the Afghan government in the eye. He gave them a solid poke, and it hurt. Now we intend to poke him back, only harder than he poked us. We will get him and his whole murderous gang of fanatics.

"A few of you in this room have been to Afghanistan. Most of us have never been there. I've been told that Afghanistan has some of the most rugged terrain on Earth, with innumerable mountains and caves. The bad guys have lots of places to hide. Despite that, we will find them, and we will make them pay for their crimes."

A reporter from the *Chicago Sun-Times* raised her hand. The president called, "Simpson, you're next."

Matilda Simpson asked, "Mr. President, this Aljibal fellow and his gang seem to have protection from the local governments. Can you comment on that?"

President Decker frowned. "I really cannot comment on whether or not Aljibal gets official protection from the locals, but he does seem to move about with impunity wherever he wants to go. Local protection for Aljibal from our nominal allies is an area that I do not wish to explore in a news conference. Our forces will not cut him any slack. If we find him, we will deal with him without mercy. We will use our technological advantage to locate him and our military advantage to neutralize him. If the local governments cannot or will not help us, we will do it on our own. Now that we are focused on Aljibal, I confidently predict that his days are numbered. I repeat my previous comment: We will get him and his outlaw band."

The news conference moved on to other questions and other pressing matters. Al'Assad Aljibal and the Haqqani Network were not the lead items in the next day's headlines. The plight of the Wilsons and the young women of the Pashto School was relegated to the inside pages of the newspapers, if it was mentioned at all.

23

UNITED STATES SENATE CHAMBER

The Capitol
Washington, D.C.
Thursday, August 2

The Vice President, in his role as President of the Senate, rapped the gavel to open the session. Congress was set to adjourn for summer recess on Friday, August 3rd.

With his duty complete, the Vice President stepped aside. Senator Chesterbrooke, the President Pro Tempore—fourth in line to the presidency and the longest-serving senator of the majority party—took the chair and called the Senate to order.

The Majority Leader had already set the agenda at President Decker's request: the confirmation vote for Ambassador Stuart Keaton as Assistant Secretary of State for Near Eastern Affairs.

Senator Lewis of Oklahoma was the first to be recognized. Rising from his seat, he declared, "Mr. President, it is my singular honor to move that the Senate approve the confirmation of Ambassador Stuart Keaton, a native son of the great State of Oklahoma, to the office of Assistant Secretary of State for Near Eastern Affairs."

Shouts of "Second!" echoed from the floor.

Chesterbrooke nodded. "A motion has been made and seconded. We will proceed with a voice vote. All in favor of confirming

Ambassador Stuart Keaton to the post of Assistant Secretary of State for Near Eastern Affairs, say 'Aye.'"

A chorus of ayes thundered through the chamber.

"All opposed, say 'Nay.'"

Silence.

"Those who wish to abstain on this matter signify by saying present."

Again, there was silence in the Senate chamber.

"There being no nay votes and no abstentions, I hereby declare it is the unanimous sense of the Senate that Stuart Keaton is confirmed as Assistant Secretary of State for Near Eastern Affairs."

Motioning with his arm to Stuart Keaton in the visitors' gallery, Sen. Chesterbrooke said, "Congratulations, Mr. Secretary Keaton, would you kindly stand to receive the praise of the Senate."

Stu Keaton, in the gallery, stood and waved. All the senators stood and applauded Stu Keaton, as did those in the visitors' gallery and the Senate staffers. It was a very pleasant way to begin his new job.

The Senate proceeded to other matters requiring votes, some urgent, some just housekeeping and procedural votes, but all necessary before they adjourned for their summer break.

After a suitable pause of about 30 minutes, Stuart and Adelle Keaton, riding on a euphoric high, quietly made their way out of the gallery.

Once outside the Senate chamber, reality pressed upon them. They needed a place to live in the Washington area, someplace with good schools for their daughter, Suzy, and decent housing for the family. Adelle would be doing most of the house hunting, with Stu having veto power over any of her choices. Stu would be busy at state, learning his new responsibilities and helping Secretary Hadley.

Within a month school would be starting again. It was time for both of them to get to work.

24

AL'ASAD ALJIBAL

Camp of the Haqqani Network
Hills of Paktika Province, Afghanistan
Sunday, August 5

Aljibal was still angry about his failed attempt to kill the American Secretary of State. Rafik had been suitably punished with fifty lashes on the bottom of each foot. His feet were so chewed up by the lashes that he couldn't walk.

Aljibal needed something to let the world know of his successes. He had promised a trial for the Wilsons. He decided to convene a council of religious elders and put the Wilsons on trial in front of live television to be broadcast to the world. He needed help from Al Jazeera.

"Jubal, I want you to call Amir and see if he can arrange for Al Jazeera to send a camera crew up here to record the trial of the two Wilson pigs, which will be held in three days' time. I would like a live feed direct to Al Jazeera and to the world."

Jubal el-Madoush looked up from his phone where he was trying to get the day's news. "Rayiys, Al Jazeera might not be able to do what you want in only three days. Would you be willing to hold the trial when the camera crew can actually get here?"

"See when they can get a crew here."

"We would need to rendezvous in Ghazni and bring them in and out blindfolded so they could not report the location of our camp."

"That is acceptable. Let them give us a date, and we will figure it out from there. Whenever they can get here, we will have the trial. Then we'll behead the prisoners."

"I don't think we should tell that to Al Jazeera before the trial. They might not come if they think it is just an execution of prisoners. There has been too much Western criticism of Al Jazeera for broadcasting news favorable to our cause."

Aljibal was losing patience. "Just get in touch with Amir and see what he can arrange for us."

"Right away," agreed Jubal and hit his speed dial for Amir.

Amir saw the caller ID and answered on the second ring with none of the usual telephone pleasantries and no names were mentioned.

"My Rayiys wants a live TV feed from Al Jazeera for the trial of our two criminals," said Jubal. "Can your contacts arrange that?"

"I think we can do something for you," answered Amir. "When do you plan to do the trial?"

"We would like everything in place in three days. If it cannot be arranged in three days' let them tell us when they can have a crew here, and we will accommodate their schedule. This would mean bringing in their crew blindfolded so they do not see where our camp is located. I propose we rendezvous in Ghazni at the bus terminal. Their vehicle will be stored at our mutual friend's garage. We will arrange transportation from Ghazni and return the camera crew to the garage when the trial is complete. We also have to collect their cell phones and leave them at the garage so they cannot be traced by the GPS feature."

"I will get back to you with an answer, and a date if they are interested," said Amir. "My guess is they will be happy to record such a trial. I will call you with an answer very soon."

25

AL JAZEERA CAMERA CREW

Camp of the Haqqani Network
The Mountains of Afghanistan
Wednesday, August 8

Three days later, a three-man camera crew from Al Jazeera arrived in the Afghan town of Ghazni. Only first names were used.

Hussein was the director of the crew and would be in overall charge of what was sent out by video. If any narration was needed, he would also do that. Ubaid (OO-bah-eed) would man the primary camera. Nusair (Nu-sah-eer) would do technical hookups and maintain the equipment. Once the equipment was functioning properly, he would also man the secondary camera. The agreement was to send out a live signal to Al Jazeera, which would immediately broadcast whatever live signal it received. In the event the signal was not received at Al Jazeera, a simultaneous videotape would be recorded of the broadcast while the crew was shooting.

The Al Jazeera crew arrived at the bus depot, the designated rendezvous location, in a pickup truck with all their equipment loaded in the truck bed. They were met at the bus depot by a member of the Haqqani Network who led them to a garage where their truck would be hidden while they were at the camp.

The men were asked to surrender their cell phones so they could not be tracked by the standby signals. The camera crew leader explained that he had to be able to call the station when it was time to broadcast. They arrived at a compromise when he was assured he could use a phone already at the camp to make his call. The three phones were left in the pickup truck in Ghazni.

A van with blacked-out windows provided transportation for the men and their equipment. Once the men were in the van, they were blindfolded, which they had been told to expect.

The van drove south for half a kilometer, then turned east a short distance, then turned northwest, then south again, southeast, north, southwest, east, did a U-turn, and went west, then northeast. It finally turned south again and left Ghazni. The Al Jazeera crew was completely disoriented as to which direction they were heading.

Once beyond Ghazni, the van turned west for three kilometers until it met an unpaved track that angled northeast into the mountains. They followed this winding dirt track for almost 5 km until they turned northeast on a curving paved road for 16 km. Then again onto an unpaved road which eventually ended 4 km from the camp. There, they were met by a group of Haqqani fighters who would serve as porters to carry the equipment to the camp. The Al Jazeera crew was given a little food and drink and allowed to rest before trekking into the hills. Never once in their meandering trip were the blindfolds removed.

Still blindfolded, each member of the crew was guided by a fighter at his side as they climbed the mountain trail to the camp of the Haqqani Network. Once in the camp, they were led to a cave and the blindfolds were removed. It took them almost an hour to fully recover their equilibrium and steady gait.

Once the crew was rested, al'Assad Aljibal greeted the Al Jazeera men in the cave.

"I am al'Assad Aljibal. Welcome to the camp of the Haqqani Network of the Islamic Caliphate. We are here to have a trial of two Americans who have committed many crimes against Islam. You are here to show the world what Islamic justice is. Whenever you have your equipment ready, we can begin our trial. The judges and the witnesses are waiting for you."

Hussein addressed Aljibal. "I am Hussein, and I am in charge of this crew. We will need to see where the trial will take place so we can set up correctly."

He motioned toward Nusair, "Nusair is our equipment expert. He will need two men to assist him in setting up his dish and recording equipment. Ubaid is our main cameraman. Our equipment is battery-powered with a safe operating time of 45 minutes. After 45 minutes, we will need to pause the trial so we can swap in fresh batteries, or parts of the trial will not be recorded. We have enough batteries for three hours of broadcasting, but the station managers would prefer to limit the telecast to 90 minutes. It will be necessary for us to begin exactly three minutes after the hour. The station will need time to break into regular programming and announce the live feed from the trial. I will have to telephone the station to let them know one hour ahead of when we are ready to begin our broadcast."

Aljibal nodded his agreement. "Alerting the station is acceptable. When you need us to pause for a battery change, draw your hand across your throat to indicate cut and we will stop for you. I do not believe we will have a lengthy trial. Our evidence is strong, and the judges know what we are hoping to accomplish."

"Then let us start setting up our equipment now," said Hussein. His unspoken thought was about the judges knowing what was expected from them. Some trial this was going to be.

Nusair and Ubaid began unpacking cases. Nusair explained, "The first thing we must do is set up our portable dish antenna aimed at Afghansat. Without the dish, no signal will be broadcast." He unfolded a tripod and set it up.

Next came a segmented parabolic dish antenna that he unfolded by rotating the segments around the center portion. The dish was then mounted on top of the tripod. He took out a hand-held device that he used to scan the sky until he picked up a signal from the satellite. Skillfully, he angled the dish until it was receiving the maximum strength signal. When he was satisfied, he used a wrench to tighten all the bolts on the dish and tripod, locking the dish in position. He again checked the signal. Satisfied, he returned the hand-held device to its case. Then he began stretching cables to connect the various elements of equipment.

While Nusair set up the backup recorder, Ubaid was setting up the two portable cameras. Shortly, all of the equipment was ready.

All three of the Al Jazeera men went to find Aljibal to get the layout of the trial.

Aljibal brought them to the clearing. "There will be five holy men as the judges at this end of the clearing. They will sit behind a table over there. The accused will be here. I will be the prosecutor, and I will stand there. The prosecution witnesses will be near the accused so they can point at the guilty party when they speak. My fighters and the camp people will stand behind the main speakers to view the trial."

Hussein nodded his understanding. "We will need to hook you up with a small wireless microphone attached to your clothing. We will need similar microphones on the accused, on the main judge, and a boom microphone for the prosecution witnesses. Will there be a person to represent the accused Americans?"

"No. They can speak for themselves."

"We will need another half hour to set up the sound equipment, and then we will be ready to go ahead."

Nusair addressed Aljibal, "I will do your microphone first and show you how to turn it on and off. Then the chief judge and finally the Americans. Ubaid will set up the boom microphone. He will need one of your men to help him. It will take me ten minutes to get the lapel microphones ready. Will you be nearby?"

"I will be here watching everything," said Aljibal.

To Ubaid, Nusair said, "Let's get the equipment we need." They both walked to another case and began unpacking it.

Shortly after 2 p.m. everything was set to go. Camera angles had been decided. Nusair would video the prosecutor and the judge, zooming in or out as needed. Ubaid would keep his camera on the two accused defendants. Hussein would sit at a small console and decide which camera's image was to be broadcast at any given moment. He could also decide to do a split screen with both cameras broadcasting simultaneously. He borrowed a phone and called the main station of Al Jazeera. He was told that they would go on the air at three minutes after 3 p.m. Hussein had 55 minutes to get everyone properly situated.

Aljibal was informed of the time requirements.

The judges, five *mullahs*, took their places. The accused Americans, Clara Wilson and Henry Wilson, were brought out and tied to folding wooden chairs placed side by side. Their microphones were switched to the on position.

Aljibal was in position, and his microphone was live. The chief judge was also wired up and turned on.

The kidnapped girls, all wearing burqas and dark veils, were milling about speaking to each other in subdued voices. Armed mujahideen stood behind the accused and in a perimeter around the girls. All of the fighters had the lower halves of their faces covered.

At 3 p.m. Al Jazeera announced the trial for its listeners. Two commentators acted as anchors, explaining the nature of the trial and identifying the participants. Particular emphasis was paid to the fact that this was a live broadcast without editing or corrections. The viewer was seeing it as it happened.

At three minutes after 3 p.m., Hussein gave Aljibal the signal to start.

Aljibal, the lower half of his face covered with a cloth, began in a loud voice, "I am al'Assad Aljibal, the Lion of the Mountains, leader of the Haqqani Network of the Islamic Caliphate. Today, we are gathered for the trial of Clara Wilson and Henry Wilson, two Americans who have violated the teachings of the Holy Koran and who have defiled the minds and bodies of Islamic virgins.

"The accused will be tried before a court of five holy men who will hear the witnesses and will decide the guilt and punishment to be delivered to the accused."

The chief judge, who was sitting at the center of the five judges, said, "Recite the charges against the accused."

Aljibal held up a sheet of paper from which he began reading. "The accused, Clara Wilson, is a Christian who pretends that she is a teacher of children. She has filled the heads of young women with ideas that are contrary to the words of the Prophet, *Sal Allaahu Alaiyhi wa Sallam*. She has taken them away from the true path of Islam by teaching the girls to read and write, teaching them arithmetic, diverting them from domesticity, and making them think they are independent of men and not subservient to men. In the words of the ancient sages, 'it is better to teach a camel to read than to waste such effort on a woman.' She has taught them immodesty. They did not cover their faces in her school, nor did they wear the burqa. They sang songs and listened to music. She did not isolate them when they were unclean in the eyes of Allah.

"The accused Henry Wilson is a Christian who pretends to be a physician and healer. He is a rapist and a defiler of virgins. He has looked upon the faces and bodies of Islamic women. He has ministered to Islamic women with improper modesty procedures. He has defiled children with his hands on their forbidden parts. He laughs and sings songs. He teaches young girls to be prostitutes.

"We ask the court to find the accused guilty of blasphemy against Islam and that a proper punishment be decreed."

The chief judge asked, "Do you have any witnesses against the accused?"

Aljibal answered, "The witnesses are present." He motioned for a small group of ten girls to step forward. Aljibal had chosen these ten at random. "These are ten of the girls who have been raped by the accused Henry Wilson and who have been taught immodest behavior by the accused Clara Wilson."

The chief judge addressed the first girl in line, "When did Henry Wilson rape you?"

The girl answered, "Dr. Wilson never raped me. The only person who ever raped me is my new husband. He beats me every day and forces sex upon me against my will."

A stunned silence greeted these words. Every sound was picked up by the boom microphone and broadcast to the world.

The other girls who were witnesses said variously, "She is right." "That is the truth." "He never hurt us in any way." Many of the girls standing in the crowd shouted their agreement.

Aljibal was livid. "See how they have all been brainwashed by these two American devils. They are afraid to confront them for their crimes. They fear retribution."

"Do you have any other witnesses?" asked the judge.

"No. I could bring every one of these girls before you, but these ten are enough to show you how they have been abused by the accused."

The judge addressed Clara, "Do you have anything to say in your defense?"

Clara sneered at the judge, "What kind of court is this? We sit here tied like goats in a slaughterhouse while he spouts lies to this court. There will be no justice here today. I have taught these girls to be prepared for life in the modern world. I have taught them that they are people who deserve respect by virtue of being human beings. I have taught them that there is no shame to be a woman. If those things are crimes, then I am guilty."

To Henry, the judge repeated his question, "Henry Wilson. Do you have anything to say in your defense?"

Henry looked at the judges and said, "Would you believe anything I would say? I have never improperly touched any of these girls. I have cared for their health with the limited means I had available. I have never raped anyone. The charges are false."

Aljibal, as prosecutor, sneered, "The accused Clara Wilson has admitted her guilt to the court. The accused Henry Wilson continues to lie to the court. Before the witness of the world, they must be found guilty of their crimes."

The judge said, "The court will convene and make a decision."

The five judges stood together behind the table. The chief judge asked each judge for their vote.

Each judge said, "guilty." The voices were all picked up on the chief judge's microphone.

"What should the punishment be?"

In turn, each judge said "death."

"Then we are agreed," said the chief judge.

All the judges resumed their places at the table. The chief judge intoned, "It is the unanimous decision of the court that the accused are guilty of having committed blasphemy against Islam. It is the unanimous decision of the court that they shall be sentenced to death by beheading."

Shouts of "NO!" "NO!" "NO!" arose from the assembled girls. Many broke into tears.

Aljibal said to the two fighters behind Clara and Henry, "You have heard the decision of the judges. Carry out the sentence on Clara Wilson."

Clara screamed, "Noooo!"

Henry shouted, "You are a coward to execute a woman who has done no harm to anyone. For this sin you shall burn in Hell. Take me instead. Let her live."

The man behind Henry grabbed his hair and turned his head toward Clara, forcing him to face his wife.

Aljibal laughed. "She will die. You will watch her die. Then you will die. Both of you will go to Hell before I do."

The man standing behind Clara grabbed her hair and pulled her head back. He took a large knife from his waist and drew it across Clara's throat. The knife severed her jugular veins and carotid arteries and her trachea. As blood and her life spurted forth, her body gave an involuntary spasm. The executioner maintained his grip on her hair.

Some of Clara's blood spurted onto Henry's face and clothing. He squeezed his eyes shut and shuddered at the horror of what his wife was suffering. The video camera captured every second of the horror.

The man behind Clara kept sawing at her lifeless body until he severed her spine and her head was no longer attached to her body. Triumphantly, he held up Clara's head by her hair, blood dripping from the neck, and shouted, "*Allahu akhbar! Allahu akhbar! Allahu akhbar!*"

Horrified screams erupted from the girls in the crowd. Aljibal's men cheered. One of the mujahideen fired off a full clip from his rifle on full automatic into the air.

Aljibal, still the prosecutor, yelled, "Carry out the sentence of death on the American defiler of women and virgins." The camera switched to focus on Henry.

The executioner behind Henry, firmly gripping Henry's hair, took his knife from his belt.

Henry screamed at Aljibal, "I curse your evil soul! You are worse…" At that moment, the executioner drew his knife across Henry's throat. Blood spurted everywhere. Henry's dying words remained unspoken.

The executioner kept sawing at Henry's neck, but the muscles and tendons were tougher than Clara's, and it took almost twice as long to sever Henry's head. When the beheading was done, he too held up his victim's head and shouted, "*Allahu akhbar! Allahu akhbar! Allahu akhbar!*" Rifles were fired into the air, and men cheered.

The girls, deeply shocked, wept and hugged their sisters.

Aljibal shouted, "This concludes the court. Justice has been done to the enemies of Islam. Allah has been avenged! *Allahu akhbar! Allahu akhbar! Allahu akhbar!*"

From start to finish, the trial and executions of Clara Wilson, Ed. D., and Henry Wilson, M.D., took less than 25 minutes. The video finished with a view of the headless bodies still tied to the two chairs. Then it faded to black and the live broadcast to the world of the trial and executions of Clara and Henry Wilson ended. Islamic justice and mercy were plain for all to see.

26

JACK & LAURA

St. Barthelémy, French West Indies
Gustavia Airport
Thursday, August 9

Jack and Laura boarded the small Winair plane bound for St. Maarten. They were the only passengers. The copilot was sitting alone at the controls, going over a checklist.

"R&R is over," groused Laura to Jack. "I could take a steady diet of this island."

"Do you realize we haven't seen a newspaper or watched a TV screen since we arrived here?" Jack observed. "I haven't missed the news one little bit. It is almost always bad news."

"What's the expression? 'No news is good news'? Sounds like it applies here."

"You've got that right," Jack agreed. "When we retire, we should plan on doing it in St. Barths so we won't have to listen to the bad news."

"It's an idea that has some merit. Could we afford a place here? It is pretty expensive."

"With two pensions, we might be able to do it. There are a lot of Americans who have homes in St. Barths. Of course, most of them are mega-wealthy. Maybe we can afford a grass hut on the beach somewhere."

"Oh yes," said Laura, "and then we would get arrested for vagrancy or littering the beach because we have our hut there."

"Well, it's a nice dream. I don't care where we retire so long as we're together."

"If we retire to a place where there are French chefs, I am bringing a bathroom scale to monitor my weight. I think I gained three kilos on this trip because the food was so over-the-top good. I'm going to have to work it off when we are back home."

The Winair pilot came aboard at that moment and interrupted them. "Fasten your seat belts folks. We'll be taking off in a few minutes."

The plane was so small that Jack and Laura could speak to the pilot. "Is this route always this busy?" Jack asked.

"In the summer, it is not unusual for us to fly with no passengers at all. Just the mail to and from St. Barths and some air freight. We are happy to see both of you. It justifies our jobs. However, in the winter months, we often have every seat occupied, and during school holidays up north, we have to make some extra runs to and from St. Maarten."

"The "approach to the airport over the hills is pretty hairy," Jack commented.

"The St. Barths airport is one of the most dangerous airports in the Caribbean, maybe in the world. We need special training to land here. The aircraft are STOL planes because of the steep descent coming into the airport and the short runway for takeoffs. We do a lot of seat-of-the-pants flying if there are crosswinds. We like doing it. Flying into St. Barths is a fun job. We get to carry some A-list celebrities in-season and interesting folks all year round. Most of our passengers are really nice people."

"Does anyone ever freak out when they see the plane making its approach to the airport?" Laura asked.

"Some people get frightened, but it is all over before they get to the point of starting to scream. So, we pretty much don't have that problem," the pilot said. "Most of our passengers have been here multiple times. They know what to expect, and they know they will survive the landing. Now you folks relax, and we'll be taking off in a few minutes. Enjoy the flight." The pilot went forward to the cockpit and went over the checklist from the copilot.

The twin engines coughed to life and the plane taxied out to the runway. In a few minutes they were airborne heading for St. Maarten to catch the flight to Miami and then on to Reagan National in Washington D.C. and home."

27

JACK & LAURA

Jack's House
Silver Spring, MD
Thursday evening, August 9

Jack and Laura exited U.S. Customs in Miami. They had to hurry to make their connecting flight to Reagan National Airport in Arlington, Virginia. Two hours and 20 minutes later, they were walking up the passenger concourse past the airline gates when they passed a newsstand selling newspapers, magazines, books, soft drinks, T-shirts, candy, and traveler's incidentals. Jack said, "Give me a minute, Laura. I want to get a newspaper. We haven't any clue as to what happened while we were on vacation."

Jack went into the shop, picked up a *New York Times* and a *Washington Post*. He looked at the headlines and stood there in shock.

Laura saw his face. "What's wrong, Jack? You look terrible."

Jack could hardly speak. "The Pashto School. The Wilsons have been executed. The executions were broadcast live on Al Jazeera. The students have been kidnapped by ISIS. Years ago, I sent Inaya and Naila there so they would be safe."

"Who are Inaya and Naila? What is the Pashto School?"

As he quickly scanned the front page of each newspaper, Jack explained the story of Inaya and Naila and his connection to them.

While Jack was standing in the shop reading the newspapers, Laura stepped up to the register and paid for them.

Jack kept reading the devastating article as Laura guided him toward the luggage carousels. Buried deep inside the *Times* was a background story on the July 27th raid—the school, the slaughter, the trail of blood left by Aljibal and his men. Then he saw the names. Inaya. Naila. The words blurred as his eyes locked on their fates. Inaya's courage was described in a single, fleeting paragraph—bravery that ended beneath Aljibal's gun.

Jack stopped cold. It was as if the floor had fallen out from beneath him. His chest hollowed, his breath caught, and the paper trembled in his hands. Tears welled, spilling faster than he could blink them away.

Laura turned and froze. His face was unrecognizable—stripped of its usual control, carved instead by grief and a fury she had never seen.

In a voice flat and unyielding, Jack said, "We are going to Afghanistan. Immediately. Tomorrow. As soon as I speak to Herb."

He reached for his phone. Dead. Of course—it hadn't been charged once in St. Barths. "Yours?" he asked, his voice tight, almost mechanical.

Laura checked hers. Black screen. "It's gone. No charge."

Jack folded the paper, his tears already drying into resolve. "Then I'll call Herb when we get home. Let's get our luggage."

The raw grief had vanished, replaced by something far more chilling. His jaw was set like stone, his eyes dark with unflinching intent. Laura shivered. She had never seen a human face carry such a frightening mix of sorrow and absolute, steely resolve.

By the time they reached the baggage area, suitcases were already spitting out onto the carousel. Their bags appeared among the first; they grabbed them and threaded through the crowd to the taxi line. The ride to Silver Spring was short but felt endless to Jack—every mile a scrape against the rawness in his chest. He wanted to read more about the Pashto School, about al'Asad Aljibal, but the night swallowed headlines and made the phone screen a black mirror.

Anger settled into him like a thing with weight. *Aljibal's days will be measured in hours,* Jack thought, the vow a cold certainty. *I'll get that son of a bitch if I die trying. He will die, and he will suffer. Every one of his men will die with him.*

Thirty-five minutes later the taxi pulled up at Jack's house. He practically ran through the door and went straight for the landline. The call to Herb Watson's home went to voicemail. "Herb, it's Jack. I just got home. We have to talk—immediately," he said, breathing too fast, then hung up and dialed Herb's private office line.

Herb answered on the first ring. "Watson," he said, suspicious but attentive when the caller ID read Jack Miller.

"Herb, it's Jack. I just saw the news about the Pashto School. We have to go—now."

"I won't object," Herb replied after a pause. "But Afghanistan isn't my patch. I'll need authorization to send you. Will Laura go, too?"

"Yes," Jack said. "We're a team."

The word steadied him more than he expected. The resolve in his voice left no room for doubt.

"I'll talk to Evan Stevens tomorrow morning. Afghanistan is his bailiwick. I'll even leave a message for him tonight. Now I want you to tell me why you need to go to Afghanistan so urgently."

Jack related the story of Inaya and Naila quickly. He explained his extended relationship with the Wilsons. He finished his narration with "I'm going to kill al'Asad Aljibal."

Herbert Watson was extremely loyal to his field people. If they needed something, he would move heaven and earth to get it for them. But more, Herb was coldly analytical, and he sensed that Jack had way too much emotion involved in this potential operation. So much emotion that Jack might not always be as coldly rational as he should be. Still, he had already promised to talk to Stevens the next morning, and he would keep his promise.

"Jack," Herb said, "I will do what I can to get you where you want to be. Give me time to work out the details and provide you with some support on the ground. You and Laura cannot take on these guys all by yourselves."

"Okay, Herb, I'll be patient. Just get it done for me." Jack hung up his phone.

He turned to Laura, "You don't have to come if you don't want to. Afghanistan can make Saudi Arabia look like a garden."

Laura looked Jack straight in the eye. "If you are going, then I am going. Someone has to keep you out of trouble. Watching your ass is my designated role in life. We go together or neither of us goes."

Jack embraced Laura, "Thank you. When things get tough, there is no one I would rather have by my side than you. We go together."

After a few moments they broke apart. Laura said, "I'll go unpack our stuff. You read the newspapers and after you are done, I will read them so we both have the same information."

Jack looked at her. "I love you, Laura."

Laura looked at Jack. "I love you, Jack." Then she turned to go unpack their luggage.

They were a team in every conceivable way.

28

ARCHER M. HADLEY

Secretary of State of the United States
State Department Headquarters
2401 C St. NW
Washington, D.C.
Friday, August 10

The televised executions of Clara and Henry Wilson cracked public complacency like glass. The Wilsons had been quietly heroic—Americans who poured time, money, and courage into feeding and schooling Afghan orphans—work that actually stitched some dignity back into lives ripped apart by war. Seeing them dragged before a sham "trial," then murdered on camera, turned shock into an almost physical hunger for justice.

Aljibal's decision to broadcast the killings to the world left decent people stunned and outraged. Even the network that carried the footage was accused of complicity. Governments that often offer only careful statements suddenly found their voices sharpened into condemnation. Western heads of state denounced the spectacle; European capitals held joint news conferences. Nations across Asia and Oceania—Japan, South Korea, India, Australia, and others—issued strong statements of support. Even Cuba pledged assistance.

Only a few Muslim-majority states added public condemnation; Morocco, Jordan, and Egypt were among them. Turkey's response was notably muted, its president wading into ambiguity with a suggestion that implied the Wilsons might somehow have provoked the attack. Major powers, including Saudi Arabia, Iran, Russia, and China, and several others, such as Pakistan and the Philippines, remained conspicuously silent.

The effect was immediate and personal: a broad swath of the world that had grown used to distant brutality now demanded that those responsible be hunted down and punished.

In response to multiple news outlets' requests for comment from the United States government, Secretary Hadley called a news conference.

Promptly at 1 p.m., Secretary Hadley stepped into the press briefing room at State Department headquarters. A deep blue velvet drapery covered the wall behind him. The flags of the United States and the Department of State stood on either side. Microphones were set up at a speaker's podium. He stood aside as an assistant announced, "Ladies and gentlemen, the Secretary of State of the United States of America, Mr. Archer M. Hadley."

Archer Hadley approached the microphones. He spoke without notes. "I have asked you all here today because of terrible news from Afghanistan. I am sure all of you have seen what has transpired.

"The founders of the Pashto School, Clara and Henry Wilson, two Americans, have been beheaded in a gruesome public atrocity which has been broadcast to the entire world by Al Jazeera.

"Civilized people everywhere are repelled by the cruelties and gross injustices that have been perpetrated by ISIS and have repeatedly been shown on Al Jazeera television.

"Dr. Clara Wilson and Dr. Henry Wilson were two selfless people bringing the light of learning and the gift of healing to Afghanistan. That they happened to be Americans is a source of pride to those who lent them moral, material, and financial support. They asked nothing for themselves other than the opportunity to do their good work in peace. Their neighbors in the little Afghan village of Sinjara accepted the Wilsons as if they were part of their community. The local economy was stimulated because of the Pashto School. The Wilsons taught young girls the rudiments of modern life so that they could one day become productive members of Afghan society.

"All of that good work has been destroyed by the brute beasts of the Haqqani Network of ISIS. Their leader, who fashions himself as al'Asad Aljibal and calls himself the Lion of the Mountains, is the inspiration for the destruction we have all witnessed. It is he who has ordered the kidnapping of the girls of the Pashto School. It is he who has ordered the murders of many innocent people at the Pashto School. It is he who has confined the young women of the Pashto School to sexual slavery and involuntary marriages. It is he who has ordered the brutal beheading of the two American founders of the school, two good and innocent people. It is he who has promised the same fate to any Americans who come after him to seek retribution. "I have conferred with President Decker, and we are in total agreement. Certain American Special Forces personnel already in Afghanistan as training advisers will be augmented by additional troops whose single aim will be to capture al'Asad Aljibal dead or alive. We expect to bring him the justice he deserves."

"Previous efforts by Afghan military forces have failed to eliminate the Haqqani Network and their bloodthirsty leader. We hope to quickly correct that situation. We will use ground forces, aircraft, drones, whatever it takes to eliminate al'Asad Aljibal from the face of the Earth. This atrocity shall not go unpunished."

Motioning to the reporters, Hadley said, "A few questions and then I must leave you."

Hands started popping up.

"Anna."

Anna Jensen from the *Associated Press* rose to her feet, "Mr. Secretary, how large will the military forces sent to get Aljibal be?"

"That determination will be made by military commanders on the ground. I can only say that the forces will be adequate to do the job." Hadley pointed to the reporter for the *Washington Post*. "Jim."

Jimmy Swarzkopf cleared his throat, "Will any action or approval be needed from Congress for this operation?"

"No. We already have all the authorization we need to combat ISIS or the Taliban wherever we find them in Afghanistan or, I might add, in Iraq. Nagle."

Charles Nagle of *The New York Times* stood up. "Mr. Secretary, has a time frame been established for how long we will chase this Mr. Aljibal?"

"The simple answer, Charlie, is: However long it takes. We will not rest until we get him. I say this to al'Asad Aljibal: You will not be able to get a good night's sleep for the rest of your awful life. America will get you no matter where you hide or how many of your mujahideen surround you. For your crimes, your days are numbered.

"No more questions. I must go now to meet with a representative of the government of Pakistan to see if they can contribute any useful intelligence in the hunt for al'Asad Aljibal. Thank you all for being here on such short notice."

With that, Secretary Hadley left the room.

Every reporter pulled out their cell phones to call in their story. America wanted revenge and America was determined to get it.

29

JACK MILLER

CIA Headquarters
Langley, VA
Friday, August 10

Jack and Laura were in Herb Watson's office. Watson turned to Jack, "I spoke to Evan Stevens. He does not want you to operate independently in his territory. I explained the nature of your connection to the Wilsons and the two girls who were murdered. His ruling is that you have too much emotional connection to this situation. You should let the Special Forces people do the job."

"What will it take to make him change his mind?" Jack asked.

"I already spoke to Greensman. The director refuses to overrule Stevens."

"So how do I get to Afghanistan?"

"Only the president can overrule Greensman, and that's not likely to happen."

"Maybe Keaton can intercede for me. I really don't want to do it, but if there is no other way I can get to Aljibal, then I will give it a try."

"Good luck with that," said Watson. "But truly, I don't think you should get involved in this fight."

"Herb, I have to go. If anyone is going to put a bullet in Aljibal it has to be me. He will die by my hand for what he did to Inaya and Naila."

"I repeat, Jack, leave this fight to others. You feel it is your fight but there are other forces that can do the job. Only if they can't get him should you go after him."

"This decision has me thoroughly pissed off. For years, I have done everything the agency or the Marines have asked of me. I have risked my ass so many times in so many places. This time the request is coming from me. I need to do this, or I will never rest. If I need to resign from the agency and resign my commission and get to Afghanistan on my own, I am going after that son of a bitch. And you know I will get him."

"Don't resign from anything. I need you. America needs you. If you are determined to pursue Aljibal, then talk to Keaton, and perhaps he can persuade the president to support you. But realize that if you go over Greensman's head, you won't be making any friends in the director's office."

"I have to get to Afghanistan," Jack said, "If the people I count on won't help me and I must step on toes to get there, then I will. This is personal. I want that animal to die."

When Jack and Laura left Herb Watson's office and were back in his car, Jack called the main switchboard at the State Department. A human answered, not a robot.

"May I have Assistant Secretary Keaton's office, please?"

A few clicks later, a young man answered, "Mr. Keaton's office. May I help you?"

"I would like to speak to Assistant Secretary Keaton, please. Tell him Pogo is calling. He will take the call."

A moment later, Stu Keaton was on the phone. "Hello there. I am pleasantly surprised that you called. Adelle and I were speaking about you and Koala last night."

"I hope it was good because I need a favor from you."

"All you have to do is ask, and I will do my best to fulfill your request," Keaton said.

"Perhaps it would be better to do this face-to-face rather than on the phone."

"How soon can you get to my office?" Keaton asked. "I have some free time right now."

"We're just leaving Langley. I estimate it will take 25-30 minutes to get to you."

"I'll be available when you arrive."

"Thank you." With that, Jack broke the connection and headed for the State Department offices in Foggy Bottom.

When Jack and Laura arrived at Keaton's office, an aide was waiting to escort Pogo and Koala through security and directly to Keaton. Keaton was on the phone when they entered his office. He motioned for them to sit in the chairs in front of his desk. When he hung up the phone, he stood and shook hands with both Jack and Laura.

"I truly appreciate that you have taken the time to see us," Jack said.

"It is the least I can do for you two. Whatever you need, I will try to get it done for you," Keaton responded.

"First, I have to give you some background." Then Jack explained the history of Inaya and Naila and what they meant to him. Then he told of his connection to the Wilsons. He told of the refusal of the CIA management to allow him to go to Afghanistan, and explained the necessity of being allowed to take down Aljibal for the crimes he had committed. Lastly, he got to the favor he wanted: "Only the president can override the decision of the director. Could you get the president to order the director to send Koala and me to Afghanistan for the purpose of tracking down Aljibal? And further, could you make it look like it was the president's idea? We could be informally attached to whatever Special Forces detachment is tasked with getting Aljibal or we could go after him on our own. Operational flexibility is always best for us."

Keaton was silent for a heartbeat. "I hesitate to overrule the director, but you have a really strong reason for going after Aljibal. I think their concerns of emotional over-involvement are a misplaced abundance of caution. I will bring your request to the president and urge him to suggest it was his idea. Between us, I think our chances of success with you two working with the SEALs or the Green Berets are better than with the Special Forces operating alone. Your special skills and innovative style might be the deciding factor between success and failure."

"Thank you, Mr. Secretary. If I could have gotten this done on my own, I would not have bothered you. But dealing with the bureaucracy is sometimes beyond my scope of expertise."

"You do what you do better than anyone I have ever met. Leave the bureaucrats to people like me. I will call the president. We'll have a decision in a day or two, and hopefully the decision will be the one you want."

"Thank you again, and please send our regards to Mrs. Keaton and to Suzy."

"I'll do that with pleasure. Write your cell phone number on this pad for me."

"Yes, sir." Jack wrote his telephone number on the pad and handed it back to Keaton.

"I will call you back as soon as I have something to report."

"Thank you, Mr. Secretary," Jack said and stood. "We won't take up any more of your time." Laura also stood.

Keaton smiled and stood to shake hands again. "It is always a pleasure to see you two. I feel like you are my guardian angels, and I am happy to be able to do something for you." Keaton pressed a buzzer, and the aide who showed Jack and Laura in reappeared.

Keaton said, "Dennis will show you out of this rabbit warren. I will do my best for you."

Back in the car, they sat for a few moments. Laura looked at Jack, "Well, it is in his hands. I never thought we would ever call in the favor he promised. It is nice to have friends who can reach the top rungs of the ladder."

"I only hope the president will do what needs to be done," Jack said. "If Keaton can pull this off for us, it will be a major achievement."

"Now all we can do is wait. Let's do it at home."

"OK," Jack said as he put the transmission in drive, and they headed for Silver Spring.

30

LAURA HALEVI

Jack's House
Silver Spring MD
Wednesday, August 15

Can you imagine living with a caged tiger? Jack has been pacing the floor and engaging in all manner of strange behaviors to keep from going crazy. He is awaiting news from Keaton. It has been five days since we met with Keaton.

Jack does not answer robocalls. But since he isn't sure what number Keaton might be calling from, every time he gets a junk telephone call on his cellphone he answers it. So far he has refused two free cruises to the Bahamas, solar powered electric cells for his roof, an all-expenses-paid-three-day-tour to Disney World, offers to repair his credit, low interest loans, an offer to invest in marijuana stocks, organic-non-GMO meals pre-cooked and delivered to his home, a service contract from an appliance repair company, and multiple warnings that the IRS will be sending the police to his door if he doesn't pay up immediately. It is safe to say that Jack is getting a bit short tempered.

"Jack, when Keaton calls, you had better not bite his head off when you answer the phone," I advised.

"Those robocalls should be outlawed," said the grumblefart-in-chief. "There are so many scam artists out there that a real business doesn't stand a chance of getting a sales call to a customer."

Finally, Keaton called today shortly after 2 p.m. Fortunately, the caller ID showed a 202 area code. He knew it was coming from Washington, D.C., so he was on good behavior when he answered. I only heard Jack's half of the conversation.

"Good afternoon, Mr. Secretary."

I could hear Keaton speaking, but could not make out what he was saying.

"Yes, sir, I've been waiting for your call."

Keaton spoke again, and Jack nodded in agreement. He turned to me and gave a thumbs-up signal.

"Thank you, that's good news, sir. I will tell Koala."

More talking from Keaton.

"Yes, sir, thank you again. We will do our best." Then Jack disconnected the call.

"Well," I asked, "what is the verdict?"

With a big grin on his face, Jack said, "Keaton just heard from the president. We'll be getting orders to deploy to Afghanistan to hunt for Aljibal. And the president agreed to make it sound like it was his idea, so no one at Langley will be pissed at us. We have to be patient a few hours until the word works its way through the proper channels. Greensman is going to have to call your boss to get this cleared from Mossad's end. Keaton wished us 'good luck and good hunting' before he hung up."

I hugged Jack, and he gave me a bear hug back. I thought of the biblical story of Ruth, who said, "Whither thou goest I will go." We'll be headed for a dangerous part of the world, going after a very bad guy, but this is something that Jack must do. He wants me with him, and I would not think of letting him go alone. As good as we may be individually, we are better together as a team.

Around 6:30, Jack's phone rang again. It was Herb Watson with orders for Jack and me. Herb told Jack to call him back on a secure phone.

Jack picked up our CIA landline and called Herb's private number.

After listening to Watson for a moment, Jack said, "Herb, I am going to put you on speaker so Laura can hear what you have for us."

Herb's voice came through the speaker, "The president has suggested to the director that it would be a good idea to send you two to Afghanistan to assist in the hunt for Aljibal. Mossad HQ has agreed that Laura should be in the deal. Greensman suspects that you had a hand in this suggestion, but he has no proof, and I didn't say anything."

Jack said, "Thanks, Herb. I appreciate your discretion."

"Now, since you'll be operating in Stevens' area, he will be the primary boss of the project. I will only be advisory and a backup if you need anything he can't or won't deliver. If, for any reason, you leave Afghanistan, you both revert to me. I expect you to copy me on all reports you send to Evan. I suggested to Evan that you go in-country at Bagram and link up with the SEAL team that has been assigned to chase Aljibal. He agreed. Instructions are being cut at CNO to the SEALs to expect you."

"Sounds good," said Jack.

I cut in with, "Will the SEALs have a problem working with a woman in a combat situation?"

"Those guys are the best of the best we have. I'll make sure that they know to treat you as an equal. They will only have your code names, which will add a note of mystery to both of you. Evan will let them know that your bona fides extend back to a recent operation in Saudi Arabia, without informing them which specific operation you were involved in. They'll figure it out on their own with no one saying anything definitive. I'm pretty sure you won't have a problem."

Jack said, "We could use those cell phones we had in Saudi land."

"You can have them. Are your shots up to date? You are going to need varicella in Afghanistan, which you didn't need for Saudi Arabia. Come into Langley tomorrow and we can have the medical people check your records and bring you up to date. Laura, do you have a record of your vaccinations?"

"Yes, I do, but it is in Hebrew. I'll have to translate it for the doctors. I had the two-shot shingles vaccine in Israel, so I am good with the varicella."

"That's good. Both of you be here at 0800 tomorrow and we'll get things rolling. Stevens will be in my office too. So, we'll only have to go over the details once."

"Thanks Herb," said Jack. Until tomorrow," I said.

"Until tomorrow," I said.

Jack hung up the phone and turned to me, "We're good to go."

"Yes," I answered, "now all we have to do is find Aljibal and kill him."

31

KOALA

Bagram Air Force Base
Afghanistan
Tuesday, August 21

August in Afghanistan is like visiting Hell on earth. Dante had this place in mind when he wrote *The Inferno*. The daytime temperatures can climb to 115° F, and nighttime temperatures drop to near freezing. Jack has been here before, but I haven't.

We landed in-country at Bagram via military airlift with our weapons and gear. Bagram is just north of Kabul and was once a Russian air force base before the Americans took it over. The destruction and misery we saw from the air on our approach is so widespread that it almost makes me nostalgic for the Saudi Arabian desert. From the air, I spotted an area of wrecked aircraft just piled up in a haphazard manner. Jack explained that it was Russian aircraft damaged and abandoned from their Afghan invasion and that the Americans had cleared them off the base and piled them up out of the way. The area was called the MIG Boneyard.

The SEAL team we were supposed to hook up with was well southeast of us, operating in the hills near the Pakistan border. We would need a vehicle for our planned activities. Back at Langley, we had requested a pickup truck as our preferred mode of transportation, mostly because a pickup would not draw undue attention to us and would be unlikely to trigger an IED under our wheels. The Taliban and ISIS would ignore us, thinking we were natives, and there weren't enough Afghan or U.S. troops in the area for us to have a problem with them. A 3-year-old Toyota 4x4 with a few dents and some rusty spots would be ideal. I hope we get what we requested.

We both had 5.56mm M-16A2s and 9mm Beretta M9s. Jack also had a Remington M40A5 sniper rifle with a 3x9 variable telescopic sight, stored in a canvas carrying case with a sling. Ammo comprised eight magazines each for the M-16s and three magazines each for the Berettas. Jack had fifty rounds of match-grade 7.62 ammo for the sniper rifle, plus detachable flash and sound suppressors. We were dressed in Marine BDUs with no name tags, but Jack wore his Marine major rank on his. Jack was wearing his favorite scuffed, hand-made-in-Italy combat boots. I wore my Israeli paratrooper boots. Various knives completed our weapons. Boonie hats topped off our outfits.

Herb Watson made sure we carried the same high-tech cell phones we'd used on our Saudi mission. On the surface, they were nothing more than ordinary Apple i15s—the kind seen everywhere in the Middle East. The screens were set to Arabic, so any curious local would dismiss them as commonplace, though a hidden keyboard allowed us to slip back into English when needed. Outwardly, they could place a normal call. But with the right coded sequence, the phones transformed into something far more valuable: radio-burst transmitters. A few taps and a whispered message would be encrypted, compressed into a one-second flash of static, and fired off before the phone erased all traces. To anyone eavesdropping, it was nothing but a blip of noise. To us, it was a lifeline—silent, untraceable, and invisible.

Other variations in our phones are that the map and photo apps have been joined so that taking a photo of a building or person can give us exact target longitude and latitude coordinates in degrees, minutes, and seconds. Wherever the camera focusing square is centered, those coordinates appear at the bottom of the screen. This feature is essential in the event that we might have to call in a drone strike on Aljibal, when we find him. As long as we have our phones in our possession, we can be tracked by satellites passing overhead. Our phones also have IFF capability, so that drones and satellites will know we are Friends and not Foes.

The batteries in these phones are special 96-hour, super-long-life lithium-ion batteries that are not yet commercially available anywhere. We might not always be near a source of power to recharge these batteries. Of course, if we have any vehicle, a car or a truck, we can charge them using the cigarette lighter port. Those techies at Langley dream up all kinds of great stuff.

Before we left Virginia, we went over to the range at Quantico and test-fired all our weapons. We were both satisfied that they were accurate and would function properly when needed.

During our check-in at Bagram, we were handed over to an Army Chief Warrant Officer whose name tag read Marcus. Marcus had a strong Boston accent. Jack looked at me and said, "Marcus probably liked the Red Sox." From what I could see, Marcus was wearing khaki socks. Sometimes Jack's reasoning escapes me.

Marcus was in the quartermaster corps. He loaded us into a Humvee and drove us over to the motor pool. There, he offered us a camouflaged SUV. I offered my opinion of the SUV, "Why not take yellow paint and write 'shoot me' on it?"

Jack agreed. We were looking around the motor pool when Jack spotted a pickup that would be OK for us. "That beige one over there," Jack pointed, "the Hyundai with the shot-out headlight."

"We can't send you out in that," Marcus said, "You would look like the Taliban."

"That's the idea. It's called blending in," Jack said. "If it runs, we'll take it."

"Give me half an hour and I'll get the headlight fixed for you."

"Don't fix the headlight. I like it just the way it is. Let's start it up and see how it sounds."

Aside from a tear in the plastic cover of the passenger seat and the shot-out headlight, the truck ran well. It wasn't a 4x4 but, hey, you don't get everything you need in any army.

"Have the mechanics check the oil and hydraulic systems, fill the tank, and if it is OK, we'll be back in 60 to 90 minutes to get our wheels. We'll need forty gallons of fuel in jerrycans. We need to head to the mess hall right now. And then we need some local threads."

"Yes, sir, Major. The truck will be waiting for you after you've chowed down," Marcus said. "By the way, Spooksville is over near HQ. It is so secret that anyone on the base can give you directions on how to get there. They will have the clothes you need."

I thanked Marcus for his help. Then we headed for the mess hall, dragging all our gear. Jack wasn't about to let go of the sniper rifle. A gun case like that has a tendency to grow legs and walk away from its rightful custodian.

The food and the choices in the mess hall were pretty good, considering it was 1500 hours. I expect this mess hall runs 24/7. After we ate and used the latrines, we asked for directions to the CIA HQ (aka Spooksville). A 12-year-old local Afghan kid overheard us asking and offered to take us there. He spoke very fluent military English—initials and acronyms instead of words, curse words liberally sprinkled into his sentences.

Questions: What was a 12-year-old local kid doing on the base? And how come he knows where everything is? What kind of security measures do we have in place here? (Note that I am already considering myself part of the American 'we' when I ask this question.) We later found out he was an orphan, and some big-hearted G.I.s had sort of adopted him.

The kid, who said everyone calls him Moe (real name Mohammed), gave us a verbal tour of the base, including pointing out the Pat Tillman USO Center. The center was named in honor of the late Arizona Cardinals football player. Pat Tillman left a successful football career to join the Army Special Forces. He was killed in action in Afghanistan in 2004 under circumstances that have yet to be fully explained—whether it was a Taliban ambush or friendly-fire—and Moe included that information in his guided tour too.

We checked in at Spooksville. Jack handed our orders to Kevin Waters, the station head. He was a fit-looking man with a completely shaved head. From the shadows on his scalp, you could see he would have a full head of hair if he let it grow. He was sitting behind a standard government-issue steel desk. Except for an American flag in a floor stand and a framed photo of President Decker, the office was as bare-bones utilitarian as an office can be. Nothing of a personal nature was evident anywhere. Maybe the CIA didn't want anyone to know who was using the office.

Waters gave us two identical packages of maps and verbal directions to the SEALs unit based near Orgun with which we would be working. Orgun was located approximately 200 km due south of Bagram. Add some twists and turns in the road, and the actual driving distance was closer to 275 km. We were also briefed on local radio protocols. "We need you guys to check in daily."

Jack smiled. "We would do so if it were feasible, but we won't be using radios. We will be operating independently unless we happen to need some support that the SEALs can't provide. Daily check-ins would be done on our phones via Afghansat."

Waters responded, "I know what your assignment is, and I understand that you need some latitude regarding formalities. But whenever and wherever possible, I would like you to check in so we can be assured you are still alive."

I added to Jack's comment, "We need a telephone number in your office or a cell number that only you have access to."

Waters then gave us his cell number and a number for daily check-ins, which we programmed into our telephones. "Try to call me at least once a day. Pogo, I know you have been deployed here before. Koala, this is a tough place with some pretty nasty characters. Be careful."

"I've been in some mean places before. We are a good team, and we cover each other's backs. He needs me. I need him. Together we will kick some butts."

Jack said, "We need a burqa and local pants and a jacket for Koala, and I will need local Afghan peasant clothing. Can you outfit us?"

"We have what you need on the second floor. Janet up there is great at helping our people blend in," Waters answered. "See her when you leave here, and she'll take care of you. I assume you can speak the local language," Waters asked, even though it was a statement, there was a question in it.

Jack answered in Pashto, "We'll get by."

In Pashto, I said, "Of course. We speak the language like spooks."

Waters laughed and said in Pashto, "You'll be OK. Do you have any questions for me?"

"No," Jack answered, still in Pashto, "I think it's time to visit with Janet upstairs."

"Good hunting," said Waters in English. "Bring that bastard's head back on a pike pole."

"We intend to get him," Jack answered, switching back to English. "He is going to pay for what he has done."

Waters suggested, "I think you should get some rest tonight and head out in the morning. Jet lag can be a bitch."

"That's a good idea," said Jack. "Where are the BOQs?"

Waters gave us directions to the Bachelor Officer Quarters.

As we turned to leave to get our local clothing from Janet upstairs, I said, "Thanks for being here for us. It's nice to know we have some support if we need it."

Waters just waved his hand. "It's our job to make sure you get back alive and in one piece if it's possible. We don't always succeed, but we always try."

32

JACK AND LAURA

South of Bagram in the Afghan hills
Wednesday, August 22

We drove our one-eyed pickup out the main gate of Bagram at 0615. We passed through two walls that were merely to block visual recon of activities within the base and a third barrier of 10-to-12-foot-high coils of razor wire. These barriers surround the entire base.

All of our gear except for weapons was in the back of the truck. We had cans of water, cans of fuel, combat rations, combat first-aid packs, a two-man tent, a sniper's spotter scope, some clean socks and underwear, and our local clothing. Our weapons were all in the cab with us.

Once we were out of the vicinity of Bagram, we pulled over behind some trees and changed from our BDUs into our local clothes. Laura donned her *tunbaan*, loose fitting pants. Then she put on a *parahaan*, a dress over the pants. She finished it off with a *chador*, a headscarf that covers her hair. (There is something about a woman's hair that makes Muslim men behave illogically if they see it. A Muslim woman showing her hair is behaving the same as if a Western woman were half naked.)

Jack was driving. Laura was reading the map and acting as navigator. Laura said, "Our SEALs are in Orgun, about 200 km south of Bagram, from point A to point B in a straight line. That translates to over 250 to 300 km on the road, plus some rivers to cross. The first 25 km seem to be on paved roads. Any shell holes and craters we encounter will probably not be filled in. We'll have to deal with them when we get to them. Once we enter the hills past Gardeyz, it will be all secondary roads, likely including some dirt roads as well. Are Afghan roadblocks any different from the roadblocks in Yemen?"

"This is ISIS country," Jack said. "Roadblocks are the major source of income to extort money from travelers. Then there is the kidnapping of foreigners for ransom and the raping of women for fun."

"So, when we see a roadblock in Afghanistan, do we shoot first and say 'Hi Guys' later?"

"Depends. If it is the Afghan government or police, we stop and talk, but we must always be ready to fight. Sometimes they're honest, sometimes they're not. If the roadblock is clearly ISIS, we turn around and hightail it out of there to a place where we can plan an attack on the roadblock, and hopefully, we'll have some survivors who can tell us where to find Aljibal."

"That's not much of a plan. But I guess it will have to do until we get to the bad guys."

They drove on in silence with only occasional directions from Laura. Around 10:00, Jack pulled off the road. They ate some of their rations and went into the scrub off the side of the road for some latrine relief. In three and a half hours of driving, they had passed through the towns of Barak and Gardeyz, which were controlled by the Afghan government. They were now on the border of contested territory. ISIS fighters could be anywhere.

Laura took over the driving. A woman driving in Afghanistan is not such an unusual sight as it would be in Saudi Arabia. The Taliban and ISIS refuse to let women drive. The Afghan government looks the other way and pretends it isn't happening.

Jack sat in the passenger seat with the muzzle of his M-16 pointing out the open window. Laura's rifle was lying across the dashboard shelf above the instrument panel. Jack had to keep it from sliding left or right whenever the truck made any turning motion.

They had been traveling at a modest pace for about an hour when they saw a roadblock up ahead. It appeared to be manned by three Afghan militiamen. The Afghan national flag, three vertical stripes black, red, and green, with a design in the center, was on a pole stuck into the ground on the right side of the road.

"I think we can get through this checkpoint OK," said Jack.

Laura eased the truck to a stop at the roadblock. Two militia men stepped out from either side of the barrier; a third lounged behind it. Rifles hung low, muzzles trained on the cab, fingers close to triggers.

"Get out of the truck," the man nearest Laura ordered.

They climbed down. The man on the right sniffed the air and squinted at her. "Why is a woman driving?"

Jack answered before she could: "She drove. I was tired."

The man scoffed. "Women shouldn't be driving. Fine—10,000 Afghani. Now."

Jack made a quick mental conversion—about a hundred dollars—and kept his hands where they could be seen.

The militiaman on the left jabbed the butt of his rifle toward Laura. "You come with me." His gesture was a command, not a question.

"My woman stays with me," Jack said.

"She will do as we tell her," the man by Jack replied, voice flat. "You keep quiet." They pushed Laura through the barrier.

Behind the hedgerow the third man—the one who had been watching from the barrier—stepped forward. He ran a thumb along the blade he had drawn from his belt. "Nice-looking," he said, leering. "You come with me."

Laura said nothing. Her face stayed still.

The man guided her between two tangles of dry brush and stopped. Close enough for the smell of sweat and rust, he thrust the knife out. "Take off your tunbaan or you'll be cut," he spat.

"No." Laura's answer was measured, a small sound in the hot wind.

He leaned in, knife flashing. "Do it now or you'll bleed."

"It's not nice to force a woman," she said.

"You are a woman. I am a man. You will do as I say," he snarled.

She smiled then—small, unreadable. A smile that had nothing to do with fear.

Laura had been a Krav Maga instructor in the IDF. Krav Maga meant neutralizing threats with phyiscal contact before they could move. As the man jutted his left foot forward, sandals scuffing the dust, Laura felt his weight, where his balance would shift, how close his blade would be when he lunged. She was already five moves ahead.

"Why are you smiling?" he demanded, leaning until the knife hovered an inch from her cheek.

She did not speak while she finished planning how she would end the conversation.

Laura slowly raised her right hand to shoulder height. His eyes followed the motion just as she wanted.

Her boot came down like a hammer on his exposed foot. The snap of breaking bones was sharp and sickening. He howled, staggering, but she was already moving. Her left arm slammed his knife hand aside while her right fist—knuckles angled forward—drove into his left eye. The scream turned raw, his blade clattering into the dirt.

He tried to cover his face, but Laura trapped his arm and cracked him in the other eye. Blinded now, he reeled. She released him just long enough to drive a brutal kick into his groin. The breath left him in a single strangled grunt as he doubled over.

His head dropped into range. She snapped her boot up and smashed his face, shattering his nose and teeth. Blood sprayed. He gurgled, helpless.

Laura closed in, clapped both palms against his ears—an explosive pop as his eardrums ruptured—then chopped his collarbone with surgical precision. The bone cracked loudly enough for Jack to hear it back at the truck.

The militiaman crumpled to the ground, writhing, ruined. His foot was crushed, eyes swollen shut, nose and mouth pouring blood, testicles destroyed, ears ringing with silence, and collarbone splintered.

He wasn't dead. But he was finished.

Laura smiled, calm as ever, and walked back toward the road.

From over by the pickup truck, Jack nodded at Laura. The militiaman with his rifle on Jack, half turned away to see what Jack was looking at. Jack stepped in sideways, grabbed the rifle from the militiaman's hands, and brought the butt end straight up under the man's chin with great force. The militiaman went down immediately.

The third man behind the roadblock was surprised to see Laura standing in the road. He was facing away from Jack. With the rifle he had just liberated, Jack fired a three-round burst that caught the last militiaman in the backs of his knees. He went down. Jack put another burst into the back of the man's head. He wouldn't be getting up again.

The man at Jack's feet, who had been so cooperative as to give Jack his rifle, let out a groan. Jack kicked him in the head to knock him out completely. Gratitude for surrendering a weapon only goes so far.

Jack went to the driver's seat and pulled the truck through the barriers to where Laura was waiting. She got in.

"That was almost fun," she said. "Beating up a would-be rapist is like dispensing instant justice."

"What did you do to him?"

Laura gave a quick summary of the injuries she had inflicted on the would-be rapist.

Jack laughed. "I was never in doubt that he was the one who was in danger and not you. As soon as I saw the knife come out, I knew he would suffer. You did a very thorough job."

"A man who thinks it's okay to rape women must receive the complete treatment. I wonder if he will ever see again? Or if he will ever admit he was beaten up by a woman. These guys are such macho pigs."

"I guess I'll drive for a while. You've had your exercise for today."

"The adrenaline rush is just starting to subside. I'm really wired now. Tell me you love me because I need to feel loved."

Jack pulled the truck to the side of the road. He reached over to Laura and hugged her. He planted tender kisses on her mouth, to which she responded with tongue and passion and hands groping at his crotch. "I need you now."

"This is a bad place for love and sex."

"I know it. I just thought you should know what I want."

"I always want you, day and night. I love you, Laura. I am really happy with the way you took care of that guy. He deserves to be crippled for life. And you are the sexiest woman I have ever known. I'll do what you need as soon as we get to a safe place to make love."

Jack pulled back onto the road. They continued driving south, holding hands, neither one saying a word, just happy to be with each other.

33

JUBAL EL-MADOUSH

Camp of the Haqqani Network
Hills of Paktika Province, Afghanistan
Friday, August 24

Jubal's phone buzzed against his thigh. He fished it out and glanced at the sender: Amir el-Madoush. He opened the message.

> Our American friend returns tomorrow. Leaves Saturday night. We still owe him a goodbye gift. Same place as last time—move fast.

Jubal dropped the phone into his pocket and went in search of Aljibal. He found him halfway inside the cave, steam rising from a chipped cup of tea.

"Rayiys," Jubal said, breath hitching with adrenaline. "Amir says Hadley comes back tomorrow and leaves Saturday night. We missed him before."

Aljibal's eyes never left the cup. "Were they ever suspicious that the first strike was meant for Hadley?"

"Amir said the press called it an attack at the airport. Nobody tied it to Hadley, at least not in Islamabad's papers."

Aljibal set the cup down like a metronome. He studied Jubal with a calmness that made Jubal's heart beat faster. "Prepare the men and the gear and move now."

Jubal felt excitement as the set of commands that followed him took shape: men, weapons, fuel, and a quick departure. "It shall be done," he said.

He left Aljibal in the cave with his tea and pecked a reply into his phone.

We are on our way.

Then he gave orders for the men he wanted. Nadjim and Anwar knew what was expected of them in this operation. He added Mahamoud. Rafik, who screwed up the last attack, was still unable to walk without crutches. Aljibal would not want him along anyway.

Within an hour, the truck, a six-man crew cab model, and five men were loaded and ready to roll. It was a little over a 400 km drive to the airport in Rawalpindi. Nadjim was to drive the first 200 km. Anwar would finish the trip, driving the last 200+ km. Aljibal would ride in the front passenger seat. Jubal and Mahamoud would ride in the back with whoever was not driving.

Aljibal was determined not to fail this time. He would settle his score with Hadley. The insults that Hadley had uttered would be atoned for by his death.

34

ARCHER M. HADLEY

United States Secretary of State
General Headquarters Pakistan Army
Rawalpindi, Pakistan
Friday & Saturday, August 24 & 25

Secretary of State Hadley stepped once more onto Pakistani soil, this time with Stuart Keaton, his freshly minted Assistant Secretary for Near Eastern Affairs, in tow. Their visit would last a mere thirty-six hours—hardly enough time before Hadley had to dash to Brussels for a NATO ministers' meeting.

His mission was blunt: introduce Keaton to Field Marshal Bouradin and then wash his hands of the man. Let the rookie handle the general's endless demands. Hadley would also have to deliver Washington's new military aid numbers—leaner than Bouradin expected. The field marshal's temper was legendary, and Hadley intended for Keaton to feel its full heat while he himself faded into the background.

Word spread fast in the papers: Hadley was coming. The smarter reporters began guessing what would be in the aid package; every one of them wrote the same fantasy line—F-35s. Bouradin already knew the truth and braced for the humiliation. When the curtain dropped, the missing fighters would be on him.

Hadley's plane, with Keaton, aides, and the NATO press cluster in tow, touched down at Nur Khan. No honor guard this time. Only Ambassador Dave Cooper waited on the tarmac. Hadley felt a small, private relief; he despised ceremonies and the way they ate time.

SUVs and a bus moved the party toward the Islamabad Marriott. Hadley and Keaton rode with Cooper. The ambassador didn't waste words.

"The papers expect squadrons of F-35s," Cooper said. "They'll blame Bouradin when he doesn't get them."

Hadley shrugged. "I told him last month he wasn't getting them. Do you think we hand over our most sensitive tech to whoever asks? Give them F-35s and in a week China and Russia will be dissecting them. We don't trust these guys as custodians of that kind of hardware."

Keaton, still new enough to say the obvious out loud, added, "Whatever we give is a gift. Stick to the plan. They'll grieve, then push for next year. China and Russia aren't handing out advanced fighters either—and we shouldn't be the first."

Hadley agreed. "Stu, after I leave tomorrow night, Bouradin will try to get you to commit to increasing the aid. Stick to the aid numbers as I have outlined them. The package is more than they have earned. Don't forget who gave Osama bin Laden a safe haven for several years. These guys are not our buddies."

The conversation between the three men covered several other topics, some speculation about the upcoming presidential election, and some Washington gossip. It was all friendly. They arrived at the Islamabad Marriott slightly after 10 p.m. Hadley and Keaton needed sleep to be sharp for the field marshal the next day, so each man retired to his room.

Saturday in Islamabad broke hot and bright. As expected, Field Marshal Bouradin swept in a few minutes past nine, his entourage trailing like banners. The Americans had been ready on time, of course—their hosts had set the hour—but Bouradin's lateness was deliberate theater, a reminder of who held the stage.

Hadley had warned Keaton it would happen. When the doors finally opened, the two Americans exchanged a small, private smile. Petty power plays lost their sting when you could see them coming.

Field Marshal Bouradin swept into the conference room. He was dressed in combat fatigues with all of his campaign ribbons colorfully displayed on his left breast. His highly polished paratrooper boots glistened in the light of the room. His Saddam Hussein mustache was neatly trimmed on his otherwise clean-shaven face. Under his left arm, he held his field marshal's swagger stick. The ebony baton had highly polished two-inch silver caps on each end. The air of command presence engulfed him like a cloud.

Hadley almost laughed at the scene Bouradin presented, but, like a professional diplomat, he managed to turn the inner hilarity into an outward smile of greeting.

Sitting next to Secretary Hadley was an embassy staffer who was fluent in Pashto and Urdu. He also had a hidden voice recorder. His purpose was to monitor any conversations in Urdu and Pashto between Bouradin and his officers and to get a real-time recording of everything that was said by everyone in the room. The aide had an iPad in front of him that was linked to similar iPads in front of Hadley and Keaton.

After perfunctory good morning greetings and introductions of all the major people who were present, the field marshal got things rolling in his Oxford-accented English. "Gentlemen, we are all very busy, so let us get down to the essentials for this meeting. We must address this year's military aid package. As you may recall, Secretary Hadley, we requested F-35 Lightning II fighter jets, and you countered with A-10 Warthogs. We requested thirty-eight high-speed coastal patrol vessels, and you countered with five boats. Other military hardware we requested is not an issue at the moment since we are in agreement on that material."

Hadley smiled. "Field Marshal, surely you realize that F-35s are for NATO members only and for other allies with which we have an extra-special relationship. The F-35 is our most advanced production fighter plane, and we will not jeopardize the technological advancements in that aircraft by exposing its secrets to an ally whose military establishment is as porous as yours. Too many people in your military are sympathetic to China and Russia, or are even on their payroll, as well as Pakistan's. The F-35s are not on the table now, nor will they be for the foreseeable future.

"The two squadrons of A-10s that we have offered will augment Pakistan's existing force of A-10s. They are a formidable weapons system of great versatility and will provide additional air support to Pakistani armor and infantry forces. I urge you to accept this offer.

"As to the patrol vessels, Pakistan's limited coastline can adequately be patrolled by as few as two of the vessels, and we have offered five fast patrol boats, which gives you backup capability for any defensive eventuality."

The field marshal smoothed his mustache with the thumb and forefinger of his left hand. Then he moved his baton with his right hand, lining it up with a few papers in front of him on the table. "My naval commanders tell me we need a minimum of ten patrol boats for adequate drug interdiction and coastal security. Five additional boats would provide us with an adequate backup force. So, the minimum number of patrol boats we can accept is fifteen."

Keaton spoke for the first time. "Field Marshal, may I suggest we raise our offer to seven patrol boats this year and an additional seven boats next year. This should satisfy the needs of your naval commanders and keep our costs within our budgetary constraints."

"I think that might be acceptable. I shall have to confer with my naval people before I accept that offer."

Both Hadley and Keaton knew the field marshal was the ultimate arbiter of what was acceptable, but they both chose not to say anything in that regard. Let Bouradin play his little games.

"I wish you would reconsider the radar targeting system we need for our fighter aircraft. I requested this the last time we met."

Hadley answered, "I turned you down last month when we met for the same reason the U.S. cannot give you F-35s. There are too many Chinese and Russian sympathizers buried within your military commands. You can do what India has done, which is to develop the system with your own engineers. Or you can buy a slightly lesser system from Israel for cash."

"Doing business with Israel is out of the question. Developing a radar targeting system with our engineers would take several years, and we need such a system now."

"I am afraid the United States cannot solve your problem," said Hadley. "You had better start the development process, even if it will take a few years, if you really want such a targeting system."

One of Bouradin's officers whispered something in Urdu to another officer.

The aide sitting next to Hadley typed a message into his iPad and sent it to Hadley and Keaton: He called us cheap bastards.

Both men noted the message but showed no facial reaction.

"That is a most unfortunate attitude on the part of the United States," said the field arshal.

"If you develop the system yourselves, then you will have the skills needed for future developmental needs. Who knows, a good system might be exported and sold to your friends," offered Hadley.

"Hmph," was all the field marshal could muster.

Keaton spoke again. "Let us find a way to conclude this business while we are here. Will Pakistan be able to use the A-10s we are offering? Will seven fast patrol boats be enough for this year, with seven more boats next year? If the answer to these questions is yes, then we have an agreement. I do not believe the U.S. government will change its position. Therefore, the decision rests with Pakistan. Do we have an agreement?"

The field marshal said, "Let me think about it overnight. I will let you know our decision in the morning."

Keaton said, "Secretary Hadley must leave Pakistan tonight for a meeting of NATO ministers. I will remain in Islamabad until Sunday to complete these talks. I hope we can have a meeting of the minds on this."

Hadley addressed the field marshal. "There is one more topic that was raised last month that we have not discussed today. The United

States would like you to rein in Directorate S. Their operations are offering too much aid to our enemies and to terror groups."

The field marshal bristled at Hadley's comment, "We have no bureau with the name of Directorate S. The organization of our government is an internal issue that will be addressed only by the government of Pakistan without outside interference from any source. The government of Pakistan does not offer aid to terror groups. It is improper even to discuss this issue."

"Well if it walks like a duck, and quacks like a duck, then we must be dealing with a duck. Directorate S is behaving like an enemy of the interests of the United States and of the publicly espoused interests of Pakistan. Since it is a clandestine branch of your ISI, then you must be able to control what it does. We expect you to curtail their operations as they affect the interests of the United States."

With Hadley's last comment, the field marshal stood up. All five of the officers in his group stood up instantly as if they were all wired together. To Hadley, Bouradin said, "Have a safe trip, Mr. Secretary." To Keaton he nodded, "Until tomorrow, here at the same time." All the Pakistani officers filed out after the field marshal without so much as a handshake or a goodbye.

After they were gone, Keaton said to Hadley, "Friendly bunch." Hadley only smiled. It was what he expected.

Once the field marshal was outside the meeting room, he motioned for one of his aides to come close.

In a quiet voice, he said, "We extend courtesies to foreign officials' aircraft when they are leaving at our airport. I want none of those courtesies for Hadley when he leaves tonight. Let his plane wait in line."

"Yes, Sir. I will get the order to the tower."

"Get Colonel Dalari to deliver the message personally. He is reliable."

"Yes, Sir. Colonel Dalari. Right away."

35

AL'ASAD ALJIBAL

Nur Khan Air Force Base/Islamabad Airport
Rawalpindi, Pakistan
Saturday, August 25

Aljibal's truck had driven through the night to arrive at the airport by 11 a.m. on Saturday morning. Jubal el-Madoush was in frequent contact with his cousin, Amir, at the airport. Once again, a rendezvous was set up between Aljibal and the colonel in charge of airport perimeter security. As before, the sentries would not be making their rounds when the secretary's plane was on runway 10R.

Aljibal rehearsed his men for the fourth time. "Three of you will stand in the bed of the truck and aim your rockets at a specific target. Anwar will aim at the passenger compartment behind the wing. Nadjim will aim at the passenger compartment immediately above the wing, and Mahamoud at the pilot's control cabin. When I give the order to fire, all three of you will fire your rockets at the same moment. When the rockets are fired, Jubal will start the truck forward, and we will escape from the airport. Everyone will reload the rocket launchers in case we are pursued. If we are pursued, Anwar will fire one rocket into the ground well in front of the pursuers, and they will stop chasing us. Any gunfire from the sentries will be over our heads. If we shoot back, it will be over the heads of the pursuers. None of the

Pakistan military is to be injured by us. If we are truly being pursued by someone who intends to harm us, I will give orders to shoot at them. But no one shoots at our pursuers unless I give the order. Does everyone understand what I am expecting from you?"

There were nods of agreement from everyone assembled and murmurs of "Yes, Rayiys."

"Good," said Aljibal. "I expect the crusader Secretary of State to go to Hell. He said I will never get a good night's rest again because the Americans are after me. We will see who sleeps well in his bed tonight."

At just after 1900 hours (7 p.m.) Lieutenant Colonel Singleton had the plane loaded and ready for takeoff. He radioed the tower. "Flight Air Force 5 requests permission for immediate departure."

The tower responded, "Air Force 5, there will be a slight delay. There are eight planes in the queue for takeoff in front of you."

Singleton responded, "Tower, I see only one aircraft moving on the taxiway and none on the runway. Where are the other seven planes?"

"Please be patient, Air Force 5. We will get you off the ground as soon as we can."

Ten minutes later, Singleton called the tower again. "I don't mean to rush you gentlemen, but we have been sitting here ten minutes. No other planes have taken off except the one that was on the taxiway. What is the delay?"

"Be patient, Air Force 5. We have our orders. We will get you off in a few more minutes," was the tower's response.

"What is the nature of your orders that you are holding us here?" Singleton asked. "I have the Secretary of State of the United States on this plane. There is almost no other traffic at this moment."

"Five more minutes, Air Force 5," was the response.

Five minutes later, the tower radioed, "Air Force 5, you are cleared for takeoff. Use runway 10R."

Singleton taxied to the end of runway 10R and paused for a moment to rev his engines to full power.

The tower radioed, "Air Force 5, hold for one minute before takeoff."

Clearly annoyed, Singleton asked, "What is the cause of this delay? I have a clear runway, and our radar shows no traffic that could interfere with my takeoff."

"45 seconds more, Air Force 5," the tower radioed.

At the fence outside runway 10R, four men were crouched in the bed of the pickup truck. Aljibal said, "Ready with the rockets."

The three men with rockets stood and shouldered their weapons.

"Aim." Aljibal waited three beats. "Fire."

All three rockets launched as one. Flames and exhaust shot out of the rear of the launch tubes. Nadjim and Anwar immediately bent down to reload. Mahamoud stood transfixed, watching the results of the rockets they had just fired. Jubal waited a second after the launch blasts and then put the truck in gear and began rolling and quickly accelerating.

All three rockets hit the right side of Hadley's plane almost at once. The rocket hitting the fuselage over the wing ignited the full load of fuel in the fuel tanks, setting off an explosion in the right-wing tank. The rocket aimed at the fuselage behind the wing, causing the rear of the plane to fall while the center section, wings, and wheels leaped upwards from the force of the explosion.

The third rocket struck the plane about 15 feet behind the cockpit, and the nose section fell forward onto the runway. Flames from burning jet fuel engulfed the middle section of the plane. A moment later, the jet fuel in the other wing tank exploded, causing the center section to leap off the ground again and tearing the explosion-damaged left wing off the airplane.

Within 30 seconds, crash crews were responding to the explosions from the fuel tanks. In less than a minute, they had arrived at the burning plane and began spraying foam on the burning fuel. Firefighters clad from head to toe in Nomex suits could be seen trying to get to the aircraft. They were driven back by the intense flaming heat. The only parts of the plane that were not burning were the tail section lying on the runway and the front 15 feet of the fuselage, which was hanging down from the center section at a 30° angle, resting on the collapsed nose wheel. The dark blue letters "UNI" were all that was left of the line of lettering that once ran along the length of the plane.

Eyewitnesses were shocked by the inferno they were seeing. Speculation that no one could possibly survive that inferno was rampant among the onlookers.

Within 18 minutes, the plane and the runway were covered in foam, and the flames were extinguished. The heat from the burning fuel remained a significant obstacle to rescue efforts. Unburned fuel and foam on the runway made walking treacherous. Any survivors were roasting alive in the wreckage or choking on inhaled smoke.

A German tourist, Gustave Manheim from Munich, waiting in the passenger terminal for his flight home, was surprised to see a plane that looked like Air Force One on the runway. Through the large glass windows of the terminal, he had been taking a video of the plane with his cell phone as it readied for takeoff. *My kids would love to see this plane,* he thought. He caught the rocket launches, the rocket strikes, the explosions, the fire, and the burning wreckage on his phone. After a shaky moment when the plane exploded, he steadied his hands and continued recording. The firefighting efforts were part of the video, but he cut it short so he would have enough battery power to email the entire video to Das Erste (Channel One), Germany's public broadcasting channel.

He took a few moments to look up their news website address, and then he emailed the video to the TV station, being careful to include his name, address, and phone number. After the video was completely transmitted, he telephoned the station to ensure they had received it and would pay him for the scoop they would have. He explained where he was, his reason for taking the video, and what he had recorded.

On the runway, military personnel from the air force base were already cordoning off the area around the wreckage. Air traffic was being diverted away from the airport. No aircraft was given permission to land.

The news spread quickly. Reporters began arriving at the airport. One enterprising reporter from *The People's Voice Daily*, a newspaper opposed to the government, telephoned the tower. The air controller, who had been in contact with the plane, reflexively answered the ringing telephone. He was in semi-shock. "Who am I speaking to?" asked the reporter.

"Salim Whamani," answered the air controller. The voice on the phone sounded authoritative. Instinctively, Salim thought he had better be cooperative.

"Did you see what happened to the plane?" the reporter asked.

"I had him holding. He was 45 seconds from takeoff," he stammered.

"Salim, don't VIP planes get immediate takeoff clearance?"

"Yes, they do," answered the air controller, "but I was ordered to delay the plane for up to half an hour if I could." Salim suddenly realized that he had to pass on the blame for the delay and the resulting carnage to someone else.

The reporter immediately sensed a scandal in what the air controller had admitted. "Salim, who gave you that order?"

"I got it from a senior military officer in Field Marshal Bouradin's office."

"Do you know the name of the officer?"

"Yes. I never saw him before. He was a full colonel. Colonel Dalari. He carried proper authority, and I didn't dare disobey him. He said he had orders from the field marshal to delay the plane." Salim began to cry when he realized how much trouble he was in. "They are going to blame me and accuse me of being part of the plot to blow up the plane. I had no idea this was going to happen." He began to blubber on the phone. Then he thought he had said too much, so he hung up the phone.

The reporter called the tower again, but no one answered. So, he called his editor and reported almost verbatim what he had just heard, including the names of the air controller and Colonel Dalari who had given the order.

"Are you sure?" the editor demanded.

"Absolutely. The air controller is petrified with fear right now," the reporter said.

"Write the story about the attack and the quotes from the air controller. We'll print it with your byline. I'll do the headline. Phone it in within the hour so we can make the morning edition." The editor hung up.

The reporter continued his inquiries. He had to get the whole story in an hour, and he had lots of work to do.

*   *   *

Al'Asad Aljibal was ecstatic when the truck pulled away after the attack. Anwar was crouching on the floor of the truck bed, facing the rear. "No one is chasing us, Rayiys."

"The whole plane has exploded," Nadjim shouted. "What an explosion! I think we must have killed everyone on board."

"I hope so," said Aljibal. "I would go to Allah's Heaven a happy man if we at least killed that pig Hadley."

Aljibal turned to Mahamoud. "Get down, you fool. You will attract too much attention standing up while holding a rocket launcher in your hands."

Mahamoud sheepishly squatted down in the bed of the truck.

Aljibal asked, "Who has a throwaway telephone? Mahamoud, happy for a chance to redeem himself, said, "I do, Rayiys."

"When we are back in camp, we will call Al Jazeera and take credit for our attack. Give me the phone."

Jubal el-Madoush had driven beyond the airport boundaries by this time. Aljibal banged on the roof of the cab with his hand. "Stop the truck and let us get inside."

To the men in the bed of the truck he said, "Stow everything under blankets. Remove the fuses from the rockets we didn't use. Bring the rifles inside the cab in case we need them. Then everyone get in the cab. Anwar, you drive the first part of the trip. We are going back to camp. You all did good work tonight. The world will fear the Haqqani Network. No one is safe from us."

Aljibal climbed out of the back of the pickup truck and sat in the front passenger's seat. He was happy with what he had done. He, al'Asad Aljibal, would sleep better than Archer M. Hadley tonight. Hadley would sleep in Hell forever.

36

STUART KEATON

Assistant Secretary of State for Near Eastern Affairs
Islamabad, Pakistan
Saturday, August 25

Bad news travels at the speed of light. Within six minutes of the strike on Secretary Hadley's plane, word reached the U.S. Embassy. Ambassador Cooper was already racing toward the airport when he phoned Stuart Keaton, who abandoned his half-finished dinner, summoned a car, and was on the road in four minutes.

Fifteen minutes after the first blast, the world was watching. A German tourist's shaky video cut into regular programming in Berlin at 3:55 p.m., then ricocheted across Europe, Asia, and beyond. By 10:55 a.m. on the U.S. East Coast, American networks had broken in with the footage, replaying the fireball again and again, the attack on Hadley's plane becoming global spectacle.

Sharp observers who viewed the video caught the rocket launches in the distant background. Speculation about who the attackers were was the initial fodder for every talking head and informed commentator.

Ambassador Cooper arrived on the scene of the attack three minutes before Secretary Keaton. They both got through the police lines to the tarmac, but at that point Pakistani military personnel would not allow them to get any closer to the airplane. A Pakistani officer,

Colonel Sandahar, linked up with the two Americans and was trying to be as cooperative as possible given the carnage that was evident on the runway.

Firefighters were beginning to remove the bodies from the plane and were laying them out in a line on the runway. All the victims had been seated, wearing their seat belts, and were easy to locate. So far, no survivors had been found.

Keaton said to Colonel Sandahar, "I want them to recover the black boxes immediately, and I want them turned over to the United States government. This plane is covered by diplomatic immunity, and I don't want any problems with the recovery and transfer. When we analyze the contents of the recorders, a representative of the Pakistan government can be present, and we will give the Pakistani representative exact copies of what the recorders reveal."

"I will have to get permission for the recovery and transfer," said Sandahar.

"Call the field marshal now and get the permission while we are here."

The colonel took out his cell phone and made the call. A conversation in Urdu ensued. The colonel finished by saying, "Yes, he is right here with me."

The colonel turned to Keaton. "Field Marshal Bouradin would like to speak to you." He handed his cell phone to Keaton.

"Yes, Field Marshal."

Bouradin said, "First, let me extend the official condolences of the Pakistan government to the government of the United States."

"Thank you, Field Marshal."

"Your request for the black boxes contravenes Pakistan aviation regulations. However, given that you are claiming diplomatic immunity for the aircraft, I think we can make an exception in this tragedy. So, when the aircraft is cool enough for mechanics to get at the black boxes, you shall have them."

"Thank you for your cooperation," said Keaton. "At a time like this, it is most appreciated."

"I am on my way to the airport as we speak. I will see you in a few moments. Please allow me to speak to Colonel Sandahar, and I will give him appropriate orders."

Keaton passed the phone back to the colonel. "The field marshal has orders for you."

Sandahar listened to Bouradin for a few moments, said, "Yes, sir," in Urdu, and disconnected the call.

"You shall have the black boxes as soon as we can safely extract them."

"By the way," said Keaton, "the boxes are orange, not black. They are in the tail of the aircraft, which did not burn. We should be able to extract them while I am here. Further, I will request a U.S. Air Force plane to transport the boxes back to Washington. Do I need special permission for the plane to land here?"

"A U.S. military plane can land here."

"Good. I will call Washington, and they will dispatch a plane from Bagram to pick up the boxes and take them to Washington. Your officer can fly on the plane if you so desire."

"I will clear that with the field marshal."

At that moment, Bouradin strode up behind Keaton, Cooper, and Sandahar. "Clear what with the field marshal?" he asked.

Colonel Sandahar snapped to attention and saluted. "Secretary Keaton wants to have a U.S. military plane transport the black boxes to Washington and has offered to have our investigating officer accompany the boxes on the flight. I believe this is an unusual offer that would require your approval before the officer undertakes such a journey."

"Find out who our expert is and get him ready to travel at a moment's notice. It would be best if he could speak English, too."

"Yes, sir," said Sandahar. He then stepped away from the group and began making phone calls.

Keaton said, "Excuse me a moment. I must call President Decker to request the transportation."

Bouradin nodded. "I had better find out what is happening here," and walked off toward the crews who were extracting the bodies from the wreckage.

Keaton called the White House. The president had been aware of the news of the attack on the Secretary of State's plane. The local time was just after 11:00 a.m. He took Keaton's call in the Oval Office. "Stu. This is awful news. I have seen the video of the attack on TV. It is awful. Are there any survivors?"

"I haven't seen any yet. Crews are extracting bodies from the wreckage. I was not aware that a video of the attack existed. A local TV station has a camera truck here, and they will be broadcasting the crash scene in a few minutes. I have made arrangements for the cockpit voice recorder and the flight recorder boxes to be retrieved and flown to Washington and need a plane to be ordered here from Bagram to take them back. A Pakistani representative may accompany the boxes to Washington. I have promised them that we will provide them with an exact copy of whatever is recorded and that their representative can be present when we analyze the contents. We will also need a C5A on standby to transport the bodies back to Dover. We will need a lot of military caskets, about fifty."

"OK, I will give the orders and get things rolling at Bagram. An Air Force officer will contact you directly to make this happen as you have promised."

"Please send my condolences to Mrs. Hadley when you speak to her. I will do it personally when I return home in a day or two."

"Good luck, Stu. I am glad it is you who are there for us. I have confidence in you."

"Thank you, Mr. President. Now I had better get back to work here."

"Goodbye, Stu, and thank you. You made the right calls for us."

"I wish I weren't forced to make these calls at all under these circumstances. Goodbye, Mr. President." With that, Stuart Keaton broke the connection. He then went to look for Ambassador Cooper so they could update each other.

37

STUART KEATON

Assistant Secretary of State for Near Eastern Affairs
Islamabad, Pakistan
Sunday, August 26

At 11 a.m. the next morning, an angry, haggard, and disheveled Stuart Keaton stood before a bank of microphones in a meeting room at the Marriott Islamabad Hotel. An equally haggard Ambassador David Cooper stood at Keaton's side. A bank of six TV cameras and the attendant bright lights faced the two men. Keaton and Cooper had been up all night at the airport. They had both just returned to the hotel.

When the body of Archer Hadley had been recovered from the wreckage, close to midnight, Keaton and Ambassador Cooper made the identification of the badly burned corpse.

They remained at the airport until the last body was removed from the wreckage. Those at the rear of the aircraft were apparently unburned. They had all died of toxic smoke inhalation.

The pilots and cabin crew had died from rocket shrapnel and injuries sustained in the collapse of the forward part of the plane onto the runway. The passengers in the central part of the fuselage suffered all manner of injuries, but mainly they had died in the fire. Some of the bodies were burned so completely that they were totally unrecognizable.

They would await DNA and dental analysis back in the United States before they could be identified.

In total, forty-eight people had been killed in the attack, including Secretary Hadley, State Department personnel, newspaper and press representatives, and the military crew of the aircraft. No one survived.

Keaton spoke first. "We all know of the terrible, cowardly attack last night at Islamabad International Airport. Forty-eight Americans died, among them Secretary of State Archer M. Hadley. Hadley was a true patriot who left a lifetime appointment on the Federal Appeals Court to serve his country. His loss is immeasurable.

"Many others perished in that inferno—men and women of the State Department, members of the press, and the military crew who flew the plane. Each was dedicated, each was brave. Not one of these brave Americans deserved the fate that befell them."

"I have been informed that it has been announced on Al Jazeera that al'Asad Aljibal of the Haqqani Network has claimed credit for the attack. He says he killed all those people because Secretary Hadley had insulted him and was an enemy of Islam. He wanted his revenge against those who insult the Haqqani Network and who insult Islam.

"Our hearts are stricken in sympathy for those who died in this senseless attack. President Decker has ordered all flags on federal buildings to be flown at half-staff for the next fourteen days in honor of Secretary Hadley and those brave Americans who died last night.

"Words are inadequate to describe the emotions that Ambassador Cooper and I are feeling. I will accompany the remains of those who perished on the flight back to the United States. President Decker has ordered a military C-17 to transport the bodies. We will be landing at Dover Air Force Base upon arrival. The families and next of kin of those who were on the secretary's plane will be notified and allowed to be present. Some of the passengers were so severely burned that positive identification has not been possible here in Pakistan. When we get home, we will be able to access dental records and, if necessary,

DNA analysis for positive identification. I would now like to turn the microphone over to Ambassador Cooper. David."

Ambassador Cooper cleared his throat. He was clearly very emotional at the moment. "Secretary Hadley made this latest trip to Pakistan to offer military aid to the government of Pakistan. It was done in the spirit of mutual benefit to an ally in the war against terror.

"Al'Asad Aljibal claims he has had his revenge against America. He does not yet know the meaning of revenge. He will find out the meaning of revenge when America wreaks its revenge upon him. Assistant Secretary Keaton and I have seen firsthand what a perverted outlaw like Aljibal can do. Unfortunately, we cannot make him die forty-eight times. But once will be more than enough. And I fervently hope that when he dies, he will die by American hands.

"The government of Pakistan has pledged its full cooperation to bring al'Asad Aljibal to justice. We are grateful for that pledge and intend to use every bit of information we obtain to find and eliminate al'Asad Aljibal and his band of killers.

"The events we witnessed last night will haunt us for the rest of our days. My sincere prayer is that we can eliminate the men who did this heinous act before they can harm anyone else. Assistant Secretary Keaton and I will take questions from the floor for the next 15 minutes, and then we have other commitments which require our undivided attention."

Mishna Zamura from *The People's Voice Daily* leaped to his feet. "*The People's Voice Daily* published a story this morning that says the air controller in the tower was ordered by Colonel Dalari to delay the takeoff of the secretary's plane. The air controller said that Colonel Dalari was acting on orders from Field Marshal Bouradin."

The reporters in the room fell silent at this news. Those who had not heard about the published story immediately realized that the government might have been involved in the attack.

Keaton responded, "We have not seen any newspapers this morning, and we have not heard of this report. If this is true, then that is a startling development. Has there been any independent verification of the claim?"

An aide to Keaton, who was standing at the side of the room, immediately left the room to get several copies of the current edition of *The People's Voice Daily*. He understood the dire implications of the reporter's comment.

The same reporter said, "We have tried contacting the air controller, whose name is Salim Whamani, but there is no answer at his telephone. We sent a reporter to his home, and there was no one there. He and his wife and family seem to have disappeared."

This comment elicited quiet murmurs of Directorate S from the assembled reporters. The reporter from *The People's Voice Daily* continued, "There is a Colonel Dalari who is attached to Field Marshal Bouradin's staff, but our efforts to reach the colonel have also failed. No one in the field marshal's office seems to know who he is."

More murmurs from the assembled reporters. They knew the colonel would never be allowed to talk, or if he was even still alive.

The reporter continued, "If it is verified that the air controllers were supposed to delay the secretary's plane, thus making it a sitting target, what implications will this have for Pakistani-U.S. relations?"

Keaton, clearly shocked by the news in the reporter's question, said, "I cannot comment on your question until we can verify the accuracy of the allegation. If it is true, it is very serious. If it is false, then it will have no effect on U.S.-Pakistani relations."

Another reporter was recognized. "How will the Americans catch Aljibal if he hides out in the Tribal Area?"

Cooper answered, "We will need the cooperation of the Pakistani military authorities if Aljibal enters Pakistani territory. In the Tribal Area, there is minimal government presence. When we locate Aljibal, we will decide how to proceed."

Question followed question from many reporters, but none had the bombshell effect of the first reporter's question.

The aide, who had left the room earlier, returned with three copies of *The People's Voice Daily* in his hands. Fortunately, as there are many newspapers in Pakistan, it was a bilingual paper, published in both Urdu and English. Both are the official languages of Pakistan. Each story ran in two languages beneath the headlines. It would still require an authoritative translation of the Urdu portions of the story, but the English version was more than sufficient to get the gist of what was being reported.

Keaton and Cooper stayed ten minutes beyond the allotted 15 minutes for questions. Cooper said. "We must apologize for leaving, but we both have official duties that must be performed now. Thank you all for coming on this very sad occasion. We must go now."

Keaton and Cooper exited the meeting room, followed by their respective aides. The reporters all began telephoning their stories to their editors. After doing their jobs, many began speaking to each other about the ramifications of what the air controller supposedly said and the disappearance of him and his family without a trace. The reporter from *The People's Voice Daily* was surrounded by other reporters trying to get more of the story.

Outside the meeting, Keaton caught Cooper's eye and steered him into a small side room. An aide followed, handing each man a newspaper before Keaton dismissed him with a curt nod. Both men bent over the article, reading in tense silence.

"If this report is accurate," Keaton said at last, "it means Pakistan itself was part of the plot to kill Secretary Hadley and the others."

Cooper shook his head. "I struggle to believe that. What possible advantage would they gain by being tied to the murder of our Secretary of State and forty-seven Americans? It makes no sense."

Keaton did not have a real answer other than, "So much in Islamic countries makes little sense to us. Get your Cultural Affairs guy working on this immediately. Let's see what his spooks can turn up. We had better get this information to Langley and the White House immediately before they read it in the newspapers."

"Shit! It's bad enough that Hadley was attacked. Now, this angle makes it look like Pakistan wants to go to war with us. What a clusterfuck this is," Dave Cooper muttered as he strode out toward the embassy.

Keaton lingered, the silence pressing in after Cooper's exit. At the U.S. Embassy, the flight recorders sat under armed Marine guard, waiting for transport to Washington. Inside those black boxes was the story no one could yet tell.

38

JACK & LAURA

The Eastern Hills of Afghanistan
Sunday, August 25

Their cell phones vibrated, showing an incoming message from Stevens. Laura was driving, so Jack punched in the codes that would decrypt the message.

Jack was stunned when he read the message. "Shit," he exclaimed. Then he sat quietly, absorbing the news.

Laura asked, "Are you going to keep the message a secret?"

"It says that Secretary of State Hadley and forty-seven others were all killed in an attack by unknown terrorists at the Islamabad Airport. They blew up his plane on the runway. There were no survivors. They suspect Aljibal was the attacker."

Laura pulled the truck over to the side of the road and came to a stop.

"What low-life animals! Does this mean Aljibal is in Pakistan, and we have to go there to get him?"

"I don't know what it means. Aljibal crosses the border as if it isn't there. We will have to get in touch with Langley."

Laura decrypted her message, and it was identical to Jack's. She immediately sent a message to Mossad headquarters asking a question in Hebrew: What do our analysts think is the most likely place for us to find Aljibal in light of the attack in Islamabad?

Jack sent the same question to Langley in English.

Twenty minutes later, when they were again on the road, Laura's phone vibrated with an incoming message. She pulled over to the side of the road again and decrypted her message. In Hebrew, it read:

> Our people believe Aljibal was the attacker. He will go back to Afghanistan. The attack on Hadley was done by a handful of jihadists firing rockets. If it was Aljibal, his larger force and the women are in Afghanistan. Stay there. He will come to you.

Laura read the message to Jack.

"I think that is the right conclusion," Jack said. "I wonder what Langley will say?"

Ten minutes later, Jack's phone vibrated with a message. Jack decrypted it.

> We have split opinions here. We are not sure the attack was carried out by Aljibal. If, in fact, it was Aljibal, some of us believe he has to go back to Afghan; others believe he may have transferred to Pak where he feels safer. Your call. If you don't find him in Afghan look for him in Pak. My personal take is stick to Afghan.
>
> Stevens

"Well, that's a lot of help," Laura observed.

"We are on our own, the way we always were," Jack said.

"Yes, but when we ask for advice, it would be nice if we could actually get some."

"Analysts analyze. Doers do. Analysts say what if's because that's their job. Doers say, 'Damn the torpedoes, full speed ahead.' I think we should continue until we link up with the SEALs and go after his camp. We'll find him there."

At that moment, a bullet crashed through the windshield, narrowly missing Laura's head. She grabbed her rifle and bailed out the driver's door.

Jack dove out of the passenger side and took cover behind a large rock on the roadside.

Laura scuttled under the truck. The engine was still idling. Another bullet hit the truck somewhere. As she was crawling under the truck, she felt the heat from the engine and the exhaust on her back. She moved faster to avoid being burned by the hot truck parts.

"I've got him," Jack whispered. "He is about 120 yards ahead on the hillside."

"I'm coming over to you," Laura said.

Jack laid down a few covering shots toward the sniper while Laura continued under the truck to the right side of the road and then scooted the four feet to Jack's large rock.

A moment later, a shot pinged off the large rock.

Laura said, "What a way to say hello."

"Since he shot first, my guess is he wanted to kill us and then rob us."

"He isn't very neighborly."

Jack said, "I want to get about 50 yards closer and see if I can get a shot at him from his flank. Can you keep him busy without letting him hit you?"

"He isn't much good with a rifle. Go and play in the rocks."

Laura popped a shot at where the sniper was hiding. When she fired, Jack moved about five yards ahead to the cover of another rock.

Things grew quiet. Jack heard another single shot from Laura, which was answered by the sniper, and then Laura fired again. The sound of bullets striking rocks at both ends was clearly heard. When Laura fired, Jack got to move again. This give and take kept up for another ten minutes, with Jack getting ever closer to the sniper.

Jack felt his phone vibrate. He softly grunted, "Yea."

Jack heard Laura's voice, "There are at least two of them up there, not one as we thought. Be careful; there may be more than two."

"Roger." Jack disconnected. Laura exchanged fire with the two snipers.

From the snipers' position, Jack heard two rifles fire together. Definitely two enemies, maybe more.

Laura fired again. A scream of pain was heard from one sniper. Laura had scored a hit. Was the injured guy badly wounded or just slightly wounded? Or was he faking it to draw them out? Jack kept moving. No one was shooting at him, but he still stayed behind cover.

He had covered about 50 yards away from Laura. He spotted the rock where the snipers had been hiding. There was a blood smear on another rock behind the sniper's position. Jack was satisfied that Laura had shot him. Now to find the son of a bitch and his partner and finish them off.

Jack continued crawling from rock to rock until he was only 25 yards away. He was on the opposite side of the road from the snipers' position. One man was shot, but was he able to move? If he could move, it meant he was still capable of fighting. *I'll just have to assume it's still one of me against two of them,* Jack thought.

Jack called Laura's phone. She answered, "Yes?"

"You hit one of them, but he has moved away from his position. I am sure they moved left, up the hill. I want to get across the road. Lay down a few three-round bursts into the area where they've probably moved to. I'll cross the road while you are firing."

"Got it. On the count of three."

Jack counted to three. Laura started firing. Four three-round bursts. Jack ran across the road in a crouch and took cover behind another big rock.

He could see the snipers' perch from his new position. He scuttled ahead on the side of the road until he was 15 yards beyond the snipers' position. Then he started to work his way up the hill.

Laura saw Jack leave the side of the road and start up the hill. She put another three-round burst into the rocks where she imagined the snipers had taken cover. In ten agonizing minutes of slow crawling, Jack was above the sniper's position, looking down on where the attackers once were. He still heard sporadic firing from the hill.

Jack kept moving to the left. A few minutes later, he was surprised to see that there were four men in the rocks. They were talking to each other in Arabic.

"That is a woman down there with the rifle," said one.

"There was a man. Where is he?" asked the second.

"We must have killed him. She is the only one firing," answered the first man.

"Maybe we can take her alive. I would like to fuck someone. Even if she is ugly, I need to fuck someone." The third man rubbed his crotch in anticipation.

"I wouldn't mind a whore either," said the fourth man.

"How can we get her to surrender? I don't want to fuck a corpse," said the second man.

Jack understood every word they said. He stood behind a large rock and gently set his fire selector to full automatic. The soft click of the fire selector was picked up by two of the men, who turned to see what it was. The noise was so soft it did not alarm either man. From behind the manly warriors who were all eager to rape the woman down below, he sprayed all four of them with 5.56 mm rifle fire.

All four went down.

He changed magazines, then on a three-shot burst he put three bullets into each man's crotch in the hope that if any of them lived, they would never bother another woman. Ever.

Jack searched the area. There were no more enemies.

Working his way back to the road, he saw a leg lying behind a rock. It wasn't moving. Cautiously, he moved until he could see the complete man. He was sprawled facedown on the ground in a small mud puddle caused by his bleeding. Jack looked around carefully to see if the guy still had any friends nearby. He didn't see anybody. Jack was now pretty sure he was the only living man on the hill.

Jack picked up a rock the size of a baseball. He threw it at the inert body. His aim was not very good. The baseball-sized rock hit the large rock near where the man was lying and bounced into the man's left arm. The body did not move. Jack thought to himself, "So much for my major league pitching career."

Jack telephoned Laura. She answered immediately. "You got him, Laura. The guy you hit is dead. There were four others. They are all finished."

"Pity. I would have liked to question them. I heard the sound of your rifle, but I didn't hear any answering clacks from AK-47s, so I knew you were alright."

"It looks like they all retreated when the one you shot got hit."

"Such loyalty among holy warriors," Laura observed. "Well, all of them are now sitting on the right hand of Allah."

"I overheard them planning on taking you alive and using you as a living inflatable sex doll."

"Maybe it's better you finished them all off."

"Would you like to pick me up on the road?"

"Yes, I would. But I caught a ricochet in my left thigh. I would like you to look at it while we are still under cover behind this big rock."

"I'm coming back to you. Make sure I don't get shot while I am on the road."

"I'll cover you. First, search the dead guys. See if they have phones or some papers or ID of any kind."

"Four of them are back up the hill. I am going to leave them there. This one guy you shot is close, so I will search him."

Jack dropped down to where the man was lying. He quickly searched his pockets, which yielded nothing more than an Algerian passport and some Afghan money. He had a small rucksack. *I'll search this later*, he thought, *taking care of Laura's leg is more important.*

He threw the rucksack over his left shoulder and clambered down from the rocks. He could see Laura's rifle above the rock up ahead, pointing into the hill from which he had just come.

When he reached Laura behind the big rock, he saw that her left pant leg was bloody. She sat back on the ground with both legs out in front of her.

"Pull up that awful skirt and I'll pull down the pants," he said.

She hiked up the skirt and leaned back onto the ground, raising her hips with her right leg. Jack reached for the waistband of the pants and gently lowered them, exposing Laura's wounded thigh.

"The bullet caught you on the outside of the muscles. Most of the bleeding has already stopped; you're just oozing a little. I'm going to put an antibiotic in there and a coagulant to stop the oozing. Then you'll get a pressure bandage wrapped around the thigh. When Dr. Jack is done, you should have a nice 4-inch scar to show our children."

"Who said I was going to have sex with Dr. Jack? What kind of medical office is this? Children! I want a second opinion."

"Here's my second opinion. I think you are totally naked underneath all your clothes, and it is Dr. Jack's job to find out if that is true, so I can do a proper examination. And underneath all his clothes, Dr. Jack is also totally naked."

"You can check under my clothes some other time. Right now, leave your pants stapled to your ass and fix my naked leg attached to the rest of my naked body that is underneath all my clothes."

Jack was so relieved the wound was not serious that he smiled and said, "OK, Here is a third opinion." He bent down and kissed her underpants on her pubic hair. "I love you, Laura. Please don't stop any more bullets this year."

"Well, you certainly have an unusual bedside manner. I am looking forward to your fourth opinion." Laura reached out and hugged Jack. Then she pulled him down on top of her and tenderly kissed him.

He kissed her back gently and said, "You scared me. No more getting hurt, please."

"I didn't do it on purpose. I was more worried about you than I was about myself."

"That's because I am an adorable kid," Jack said with a smile.

"Hang in there, fella. Tonight, I'll make you feel like an adorable man."

Jack completed his first-aid ministrations on Laura in about five minutes.

Laura stood up and winced when she put her weight on her left leg. She brushed the dirt and pebbles off the back of her underwear, pulled up her trousers, and lowered her skirt. She picked up her rifle and the sniper's rucksack, limped over to the passenger side of the truck, and got in. "We'll check out the rucksack later. Right now, I think we should get out of here. It's a low-class neighborhood."

Jack went around to the driver's side. The windshield had a sizable bullet hole in it with cracks radiating outwards. There was a bullet hole in the upholstery near where a person's right shoulder might be. From the angle up on the hill at which it was fired, the glass must have deflected the bullet enough that it missed the driver.

"It's going to be fun driving this truck with the windshield in such bad shape. We should have brought some duct tape."

"Hey fella. I'm not in such great shape either. Have a little *rachmunnes* for the truck and for me."

"What's *rachmunnes*?" Jack asked.

Laura explained, "It's Yiddish. It means sympathy or compassion. The nearest English expression is give me a break!"

"From now on, I will be the soul of *rachmunnes* until you are sick of me."

"I'll try to bear up under the strain." Laura smiled and held Jack's hand while he drove down the road with the wind whistling through the hole in the windshield. The noise was weird.

39

AL'ASAD ALJIBAL

Camp of the Haqqani Network
Eastern Hills of Afghanistan
Monday, August 27

"Bring the camera. We'll send a message to Al Jazeera. Gather everyone in the clearing."

Aljibal and his band had just returned from Rawalpindi. Within twenty minutes, the camp assembled: girls shrouded head to toe in burqas, faces hidden behind veils, and fighters forming a loose ring of rifles and hard eyes around them.

Climbing onto the bed of the battered pickup, Aljibal faced the crowd. A scarf hid the lower half of his face as the camera's red light blinked to life.

The air tightened. The men braced for news of triumph. The girls, silent and rigid, sensed another death and feared what would follow.

Once the cameraman gave the signal, Aljibal began.

"I am al'Asad Aljibal, the Lion of the Mountains, leader of the Haqqani Network of the Islamic Caliphate. Yesterday, I sent the crusader Secretary of State of the accursed United States to Hell along with all his aides and staff and the accompanying news reporters. It was we who blew up his plane, and it is we who have earned the credit for doing the will of the Prophet, *Sal Allaahu Alaiyhi wa Sallam.*"

At this announcement, the mujahideen began cheering and dancing and firing their rifles into the sky. The video camera panned the crowd of mujahideen who were celebrating. There was almost no reaction other than a numbed silence from the assembled girls. The mujahideen continued their celebration until Aljibal held up his hands. They quieted down to listen again. The camera returned to Aljibal.

"The infidel Archer M. Hadley, who was once the crusader Secretary of State, is no more. He sleeps in Hell. He who promised to find us and eliminate us has himself been eliminated, *Subhan Allah* (Glory to God)."

More cheering and gunfire followed this announcement.

"He who said I would never find another night of peaceful sleep is now sleeping for eternity."

More cheering from the mujahideen.

"Yesterday, our rockets sent everyone on the damned Hadley's plane to their deaths in the flames of Hell on earth. All forty-eight of them."

The mujahideen were unsure what Aljibal was referring to, but they cheered anyway.

"Forty-eight crusaders died at the hands of the faithful on the runway at Rawalpindi. The Haqqani Network is invincible for Allah is with us!" screamed Aljibal. "Jihad shall be triumphant! *Allahu Akbar. Allahu Akbar. Allahu Akbar.*"

Cheering, dancing, and much gunfire in the air followed. The video camera panned across the crowd and eventually faded to black.

Aljibal was very pleased with himself as he got down from the back of the pickup truck. He called the video operator to him. "Can you get that video to Al Jazeera quickly?"

"Yes, Rayiys. The Al Jazeera men left us their dish antenna. It is pointed at the satellite. All I have to do is play it back on their connections, and they will have it. First, I must telephone them to alert them that the video will arrive."

"Do it right away."

"Yes, Rayiys, it shall be done."

Within the hour Al Jazeera had broadcast the video of Aljbal's triumphant announcement and the celebration that it sparked. No terrorist attack is complete until the perpetrators proudly and publicly announce that they have performed the despicable murder of many innocent people.

40

NSA HEADQUARTERS

Bethesda, MD
Monday, August 27

Robert Bailey studied the satellite feeds of Pakistan, eyes fixed on the attack that had brought down the Secretary of State's plane at Islamabad International Airport. Four large monitors glowed across his desk as he scrolled through images from noon to eight p.m., Local Rawalpindi time.

At 15:10 a pickup appeared, meeting briefly with a military 4x4 near the fence. After a short exchange, both vehicles pulled away. At 18:50 the same truck returned, rolling toward the end of runway 10R. At 19:18 three streaks arced skyward. Bailey watched the rockets strike, the aircraft erupt in flame, and the pickup vanish into the night— the grainy images even catching the attackers in their moment of celebration.

By 19:20 fire crews swarmed the wreckage. Flames, confusion, bodies carried from the blackened shell. After midnight, the orange flight recorders were lifted from the debris. From first movement to final recovery, Bailey had the entire attack laid bare before him.

Bobby had a hunch. Because the secretary's plane was at Islamabad a month ago when there was a terrorist attack at the airport, he decided to look back on that event as well.

After a careful review of the images, he realized that the secretary's plane was the intended target in that attack, too. When he thought he had the complete picture of what had transpired, he picked up the phone on his desk and dialed.

"Major Schwartzman," answered the woman he was calling.

"Major, I have an issue that needs your urgent attention in yesterday's downloads of Saturday's attack on Secretary Hadley."

I'll be right there, Bobby. Hold the images on the screens."

A few minutes later, Major Anita Schwartzman, U.S. Army Intelligence, entered Robert Bailey's cubicle. They had been working together for almost two years. She was a tall brunette, extremely intelligent, in terrific physical shape, and quite attractive. Bob was always asking her to have dinner with him, and she always refused, citing the impropriety of what it would do to their working relationship. "What have you got for me, Bobby?" she asked.

"I will ignore the possible ramifications of that question and stick to business instead," Bobby said. "Take a look at this sequence."

He started the sequence of images from the surveillance satellites. He zoomed in on the pertinent section of the image. The pickup truck could be seen driving down the road next to the runway. When the truck arrived at the end of the runway, the designation 10R could clearly be seen painted on the runway. The truck stopped moving. The four men crouched in the back of the truck were clearly visible.

Bob zoomed out for a wider view. The plane, with its blue and white color scheme and the words "United States of America" painted on both sides of the fuselage, could be seen taxiing to the end of runway 10R.

"That's Secretary Hadley's plane getting ready to take off," Bailey explains. "It pauses for a few seconds instead of going into the immediate takeoff sequence."

Bailey then zoomed in again on the back of the pickup truck. The four attackers stood up in the truck. Three of them held rocket launchers to their shoulders, aiming toward the plane on the runway. Immediately after the attackers fire their rockets, the truck moves forward. The rockets hit the plane, and the explosions follow.

"Why was there no perimeter security?" observed Major Schwartzman.

"I had the same question in my mind, so I went backward a few hours to see what the security schedule was. Look at this third screen. This is the afternoon of the attack. You see the pickup truck driving down the road next to 10R, meeting a military vehicle by the fence. Just one occupant, whom I cannot identify. They have a brief conversation and then they each drive back the way they came."

Bailey leaned forward. "Watch this. Normally, a perimeter patrol passes along this dirt road every eight to ten minutes. But in the thirty minutes before the secretary's plane was scheduled to take off, the patrols stop. Three rotations simply don't happen. Then, after the attack, instead of pursuing the assailants, the patrol drives straight onto the tarmac to the burning plane. No one goes after the attackers. To me, it looks deliberate—like the security was stood down before and after the strike."

"That means that there was complicity from the Pakistani military to assist the attackers," said Major Schwartzman. "Dammit, they're supposed to be our allies. Once again, they prove they aren't reliable friends."

"I had a strange hunch when I saw this. Now let's look at the terrorist attack from a month ago. That's Secretary Hadley's plane getting ready to take off," Bob explains. "It taxis to the end of the runway and does not pause at all but goes into immediate takeoff sequence. Note that again there is a pickup truck near the fence of 10R."

Bailey then zoomed in again on the back of the pickup truck. The four attackers stood up in the truck. One of them held a rocket launcher to his shoulder, aiming toward the plane on the runway. Just as the attacker fires his rocket, the truck lurches forward, and the smoke trail of the rocket sails over the top of the plane. A miss. The rocket strikes the wall of the terminal building.

A moment later, a second attacker raises his rocket launcher and fires at the departing plane while the truck is bouncing over the dirt road. This rocket is also too high and misses the plane. The rocket's smoke trail shows it hitting a baggage wagon about 900 meters away.

Major Schwartzman said, "Dammit Bob! The terrorist attack was not intended for the airport terminal at all. It was an earlier attempt to kill the Secretary of State."

"That's the way I see it."

"What a shit storm!" said the major.

"It seems so," Robert Bailey observed. "On the day of the fatal attack, the same identical sequence of events occurred, and the same patrols were not made by the security people. I have the pictures of the rendezvous with the military 4x4 and the perimeter patrols that do not get made."

"OK Bob. I will need a video summary with timestamps and labels that explain your observations. Leave the conclusions to the big brass, but do a separate write-up of your conclusions as well."

"The implications of what is here leave me wondering about our good friends in Pakistan."

"You did good work, Bobby. Now, let's wrap it up with what I need to show to the big boys. Thanks, Bob."

"Just doing my job, Major. This stuff is the reason we get paid the big bucks."

"Yeah, just don't spend it all buying a candy bar at the PX."

Major Schwartzman turned to go. "Can we get your material within 30 minutes?"

Bob Bailey said, "For you, Major, I'll get it done in 25. In fact, I'm already part way done."

Major Anita Schwartzman left to alert her immediate superior that a serious situation needed to be addressed. Secretary Hadley had been murdered with complicity from the Pakistani military. They tried it once and screwed up. They had a second chance and succeeded. The president and the ranking members of Congress would have to know about the Pakistanis. This issue would be: What effective action should be taken? Lesser provocations had previously resulted in military retaliation. This was heavy.

41

JACK & LAURA

Near Orgun, Afghanistan
Monday, August 27

Jack stopped the truck in the middle of the road. There wasn't any traffic to worry about. They were pretty much alone.

"I'm going to call the lieutenant commanding the SEAL team to let him know we are here. I don't want to get shot by our own guys."

Jack dialed the pre-set number in his phone's favorites list. The call went to voicemail. Jack left a message explaining they are Pogo and Koala. We are nearby and want to link up without getting shot. Jack also explained that they were dressed as Afghan peasants.

Within a minute of completing the call, Jack's phone vibrated. He answered it. Lieutenant Cosgrove introduced himself. "I apologize for not answering your call, but I didn't recognize the number. I let you go to voicemail."

"Not a problem," said Jack. "I'm sure you have perimeter lookouts, and I don't want them shooting us. We are supposed to link up with you to chase down Aljibal. We are driving a pickup with a shot-out right headlight and a bullet hole in the windshield. We are dressed like Afghan peasants."

"Describe where you are now."

"Give me a second, and I will send you our coordinates."

"Laura," Jack said, "take a picture of the truck and get the coordinates at the bottom of the screen. Then send the photo to number 6 on your favorites list."

"Back on the phone, Jack spoke to Lieutenant Cosgrove, "Koala, my partner, is going to send you a photo of our truck, which will have our map coordinates at the bottom. You will know what our truck looks like and where we are."

"That'll work," said the lieutenant.

Laura said to Jack, "The photo has been sent."

A few beats later, Lieutenant Cosgrove said, "I have the photo with the coordinates. That is a very cool phone you have there. Anyway, you are about 12 to 15 minutes away from us. My guys will spread a small blue cloth on a large rock on the right side of the road. Stop when you get there, and we will lead you the rest of the way."

"Roger, a small blue cloth on a large rock, right side of the road. We'll be there in 12 to 15 minutes." Both Jack and Cosgrove broke the connection at the same time.

Jack and Laura were now Pogo and Koala. Operational names only for the foreseeable future.

Jack drove on. In 12 minutes, he saw the blue cloth up ahead. He slowed down to about 20 km per hour. When he got to the big rock with the blue cloth, he stopped.

A voice called out, "Drive another 30 meters."

Jack did so.

A SEAL stepped out onto the side of the road in front of the truck. His rifle was ready. Two more SEALs stepped out behind the truck. Pogo and Koala were covered front and back.

"Hi guys, I am Pogo. My partner is Koala. I believe you have been expecting us."

The man in front said, "The lieutenant wants me to bring you into camp. First, we have to hide your truck. Follow me slowly, and I'll show you where to park, and then we'll cover the truck with netting."

Twenty minutes later, the truck was parked off the road next to four armored Humvees. It was covered with camouflage netting and was virtually invisible. The three of them hiked into the SEALs' camp, Pogo carrying most of their weapons and gear and Koala slightly limping.

Lieutenant Cosgrove approached to greet them. "We've been expecting you. I didn't know there would be a woman in your group. My guys' language can get pretty coarse sometimes."

Koala laughed. "I've heard it all at one time or another. Don't be concerned about my delicate sensibilities."

"Jack said, "For this operation, I'm Pogo, and she's Koala. It is better for everyone if you don't know our names."

"That's OK with us. If we accomplish our objective, then we'll all be happy." Cosgrove asked, "Have you seen Aljibal's latest video claiming the credit for killing Secretary of State Hadley?"

"No," said Koala. "Have you got it where we can see it?"

"Step into my office," said Cosgrove as he motioned them toward a log on the ground.

Pogo sat on Cosgrove's left, and Koala sat on his right. He pulled out his cell phone and played the video of Aljibal claiming the credit for killing Hadley.

They all watched Aljibal perform for the camera. When the video was done, Koala asked, "Do we have any idea where he is hiding?"

"The son of a bitch is somewhere in this area. But we haven't been able to track him down. Any locals who might know where he is are too afraid of retaliation to give us any leads."

Koala said, "Could you play that video one more time, please?"

"Sure." Cosgrove played the video on his phone again.

Just before the video ended, Koala said, "Stop the video, back it up a few seconds."

Cosgrove did as she asked.

"There, stop the video."

Clearly seen on the screen was the assembled crowd in the clearing with mujahideen shooting rifles in the air. "In the distance behind the camp, there are three mountains that are almost all the same height. We need NSA to do some work for us to find those three mountains. When we do, we will find Aljibal."

"I'll get on the phone with home," Pogo said. "What is the time showing on the video where the picture is?"

Cosgrove looked at his phone. "Six minutes, 22 seconds."

"I will get a message to the right person who can help us find those mountains."

Pogo took out his cell phone and composed a message to Stevens and Watson:

Have linked up with SEALs. In Aljibal's latest video claiming credit for the attack on SecState Hadley at 6 min 22 seconds, Koala has noticed that there is a clear view of three mountains in the background. All three mountains are almost identical in height. We need someone at NSA to research the satellite data to find location(s) in Afghan near Orgun where there are three mountains of same height. Check out video to see what we need.

Pogo

Pogo pressed the send code. The message disappeared, and there was a quiet ping. "It's sent."

"How did that happen?" Cosgrove asked. "That was fast."

"The message was encrypted and compressed into a one-second radio burst. They'll reverse the process at the other end. Let's hope they get us some results."

We'll be chowing down in an hour. MRE's. Do you guys have a shelter? It gets pretty cold here at night."

"We have a tent. We know what to do. I have another request. We had a firefight earlier today. Koala caught a ricochet round in her left thigh. We'd appreciate it if your medic could take a look at her leg."

"Chief Williams is our medic. I'll get him to take a look."

Twenty minutes later, a giant black Master Chief Petty Officer carrying a backpack stopped by to see Jack and Laura. "Who is Koala?" he asked.

"I am," answered Laura.

"I am Master Chief Warren Williams. If you don't mind, Ma'am, the lieutenant told me to take a look at your leg wound."

"I don't mind. I caught a ricochet in my left thigh. Pogo did first-aid, but his medical skills are sort of rudimentary."

"I resent that. I have a medical degree in basic first-aid from Quacksville College."

The chief smiled, "If it walks like a duck, and treats wounds like a duck, then it must be a Quacksville graduate. Let's see the leg."

Laura rolled up her pant leg to the top of her thigh.

The chief removed the bandage from the wound. "You are lucky this was a ricochet, Koala. Most of the bullet's force was spent when it hit the rock first. I would like to inject an antibiotic to prevent any possibility of infection. Then, I would like to suture it closed so you don't injure it if you must run or fight. If I suture the wound, that will lessen the width of the scar so it will just be a narrow line."

Koala said, "What you propose makes sense. Do it, please."

Chief Williams set to work. His big hands were surprisingly gentle. First, he sprayed an anesthetizing agent onto the wound. Then he injected antibiotics. Finally, he started sewing. Twenty-four sutures later, he was done. He covered the wound with a clean bandage and applied a generous amount of adhesive tape. "It isn't plastic surgery, but it will be much neater than letting the wound remain open and leaving a scar one inch wide."

Koala looked at the big man. "Thank you so much for your care. Right now, the leg is something I no longer have to worry about."

"Those stitches will have to come out in about two weeks. Any doctor or medic can do it for you."

"I'll get it done," Laura replied.

Chief Williams said, "It is nice to do some medicine without someone shooting at me. Every now and then, I get to feel like a real corpsman. I would advise you to stay off the leg for a few days, but my gut tells me you won't listen. So, all I can tell you is not to lift anything too heavy. Logs, anvils, and small horses are definitely out."

"Your gut is right. There is no way I can stay off the leg until we get Aljibal. After he is dead, then I can rest."

The chief stood, picked up his backpack of supplies, "I'll be around camp if you need me. You are lucky with that wound. It could have been a lot worse."

42

STUART KEATON

The White House
Washington, D.C.
Wednesday, August 29

Assistant Secretary of State Stuart Keaton was shown into the Oval Office. President Decker stood up from behind his desk and walked around to shake Keaton's hand. "Stu, it's good to see you. The job you and Dave did in Islamabad was flawless. The flight data recorders came in yesterday and have already been analyzed by the experts. A copy has been made for the Pakistanis and is already on its way back to Islamabad. Their expert was a witness to the copying process, and then he flew back with the copies. We had him attest to the accuracy of what we did."

"Thank you, Mr. President. Sometimes, in the crush of events, you overlook or forget to do some essential things. I hope I didn't miss something important."

"At this moment, no one can fault anything you and Dave did, and no one has thought of anything you didn't do. Flying home with the victims yesterday was also the right thing to do. It showed respect, caring, and honor to those who perished. It was important that all the victims received the same caring treatment that Archer did. Even the five unidentified remains were handled correctly."

Keaton was embarrassed by the president's praise. "The airmen who received us at Dover were unbelievably compassionate in the way they handled each coffin. When I saw the flag-draped coffins lined up in the hangar in a rectangle of four rows of twelve, I cried at the waste of human life."

"You may not know this, but your tears and your salute to the victims were caught by a TV camera crew that was there. When you thought you were alone, they filmed you walking the rows and touching each coffin with your hand. It was one of the most moving things anyone has ever witnessed. The sincerity of your feelings was seen in every home in America and around the world as well. The entire nation wants us to get Aljibal and make him pay for what he has done."

"I didn't know that I was caught on video. I didn't do that for the cameras. I was overcome with emotion."

"I know that. And so does every person who saw what you did. That you are a good man is now known to all Americans. Now I have to ask you a favor. When the 14 days of mourning for the victims are over, I want to nominate you to be the next Secretary of State."

"Surely there must be someone better qualified than I am. I have only had this job for a month."

"You have all the right instincts. After what the nation has seen of your inner heart, there is no one better qualified than you are for this vital position."

"I am honored, Mr. President. Let me get Adelle's approval before I say yes."

"There is much more to tell you. You will be in line of succession for my job. After what happened to Archer, the Secret Service will want to offer you the same protection that the Speaker of the House receives. First in succession is the Vice President. The speaker is next in succession after the Vice President. The third in succession is the President Pro Tempore of the Senate. If we should all get wiped out together, tag, you are it."

"That is a heavy burden to carry. So far, it hasn't fallen on anyone other than a few vice presidents. I think I'll be able to handle that."

"Now I have to tell you what we discovered in the cockpit voice recorder and what the NSA has found in satellite images. It would be best if you hear and see it for yourself. I had the staff set up the data on one of my TVs over here."

The president picked up a remote control from his desk and pointed it at one of the television sets in his office. He switched the set on, and the exchange between Lieutenant Colonel Singleton and the tower came out of the speakers. Both men were standing, looking at the TV set and just listening to the audio. Keaton heard the air controller say he had orders to delay the flight on the ground just seconds before the attack. At the moment of the attack, the screaming of the injured crewmen could be heard, and then silence.

Keaton was not surprised by what he had heard. "This means the Pakistanis were really part of the plan to kill our Secretary of State, as the newspaper article alleged."

"Wait," said the president, "there is more. These are satellite images from Sunday, July 29th." The president initiated the sequence of satellite images of the rendezvous between the Pakistani military Range Rover and the attacker's pickup truck. The president explained the lack of perimeter security patrols. Then, the images of the rockets fired at the plane appeared, and the missiles caused damage to the terminal building and baggage cart.

"So, the attack at the airport was not directed at the airport itself but was an unsuccessful attempt to kill Hadley," Keaton said. "Further, it appears the attackers had the cooperation of the Pakistani military in removing the perimeter security."

"Now let us advance to August 25th. You will see the same sequence of a meeting by the attackers with a Pakistani officer, the absence of perimeter patrols, only now the plane is subject to multiple delays on the ground. For proof, we have the cockpit voice recorder audio and the air controller saying he had been ordered to delay the flight. At 7:18 p.m. local time, the successful attack takes place, and everyone on the plane is killed. We have images of the attacker's pickup truck driving away with no pursuit by any Pakistani military patrols. We have synchronized the cockpit audio to satellite images of the last 20 minutes before Aljibal's attackers destroyed the plane. The story written by the reporter for *The People's Voice Daily* was true. Plus, the air traffic controller, Salim Whamani, and his wife and children have disappeared without a trace. Colonel Dalari, who supposedly ordered Whamani to delay the flight, has also not surfaced anywhere."

Keaton said, "This whole thing has the stench of Directorate S about it. It could not have happened without the connivance of our noble ally, Field Marshal Bouradin. Bouradin was pissed off at Archer during the aid negotiations because we wouldn't give them any of the technologically advanced weaponry they wanted."

"My problem is: What does the United States do about this now that we have irrefutable evidence of the Pakistan government's involvement in the murders of forty-eight Americans?"

Keaton paused, collecting himself. "The world has already seen the destruction of the secretary's plane and the murder of forty-eight people. We should go public with the evidence you've shown me before anyone can tamper with the cockpit recorders. Win the court of world opinion first, then put clear demands to President Harraf: Bouradin must be retired and stripped of command. Give them the recorders and make it plain that removing Bouradin is the price of peace.

"If Harraf resists, we escalate. Cut off military and foreign aid. Treat any obstruction to our operations in Afghanistan as hostile—we will consider military options against Pakistan. I'd even position a carrier group and a Marine Expeditionary Force offshore to make our resolve unmistakable.

"Still, leave them a face-saving exit: once Bouradin is gone, invite Harraf for a state visit to re-establish relations. Give them a way to step back without losing everything."

"Stu, you have just reinforced my decision to make you our Secretary of State. You will be the special envoy that I will send to Harraf. I will call an emergency cabinet meeting this afternoon to show all of them the evidence, and then I will release the recordings to the media. I will include the Senate and House leaders from both parties. At the cabinet meeting, I will order the naval forces to the Arabian Sea off Karachi. I want you to convey my message to Harraf as soon as I make contact with him, to let him know that you are coming and that you speak on my behalf. I think you should travel on a military jet for your own safety. I don't want a repeat of last Saturday."

"Yes, Sir. I'd better let Adelle know I am leaving again."

43

NSA HEADQUARTERS

Bethesda, MD
Wednesday, August 29

While the president was meeting with his Washington Cabinet, in nearby Bethesda, Bobby Bailey was searching through thousands of images to find three mountains of the same height near Orgun, Afghanistan. So far, he had found four possible locations that met the criteria requested from the CIA operatives in the field. The spook who spotted these three hills had to be pretty sharp to have picked up on the landmark.

Bailey called Major Anita Schwartzman. She picked up on the second ring. "Major Schwartzman."

"Major, it's Bobby. I've got four possible candidates for the latest request from the spook works. I would like you to review them, and if you think they fill the bill, we could send them the info."

"I'll be there in ten minutes, Bob. I could use a cup of coffee. Today has been like a zoo up here."

"The coffee and some quiet time with a sincere admirer will await your arrival in ten minutes."

Eight minutes later, Bailey brought a large 16 oz. styrofoam cup of hot coffee, light, with two Splendas, into his cubicle. To the cup of coffee, Bailey said, "Stay hot until the major gets here."

Three minutes later, Major Anita Schwartzman arrived and plunked herself down in Bob's guest chair. "Is that coffee for me?" she asked.

"Whatever you need whenever or wherever you need it. That's the service I provide."

"I wish I could take you up on that offer. But not in this puzzle palace. But thanks for the coffee. I really need a break today." Changing the subject, Major Schwartzman asked Bob, "What have you found?"

"I've got four locations that might satisfy the search criteria I put through the computer. There were two more that were too far out of the area where they expect to locate Aljibal, so I am offering them as alternates if he doesn't turn up in one of the four I think are the most likely."

"Get me the picture from Aljibal's video on screen one, then, let's look at your candidates." Major Schwartzman took a sip of her coffee. "Ahhh, that's just what I needed."

While Bailey was punching keys on his keyboard, he said, "I'm happy that you got what you need. Now, how about considering your friend Bobby's needs?" A picture appeared on Bob's second monitor, followed by two more on the other monitors. "Here are the first three places I found."

Holding the cup of coffee, Major Schwartzman stood up behind Bailey and visually compared the three satellite pictures to the blown-up Aljibal video. "Hmm, they all look promising. Let's see the fourth picture."

Bobby replaced the picture on the last screen with his fourth-choice location. "The center hill is taller and further away, but because of the perspective, it looks like it's the same height as the two closer hills."

"Let me see your backup choices."

Bobby tapped some more keys on his keyboard, and the pictures on screens two and three changed. "Those look good also, but they are too far south. I think the first four are the best bets."

"I think you are right, Bob. Get me a thumb drive with the pictures and GPS coordinates, and I will send it down to Langley."

Bob held up a thumb drive, "You mean like this one, which I made especially for my favorite major?"

"Bobby, sometimes you are too cute for words."

Major Schwartzman took the proffered thumb drive and her cup of coffee with her. As she turned to leave, she gave Bob a friendly pat on the shoulder. "Thanks, Bobby. You are literally the best."

"You are always welcome to visit anytime the mood moves you. I'll keep the coffee hot for you. It just won't be as hot for you as I am."

44

AL'ASAD ALJIBAL

Camp of the Haqqani Network
Eastern Hills of Afghanistan
Thursday, August 30

Malik hated sentry duty. Cold found every seam of his clothing; breath came out in white puffs. Night turned the world into suspect shapes, and the old stories about jinns crowded his head—invisible things that went about in darkness snatching souls and causing mischief. You cannot shoot a jinn. They are spirit creatures.

He'd rather be back in the camp with the others, but dawn was still two hours away. Behind his big rock, he watched the road, rifle slung, listening for a sound that might be real. The moon had set hours before; darkness pressed in like a thing with teeth.

Malik reacted in alarm. He heard something moving in the darkness. *Allah protect me! The sound was coming my way!* By starlight, he could see a shadowy form in the darkness. *A jinn! I am doomed! It will eat my soul!* Malik thought, so frightened he could not move a muscle. He stood behind his rock like an ancient tree rooted to the ground. The shape came closer. *Allah, I don't want to die! Save me!*

Suddenly, the shape passed his rock outpost. It was a woman in a burqa. She was leaving the camp in the darkness. It is not a jinn. Allah has saved me.

Strength returned to Malik's legs; he could move. The woman slipped past him in the dark. He stepped out from behind the rock and barked, "Where are you going? Stop—or I'll shoot!"

She tried to run, her burqa snagging, slowing her to a stumbling sprint. Malik gave chase. Seventy meters later he grabbed her arm; she pulled free, and he took her down in a rough bear hug. She twisted and kicked until he hauled her upright and slammed her onto the dirt, where she lay stunned.

He unslung his rifle and pushed the barrel into her face. "Don't move. You'll die right here."

They both breathed hard for a long minute. Up close, the cloth at her throat and the shape of her face told him the truth: she wasn't a woman at all but a girl. Malik kept the muzzle two inches from her mouth. "Stand up. Turn around. Start walking," he ordered, forcing her back toward the camp.

Slowly, they both returned to the camp. Malik grabbed the subdued girl by the arm and led her to where Jubal was asleep. Jubal sensed their presence and immediately became wide awake.

"Jubal, this girl tried to leave the camp. I caught her."

"Tie her up to the post in the clearing," Jubal ordered. "Stay with her so that no one sets her free. When it is light, our Rayiys will deal with her."

*   *   *

Aljibal awoke at dawn, as was his habit. Jubal was waiting for him. "One of the girls tried to run away last night. Malik was on duty and caught her. She is tied to the post in the clearing. How shall we punish her?"

"It is not for us to decide. She has dishonored her husband. He must decide how to punish her. Who is her husband?"

"I don't know. I haven't spoken to her yet. I will find out and then get her husband."

Jubal went to the clearing where Malik was guarding the girl. "Who is your husband?"

Softly she said, "Qadir."

"What? I did not hear you. Who is your husband?"

"Qadir. My husband is the pig Qadir. He beats me and rapes me every day. Sometimes he rapes me twice in one day. I hate him!"

To Malik, Jubal said, "Get Qadir."

By now, most of the camp was awake. They all saw the girl tied to the post, and the other girls realized it was Parisa.

In a few moments, Qadir appeared. A crowd of men gathered around the post.

Aljibal stepped forward. "Qadir," he said, "this wretch tried to run. You were the one offended, how do you want to punish her?"

"She's been nothing but trouble," Qadir spat. "I hate her. I want her dead to restore my honor."

Aljibal nodded. "She will die by your hand. And I want it done as an example, so no other girl thinks of escaping."

"That suits me," Qadir said, eyes cold. "Just see that she dies."

Aljibal turned, addressing the crowd as if issuing an order of state. "Make it public. Let every woman here know what happens to those who defy us. There are two young trees just outside the camp. Bend them and tie them in an X. Then tie this bitch to the trees and let her die there. You can cut her however you want to punish her."

Qadir, who was truly a sadist, readily agreed to Aljibal's plan.

*   *   *

Parisa was untied from the post. The rope was tied around her neck, and she was led like a goat to the two saplings just outside the camp.

The trees were about two meters apart. Four men, two on each tree, forced the saplings sideways until the trunks crossed each other.

"Tie them tightly," Aljibal ordered. "I don't want the rope breaking and allowing the trees to snap upwards."

The men did as Aljibal ordered.

When the trees were shaped like an X, Aljibal said to Qadir, "Strip her naked. Then tie her wrists and ankles to the trees."

Parisa began to sob when she heard her fate.

Qadir laughed as he followed Aljibal's orders. Clearly, he was enjoying himself. While he was stripping off her clothing, he hit her several times as hard as he could. When Parisa was naked, he said to two of the men, "Help me lift her up so that she will be hanging from her arms and legs."

As the two men held her up against the trees so her wrists and ankles could be tied, one man commented, "She is so light. I don't think she even weighs forty-five kilos (99 pounds)."

Twelve-year-old Parisa continued to cry and beg for mercy while she was being tied up. Within minutes, she was hanging in an X from the two trees and her sobbing continued unabated.

"How do you want to cut her?" Aljibal asked, for Aljibal wanted to inflict as much suffering as possible on this girl.

Qadir took out his razor-sharp dagger. "I think I will cut off her ears. Maybe I will cut open her belly too. She always ate too much. I want to see where the food went."

Qadir stepped up to his young wife and grabbed her right ear.

She pulled her head out of his grip and screamed. He hit her in the mouth with the butt end of his knife, splitting her lip and breaking two front teeth. She was momentarily stunned and motionless. So, he grabbed her ear again and crudely sliced it off.

Parisa screamed through her bloody mouth.

Qadir grabbed her left ear and hacked that off, too. He held the two ears in front of her eyes and then he threw them on the dirt and ground them into the earth.

Parisa fainted. Her head fell forward. She hung limply from her wrists. Her shoulder joints carried all of her weight as she bled profusely from both sides of her head.

One of the men watching Parisa's torture asked, "Why don't you cut off her tits too?"

Qadir sneered, "Look at this useless bitch. She doesn't even have tits yet. There's nothing to grab, so I could cut it off. I'll take off her nipples instead." He made two circular cuts in her chest.

Aljibal said, "Cut off her eyelids, but don't cut her eyes."

So Qadir delicately slit both eyelids from the unconscious girl.

"And now I will see where all that food went that she ate," Qadir laughed. He cut an upside-down U in her lower abdomen and peeled the flap of skin and muscle downwards.

Parisa's entrails oozed out of her belly. Her small intestine fell loose and was dangling as far as the ground while it was still part of her body.

Qadir took the intestine and looped it over her head, around the back of her neck. He looked at Parisa and laughed at the effect of his handiwork.

"Now my honor is restored," Qadir stated.

"Yes, it is," agreed Aljibal, "you have done well."

Parisa hung from the X by her wrists and ankles, bleeding from her ears, her face, her eyes, her breasts, and her abdomen. Insects were already gathering on her body to feast on her flesh.

Aljibal ordered, "Bring the other girls out here to see what happens to anyone who tries to run away from the warriors of the Haqqani Network."

For the next 30 minutes, every girl in the camp was led out to the two trees and forced to see what had happened to Parisa. Each of them cried, for Parisa had been a friend at the school. Most were too shocked to say anything. Three of the girls threw up the food they had eaten for breakfast.

All the mujahideen greatly enjoyed the discomfort of the young girls. They stood around looking at the girl tied to the trees, smoking and having a sociable time. Qadir had his honor. Parisa had less than nothing.

45

POGO AND KOALA

Near Orgun, Afghanistan
Thursday & Friday, August 30 & 31

Pogo's phone vibrated with an incoming message and saw it was from Stevens. *Maybe NSA has come through for us,* he thought. He decrypted the message:

> NSA has come up with four (4) possible sites that meet Koala's request. Satellite pictures and GPS coordinates attached. Also, two (2) sites a little too far south as alternates if the first four do not work out. Good hunting.
>
> Stevens

Jack got Laura and together they went to locate Lieutenant Cosgrove. They found him cleaning his rifle.

"I just received a message from home. Koala's observation and the NSA's search identified four possible nearby sites as potential locations for Aljibal's camp. They also included two sites further south in case the first four don't produce our target."

Pogo, Koala, and Cosgrove all examined the pictures on Jack's phone together.

Cosgrove was first to speak. "I have a platoon of sixteen SEALs. I will send out eight men in two-man teams to reconnoiter the first four sites. If the teams find Aljibal, they will not make contact but will survey the target area for an attack in force."

Koala said, "That sounds good. Except that Pogo and I should be one of those teams. So you will only have six men out."

"If we are all going to attack Aljibal, I will need to have confidence in the intelligence that comes back here. Therefore, I would like my ensign to accompany you. He will know our way of fighting and how we would plan any attack."

Jack considered telling Cosgrove that he had enough experience to do the job, but then thought better of it. Instead, he said, "That is fine with us. We want you to be comfortable with our abilities, and if you need to verify anything we propose, we are amenable to that."

"Good. The teams will deploy at 0500 tomorrow and rendezvous back here whenever the job is done. You will be with Ensign Luke Irwin. Do you both know basic infantry sign language?"

"We were both infantry at one time. We know the signals."

"Until tomorrow at 0500."

After Cosgrove had left them, Jack looked at Laura. "You can stay home tomorrow. That wounded leg will slow you down. Since this is a recon mission, I would rather have you ready for the actual attack on Aljibal when we find him."

"We are a team," Laura answered. "If you had this scratch, would you stay home and let me go out without you?"

"You got me there. OK. We'll both go tomorrow. We will travel light. Let's get our packs ready, get some chow, and then some rest. Maximum ammo, just in case. I think we should wear our BDUs tomorrow."

*   *   *

The temperature hovered just above freezing at 0500. Cosgrove assigned us to the third potential location, which was the location closest to the

SEALs camp. The other three teams were moving further away and used armored Humvees for the first leg of their reconnaissance. Hands, faces, and any exposed skin were painted green and brown with camouflage grease paint sticks.

One of the Humvees dropped our team of three off about 4 km down the road from the SEALs' camp. We then went cross-country in a single file with Ensign Luke Irwin leading the way. Irwin set a rapid pace, but both Jack and Laura were able to keep up easily. As they got closer to the possible site indicated on their GPS phones, everything slowed down a bit, for which Laura was grateful. Her wounded left leg was starting to ache.

They took a break after one hour of hiking and sat in a loose triangle, facing outwards, back-to-back. Jack took out his map and noted where he had marked the location coordinates with an X. "There is a dirt road about a kilometer ahead. I think we should cross it and go east parallel to the road for another kilometer, and then go south. We'll be getting close to the border there. What do you think?"

Irwin and Koala were each checking their own maps. Koala offered, "When we are paralleling the dirt road, we will come to a stream after about a little more than half a klick. I think we should follow the stream southeast. If the camp is in this area, they would probably be somewhere near a source of fresh water, and that is the only sizable source of water in this area. They have a lot of people there."

The ensign said, "Koala has a good point. Let's do it her way."

Jack said, "OK," and five minutes later, they were moving again.

They crossed the dirt road and pushed about two hundred meters into the hills before turning east, moving parallel to the road until they reached a stream. The water ran fast and southeast, toward the Pakistan border. It was deeper than their boots, so they kept to the banks—Ensign Irwin on one side, Pogo trailing fifteen meters behind on the opposite bank, and Koala another fifteen meters behind Pogo, on Irwin's side.

The banks were rocky and shaded by overhanging trees and bushes. Progress was slow. Each man picked his steps with care, avoiding loose stones and any sound that might carry. No one spoke. The only noise was the stream itself, and even after the climb into the hills, their breathing remained steady and quiet.

In his own mind, Ensign Irwin was satisfied with the skills of the two spooks he was leading. They were showing themselves to be capable soldiers, and his confidence in them was rising. Their tactics were solid, and their thinking was sound.

The three had been following the stream for about half an hour when Irwin signaled stop with his hand extended behind him, palm visible. Then he signaled go prone. Everyone quietly hit the dirt. After a few minutes frozen in place, Irwin motioned for them to crawl up adjacent to him. They silently crawled up to the SEAL. They were at a spot where the streambed got wider; the water flowed more slowly, and meandered about 5-6 meters left and right.

About 250 meters ahead, among the trees and bushes, four women wearing burqas could be seen filling water containers from the stream. When they were done, they each hefted two containers and walked southeast away from the stream. No one else was in sight. Ensign Irwin motioned for Pogo to cross the stream and join him and Koala.

The ensign whispered, "Either we have found them, or there is a farm nearby. I didn't see any farms noted on the satmap. We must be very cautious and quiet. My gut tells me that we have the camp close ahead."

Koala pointed ahead between the trees and whispered, "There are the three mountains in the middle distance. If the camp is near, it will be to our right." She took out her map. "There is another dirt track further to the southeast running into the Pakistan Tribal Area. It is almost not even a road. Just a dirt track."

Pogo whispered, "If the camp is there, let's cross the stream and go through the hills until we can get above the camp. Be on the lookout for sentries. They have been here a while, and they feel safe. The sentries will be careless, but we shouldn't be."

Irwin liked his thinking. "Let's move out. Keep 15 meters apart. Pogo, you have the point. I'm astern."

Jack was first across the stream, heading up into the hills. Laura followed. Ensign Luke Irwin was last. They climbed carefully and silently. Soon, they were about 100 meters above the level they imagined the camp might be located.

Jack signaled, and everyone hit the ground. He pointed down below. Laura signaled I see what you are pointing at.

A lone sentry was in the woods, sitting on a rock, looking toward the camp, which was the wrong direction for a sentry to be facing. His rifle lay across his legs, but he was not holding it with either hand.

Luke Irwin crawled up to Koala.

"Sentry," she whispered, pointing at the man on the rock.

He nodded, he saw the man.

Ensign Irwin motioned to Pogo to put more space between the camp and the path they were tracking through the undergrowth.

Pogo made a circle with his thumb and forefinger with the other three fingers raised, signifying that he understood.

They proceeded higher up the hill. The camouflage pattern of their BDUs made them virtually invisible in the bushes. Their progress, so far, had been as silent as a wild deer.

Higher on the hill, the undergrowth got sparser. They arrived at a point where they could see the entire camp laid out before them. They saw the cave openings on the far hillside. The clearing where the Wilsons had been executed was mostly visible. A few small cooking fires for the midday meal were going. The winds were rapidly dispersing what little smoke the fires were giving off.

All three of them locked what they saw in their memories. Koala took out her cell phone and photographed the hillside with the cave openings. The photo registered the latitude and longitude of the hill in degrees, minutes, and seconds. She took several other shots of the camp, some closeups, and some wide-angle shots.

Then Pogo continued to lead them southeastward. The hill began curving south. They had no choice but to follow the hill, or they risked getting too close to any sentries. After following the hill for another 15 to 20 minutes, they saw the dirt track below them. Something dark was moving and pulsing on the side of the track.

Pogo motioned for the others to come up closer to him. Silently, he pointed to the dark X-shaped object.

Koala was the first to recognize what they were looking at with a sudden intake of breath. She whispered, "That is a small person, probably a girl. She is tied to the two trees in a primitive crucifixion. The black pulsing is flies all over her body. I pray that she is dead and cannot feel the same revulsion I am feeling from looking at her."

Ensign Irwin whispered, "What ugly animals these people are. That is a terrible way to die. And then to leave her there like that. These bastards must die. Sooner is better than later."

"There is another sentry down there on the near side of the road," Pogo whispered.

Ensign Irwin whispered, "I marked the first sentry on my map. Now this makes two. My gut says that there will be others. Maybe two or three more. Let's get out of here and report back to Lieutenant Cosgrove."

"First, I have to take a very short video of that poor creature. Unless you see this, you cannot truly believe the horror of it," Koala whispered.

Slowly, they retraced their path across the hill until they came to the stream. They marked this on their maps as point Beta. Then they silently exfiltrated the way they had come in. Exiting was a bit faster than entering the area. Fifty-five minutes later, they were back in the spot where they had taken their first break. This was now Point Alpha.

Ensign Irwin got on his radio and called the lieutenant. "Team 3 has located the Haqqani camp." Then he read off the coordinates of the photo from Koala's camera. If, for any reason none of them made it back to the SEALs camp, the platoon would know where Aljibal's camp was located.

All three of them felt satisfied with their accomplishment that day. Laura felt vindicated in her observation of the three hills of similar height. Jack felt he was close to getting his revenge for Inaya and Naila. Ensign Irwin intended to inform the lieutenant that the two spooks possessed reliable skills and could be integrated into their attack when it occurred. Each one, without saying anything to the others, had made a vow to cut the crucified girl down from the X trees and give her a proper burial.

They began the trek back to the SEAL encampment. Each of them wrapped in his own thoughts of how to mount an attack on the camp, free the girls, and kill Aljibal.

46

POGO AND KOALA

SEALs Camp
Near Orgun, Afghanistan
Friday, August 31

Lieutenant Cosgrove had recalled his other three teams now that Team 3 had found Aljibal's camp. Now, the task before him was to plan and execute an attack on the Haqqani Network camp.

Ensign Irwin, Pogo, and Koala hiked all the way back to camp. The Humvee that had dropped them off earlier was now far away with Team 1.

Team 3 reported in. "Koala took some photos of the camp," Ensign Irwin reported. They can put them up on their laptop, and we can plan our attack."

Cosgrove agreed. "Let's wait until everyone has returned. I want the chief here for the planning."

Laura and Jack were sitting alone, waiting for Chief Williams to return to camp. Laura asked Jack, "How much training have these SEALs received? Are these sixteen men enough to take on over forty of Aljibal's fighters?"

"Each of these men has had four to six years of very intense training before they are assigned to a field operation. Each SEAL is physically and mentally tough, capable of driving himself beyond what a normal person can endure and still produce the highest level of combat performance. There are sixteen SEALs here to Aljibal's forty-plus men. Aljibal is outnumbered as to quality and quantity. These guys will cream Aljibal's gang and will probably all survive while the mujahideen will not."

Laura was satisfied with Jack's answer.

By 1630, all the teams had returned to camp. Cosgrove called Ensign Irwin and Chief Williams for a planning session. They squatted down on the ground. "If you both agree, I want to include the two spooks in planning this attack," Cosgrove stated.

Ensign Irwin said to Master Chief Williams, "I already told the lieutenant—I had those two with me. I pushed a hard pace, and they kept up. She's carrying a wounded thigh and never made a sound. Both show solid infantry skills, sharp judgment under pressure, and good tactical instincts. They're tough. We'll have no problem integrating them with our guys."

Chief Williams said, "The spooks haven't said a word, but the guys are convinced that these two are the ones who rescued the kidnapped ambassador in Sandland. If we take them along, I want to pair each of them up with one of our more experienced men."

"That's not an option," said Irwin. "They are a team. I've been watching them closely. They are in sync mentally and physically. They anticipate each other's needs and have each other's backs. Separating them would reduce their effectiveness, and separating our guys to cover them would reduce our effectiveness."

"OK. Let's get them over here so we can get started," said Cosgrove.

Ensign Irwin saw Koala on the other side of the camp. He made a circular motion in the air with his hand, then held up two fingers. Within a minute, both Koala and Pogo arrived.

Lieutenant Cosgrove got things started. "We're planning our attack on Aljibal's camp. We need your thoughts."

Both Pogo and Koala nodded agreement.

Lieutenant Cosgrove laid out a map on the ground. "Their camp is here. I would like to hit them at first light. We know the locations of two sentries. There are probably two or three more on the other side of the camp. Two-man teams will take out the sentries with Ka-Bars. I would like to set demolition charges at the cave entrances and blow them all at once. Then we will just have a mopping up operation."

Pogo offered a thought, "Our twin assignments are to kill Aljibal and to rescue as many girls as possible. Blowing the cave entrances will trap Aljibal's men as well as any of the girls that are in there, and might kill the girls as well. I have a tripod-mounted sniper scope with us. It is in the truck with my M40A5. Let's set up an observation post to spy on the camp for 6 to 10 hours until we know where Aljibal and his fighters sleep and where they gather during the day. Any girl or anyone wearing a burqa is not a target. Do we have any night-vision equipment?"

"Each man has his own on his helmet," Cosgrove said.

"Good. Once we know where everything is in the camp, then we can attack with more assurance and less risk of injuring our own guys with friendly-fire. May I suggest that we hit them at 0300 the day after tomorrow? At 0300, they will be in the deepest part of sleep. There won't be any daylight or artificial lighting, so the advantage will all be with us."

Cosgrove thought for a moment, then said, "The plan is feasible. I just thought of something else. When the men eat the morning meal, they probably all eat together. The women will most likely be serving them. After we take out the sentries, we infiltrate close to the camp, wait until they are eating breakfast, and kill the men with a concentrated volley of semi-auto fire. Anyone left after the initial attack will be dealt with by my men. I like the idea of a day of recon to find out the who, what, and where of the camp. I would send two recon teams on opposite sides of the camp."

Koala said, "I think two teams are best, but keep them there from dawn to dark so we get the complete picture. We'll be able to locate all the sentries when they change the watch. We'll see where they sleep, when and where they eat, where the latrines are, and when they screw. Let's get the observer teams in place before first light tomorrow. Watch them until after dark. Pull the teams back here to report and to do another planning meet. With phones, our observers can text each other and us simultaneously. If they do eat together, that would be the best time to ambush the camp. If they don't eat together, then I would hit them at 0300. But first, we have to know. We have an urgent pressure to get this job done, but rushing in is not the answer. Assumptions can get us killed."

Ensign Irwin and Chief Williams both nodded approval at Koala's recommendation.

Ensign Irwin finally spoke. "I think her plan is the best one. We'll just hit them Sunday morning instead of Saturday morning."

Chief Williams said, "There is no substitute for good intel. At least until the first shot gets fired, then every plan goes to hell in a hurry. We are better off with a day of observation than we are without it. We'll have to allow Aljibal one extra day to defile the human race by his presence."

Ensign Irwin said, "There is one last thing we all need to see. I think the men should see it too, so they know what kind of low-life animals we are dealing with here. Koala, would you show us the video you took, please?"

Koala took out her phone and scrolled to the video of the crucified girl. Her phone got passed from hand to hand. Chief Warren Williams asked, "Why is the person all black?"

Pogo said, "She isn't black. The flies covering every square inch of her body are black."

The group was silent as they absorbed the horror of what the video showed.

Lieutenant Cosgrove said to Koala, "I want you to send that video to my phone. I will make sure every man in the platoon sees it and understands what kind of people we are dealing with."

Cosgrove stood. "Chief, get the observer teams organized and send them out."

"Aye-aye, Lieutenant."

To Pogo, the chief said, "We won't need your sniper scope. We have enough high-powered binoculars for the job."

"Sounds good. I really didn't want to let the scope out of my possession unless it was the only way to get the job done."

Everyone stood, and Cosgrove folded his map.

The SEALs camp had been eerily quiet when Pogo and Koala first arrived. Now, because all the men were aware of the planning confab taking place, it was even quieter. It was what one would expect from professionals like the SEALs.

47

STUART KEATON

Assistant Secretary of State for Near Eastern Affairs
Joint Base Andrews
Prince George County, MD
Saturday, September 1

K eaton paused in the morning heat and humidity. Washington was going to get par-boiled today.

An Air Force master sergeant approached Keaton. "Mr. Secretary, we are ready for you to board."

"Thank you, Sergeant. Lead the way."

Keaton and three aides followed the sergeant across the tarmac to a movable steel stairway at the front door of a C5A. All four passengers mounted the stairs and found seats in the giant airplane. About a dozen Air Force and Army officers, ranging in rank from brigadier general down to major, were the only other passengers. The balance of the fuselage was filled with military freight bound for Germany. At Ramstein, Keaton's party would transfer to a smaller aircraft to continue to Afghanistan and then to Pakistan.

The interior of the plane was huge. Keaton confided in Jerry Robertson, one of his aides, "Sometimes I wonder how they ever get this much weight off the ground."

Jerry laughed. "Well, I hope they succeed this time. The alternative is too unpleasant to contemplate. My dad was a Navy pilot. He always said that takeoffs are optional, landings are mandatory. I hope the pilot of this bird is aware of the way he'll wreck our weekend plans if he screws up the landing."

"Have faith. The Air Force will get us wherever we're going in one piece."

"I have such faith in this pilot that I intend to sleep all the way over."

"Sounds like a plan," Keaton said. "Maybe I'll try to sleep too."

✳ ✳ ✳

After nineteen hours of travel, Keaton and his three aides finally reached Islamabad. They'd managed some sleep along the way, but all four were still in a sour mood.

It was after 10 p.m. local time in Islamabad. Ambassador Dave Cooper was at the airport to greet Keaton. No official representative of the Pakistani government bothered to show up. It was just as well. Keaton was not in the mood for hypocritical pleasantries. He was there to ream Bouradin's ass.

Keaton and Cooper rode together in one limo. The three aides went in a second embassy limo, and the few pieces of luggage in a small van.

On the way to the embassy, Keaton got down to business. "Is the appointment set up with President Harraf?"

"Yes. You are on for tomorrow at 1:00 p.m.," Cooper said.

"Does Harraf know I am a special envoy from the United States and that I speak for the president and the Congress?"

"He has been informed of your status and your authority. He knows what happened to Hadley, and he knows of his government's involvement. Frankly, I think he is scared out of his head."

"Will Bouradin be present?"

"No. He apologizes because his official duties will keep him away."

"Chickenshit coward. By now, he's heard the cockpit recorder and seen the piece in *The People's Voice Daily*—he knows he's in deep shit. Two carrier strike groups, the *Stennis* and the *Kennedy*, are due off the coast tomorrow. The *Wasp* group with a Marine Expeditionary Force and the *Reagan* group arrive the next day. Nuclear subs will be in the area, unseen. Sixty warships total. The president is furious; he wants our jets breaking the sound barrier over Karachi while I meet Harraf. The hawks in Congress are baying for war. President Decker has ordered that any hostile move by Pakistani forces be met with force: defend our people, down any hostile aircraft, neutralize anti-aircraft sites. Who's our military liaison?"

"Rear Admiral Charles Denison, commander of the Stennis strike group. He is the fleet commander for this entire operation."

"Has he been briefed on the circumstances regarding the murders of the Secretary of State and forty-seven other Americans and the destruction of Secretary Archer's plane?"

"He has seen and heard what you will be presenting to President Harraf. He knows we want Bouradin gone."

"I want to contact Admiral Denison when I get to the embassy."

"No problem."

"This situation stinks. That the top echelon of the Pakistan military is cooperating with a terrorist like Aljibal is unconscionable for any responsible government."

"Islamic politics makes strange bedfellows," Cooper muttered.

"Did these fools really think their involvement in this attack would remain a secret? Did they really think they could murder a high American official and forty-seven other Americans and we would let them get away with it?"

Cooper had no answer. None was needed.

Keaton continued, "Does Harraf know we will need a TV and a computer link when I am there?"

"I have personally informed him of what you need, and he has assured me it will be ready. Just in case it is not, I am bringing our technical maven with our own computer and connectors. I know Harraf has a large-screen TV in his office. I have seen it myself."

"Once I speak to Admiral Denison and inform him of the timing, we will be set for tomorrow."

"This had better work," Cooper said. "A war with Pakistan could go nuclear."

The limo arrived at the embassy. Keaton and Cooper exited the limo and immediately went to make the call to the admiral.

48

MASTER CHIEF WARREN WILLIAMS

Camp of the Haqqani Network
Eastern Hills of Afghanistan
Saturday, September 1

An effective leader will not ask his men to do anything that he himself would not do. Master Chief Warren Williams lived by that belief. Williams felt that if he was going to lead his men into a firefight based on the intel gathered in this reconnaissance, then it had better be reliable. There was no one whose judgment he trusted more than his own. The reconnaissance of the Haqqani Network camp was going to last from 0500 to 2100, essentially lying in one place for 16 hours. If the observers were discovered, the entire attack would never happen.

Chief Williams chose three of the sharpest minds in the platoon to accompany him on this recon. Bosun's Mate Adam 'Boots' McGuiness, Electronics Technician Alan 'Allie' Vargas, and Machinist's Mate Jake Duschene were his choice of operators for this detail. Williams would team with Allie Vargas. Boots McGuiness and Jake Duschene would be the other team.

The four SEALs pushed off at 0330. The plan was to be in position before 0500 and then wait for dawn to break. Since they knew the camp's location, they could plot a more direct route and save themselves some of the hiking effort.

Boots was the point man. They were spread out 15 meters apart. Using their night-vision goggles, they were able to maintain formation even though they were spread out over almost 50 meters. Chief Williams brought up the rear.

Each special warfare operator carried a variety of equipment, including weapons, ammunition, body armor, rations, binoculars, a cell phone, ground cloth, camouflage netting, an entrenching tool, first-aid supplies, insect repellent, and line-of-sight radios with whisper mikes attached to their helmet chin straps. Camouflage grease paint covered their faces and any exposed skin. The four big men moved through the darkness like silent ghosts.

At 0450, they reached their goal in the hills and underbrush above the Haqqani Network camp. The chief said to Boots and Jake, "You two find a good observation spot in the thick undergrowth and settle in for the day. Allie and I will go to the hills on the other side of the camp. Separate from each other, but maintain visual contact. Once we are set, we will click the radios to let you know. Communicate via text if the message is too complex for radio clicks."

Allie motioned downwards. "My body heat sensors are picking up four sentries spread out around the camp. We'd better mark their locations."

"We all saw them. Note the locations and mark your maps. We have to get to the other side before first light," said the chief. To Allie, he said, "Let's get going."

Silently, they circled through the hills to the other side of the camp. Once there, they separated by about 10 meters. Each man spread out a ground cloth beneath some heavy undergrowth and covered themselves with camo netting. In the darkness, they hunkered down to wait and observe the actions in the camp.

Daylight arrived at about 0700, before the sun made its appearance over the hills. Women in burqas were moving while it was still dark, preparing a meal for the men. Immediately before daylight, the men gathered to say their prayers. They all knelt on small prayer rugs facing southwest toward Mecca. With full early daylight, they all gathered in the clearing for the morning meal. By 0800, the entire camp was awake.

None of the SEALs knew what Aljibal looked like. There were no photos. Eventually, they figured out who he was because men continued to come to him for advice and decisions. Allie Vargas was the first one to get a photo of Aljibal. During the day, each watcher managed a photo of who they thought was Aljibal. In the end, they all chose the same man.

At one point, around noon, Aljibal must have gotten angry because he hit the man in front of him, and the man did nothing to retaliate. There was no longer any doubt which man was Aljibal.

Noon prayers were the same as morning prayers, with every man and many women on prayer rugs in the central clearing. Again, the men gathered for the midday meal, served by the women.

Now and then, a man would leave the camp for a trip into the bushes where the hole in the ground that served as a latrine was located. When the girls needed to use the latrine, they had to go much further away. An armed man accompanied every girl to ensure she did not run away from the camp. Some guards did not always turn their backs on the girls when they hoisted up their burqas. Islamic modesty be damned, the men wanted to look at the girl's anatomy and watch what she was doing. Several girls screamed at the men, but the guards laughed and ignored them, continuing to watch. It was the guards who had guns, not the girls.

Many times during the observations, men could be seen hitting burqa-clad women. Sometimes the women got hit for no apparent reason or act.

Around 1500, the chief sent a text to the watchers.

Time to pull out. Very *slow* movements! Police your area. Leave no traces of your having been there. Join up at point Beta.

Forty-five minutes later, the four SEALs were well away from the camp at point Beta, the place where they had started following the stream. They were satisfied that they had accomplished their mission. All four of them were stiff from having lain in one place all those hours.

"Keep it quiet for the next three klicks," said the chief in a soft voice.

By the time the men returned to base, they were relaxed and feeling good. They combined their observations, and the chief planned a report he would deliver to Lieutennant Cosgrove. Allie's first photo of Aljibal turned out to be the best one, and they decided to use that photo in their summary.

All the key people knew that the chief was back in camp as soon as the men returned. They naturally gravitated to Lieutenant Cosgrove and Chief Williams. All five of them hunkered down in a circle. The chief spread his map on the ground so all could see it.

"We accomplished the mission and all hands are back at base," Chief Williams said. "We located the sentries, four in total, marked with Xs on the map. The men gather for morning prayers at 06:50, just before sunrise at 07:00, then eat together in the clearing. Women attend the morning meal but are not present for prayers. At the end of prayers, they rise together and roll up their prayer rugs; most sling their rifles rather than being ready to fire. We counted forty-two fighters and more than 120 girls and women. At prayer time, there were thirty-eight men arranged in three rows: fourteen in the front, thirteen in the second, and eleven in the third. That pattern may not hold tomorrow, but my gut says they'll pray in three rows again. The four sentries bring the Haqqani camp total to forty-two. My recommendation: neutralize the sentries just before prayers so all our teams are available for the main action."

"I think it is a good plan," Cosgrove said. "Does anyone have any other suggestions?"

Pogo motioned with his hand. "I think we should take out the sentries even earlier than just before prayers. The timing is pretty thin for our guys to get into position for the main attack without rushing. If we move silently, they won't suspect anything, but if we rush, there is a chance of giving ourselves away before the first shots get fired."

"Good point. All our guys will be in place by 0630. We'll take out the sentries at 0620. That will give our guys 20-30 minutes to get into position for the big bang. I want half the men facing the caves and the other half on the right flank at 90 degrees to the first line. The fronts of the caves face southeast. We'll be firing to the northwest. The men on the right flank will be firing southwest to west. I don't want any chance of our guys getting hit by friendly-fire. The range will be about 120 to 140 meters. Our weapons are accurate at that range; their AK-47s are not. The first magazine will be on full auto; the second magazine will be three-shot aimed bursts. After that, each man chooses what he thinks is best. We should be able to take these guys completely by surprise. Anyone with a burqa is not a target."

All five people in the circle nodded their agreement. The three SEALs stood and called the platoon together. Three men were on watch down by the road. They would get the word later.

The SEAL platoon stood in a loose group facing the lieutenant. There was no idle chatter among the men. These guys knew their jobs.

Lieutenant Cosgrove spoke. "Tomorrow we push off at 0330. We are going to attack the Haqqani camp. These are really bad hombres. We have three major objectives. First and foremost is to kill al'Asad Aljibal. Second is to kill as many of his men as possible. Third is to free the kidnapped schoolgirls. Anyone wearing a burqa is not a target.

"They have four sentries posted in locations that we have mapped. Four two-man teams will take out the sentries at 0620 with Ka-Bars. It must be done silently, with no alarm raised. The sentry teams will then have 20 to 30 minutes to join up with the rest of the platoon. The tangos do their first prayers from about 0650 until 0700. They all pray with their weapons by their sides. They will be in three rows in the cleared area facing toward Mecca to the southwest. We will be on their left flank and behind them. We will be forming up with one squad facing the caves on the tango left flank. The second squad, along with our two guests, will be positioned astern of the tangos on our right flank at a 90-degree angle. We'll be in the hills and underbrush about 120 to 140 meters from the clearing. Fire from cover, prone position. They will finish their prayers at about 0700. They will then stand to roll up their prayer mats. Most will have their weapons slung over their shoulders while they roll up the mats. Commence firing when you hear two clicks on your radios. I want the first magazine fired on full auto. The second magazine on three-shot bursts. After that, it is your choice. I do not want any friendly-fire injuries. There is enough room so that should not happen. Cease-fire command is three clicks on the radio. When we are done, I want this to go down in history as The Great Haqqani Turkey Shoot. Are there any questions?"

Each man had absorbed the information. The plan was clear. Now all they had to do was wait until 0330 tomorrow.

49

POGO, KOALA & SEALS

Camp of the Haqqani Network
Eastern Hills of Afghanistan
Sunday, September 2

The night was pitch black; 0330 had come. Clouds obscured the stars. There was no moonlight because it was the second day of the new moon, the beginning of the lunar cycle. Earlier, the thinnest sliver of moon showed, but it had already set. There was no natural light of any kind.

At 0330, the SEALs were ready. They bumped fists, said "Hooyah" with quiet intensity, and set off.

Each operator was using his night-vision goggles. By 0500, they reached the stream, point Beta. They had been quiet up to this point; from here on, they were silent angels of death.

The column was led by Chief Williams. The four two-man teams that would take out the sentries were immediately behind him. Pogo and Koala brought up the rear.

By 0610, the SEAL operators were in position on two sides of the camp. Concealed in the bushes and hiding behind rocks. On their radios they heard click-pause-click. One sentry down. In two minutes, there were two more click-pause-click messages. Three down. The fourth sentry was still unaccounted for.

Finally, at 0621, they heard the last click-pause-click on the radios. All four sentries down. Now they waited for the last two operators to rejoin their mates. Within seven minutes, two silent ghosts materialized out of the darkness. All present and accounted for. Now came the hardest part: waiting for a double click on the radios.

Allie Vargas was lying under a bush, his vision focused on the middle distance. He became aware of a small movement about twelve inches from his face. A four-inch-long scorpion was advancing toward him. Slowly, he backed up, reached down to his boot for his knife. The scorpion was six inches away from him, its tail curled over its back, ready to strike whatever was in its way. Allie stabbed his knife down through the scorpion's shell and pinned it to the ground. The scorpion's tail struck the knife blade three times. It wriggled and struggled to get free until it finally stopped moving. *This is just great,* he thought, *how many of his friends will show up for his funeral? Shit!* The idea of lying on the ground where scorpions were hanging out did not appeal to him. Still, he held his post. But he looked around in case there were more.

At 0651, one fighter, who was also a self-styled holy man, made the call to prayer. Mujahideen straggled out of their caves and tents with their prayer rugs and gathered in the clearing. They formed up into three irregular rows. Aljibal was at the center of the front row. From behind, Pogo had his M40A5 sniper rifle sighted in on Aljibal's body mass. When Aljibal stands up later, the aim will shift to his head.

One of the last mujahideen to arrive for prayers shouted, "Rayiys! There is someone on the hill!" Men on the prayer mats reached for their rifles.

Two clicks sounded on every SEAL's radio. A volley of automatic M-16 fire rolled across the hillsides from the left and the rear.

Mujahideen fell where they would have offered their prayers to Allah for success in murdering the infidels.

Some Haqqani men got to their feet and sprinted for the caves. Some made it, but most were cut down before they arrived. Some of the Haqqani men actually got off a few rounds before being shot by the fire from the hills.

Jack cursed and said to Laura, "I didn't get him. The man behind him stood up and took my bullet. I don't think anyone got him. The light conditions right now are the worst for accurately aimed fire. He might have escaped to the caves. We won't know whether he is alive or dead until we get down there."

Laura commented, "I wonder who moved to give the ambush away. I doubt we'll ever know. How that guy could see someone over 120 meters away in these light conditions is amazing to me. But he saw something and ruined the ambush."

"There are a lot of bad guys lying down there. I hope they are dead and not just wounded. If they are wounded, we will have to nurse them back to health and then keep them in prison for the rest of their lives."

Slowly, the SEALs began filtering down to the clearing and examining the results of their attack. There were twenty-six dead men, three men with multiple gunshot wounds. Nine men were unaccounted for and had escaped to the caves in the semi-darkness. The search was on for the body of Aljibal.

Laura said, "They're looking for Aljibal."

Jack grimaced. "I'm pretty sure they won't find him. Evil bastards like him have a way of escaping to do more harm to more innocent people. Justice seldom catches up with them in any easy way."

Ensign Irwin led eight SEALs toward the caves to track down the few who escaped. They had no idea what to expect when they entered a cave. Would some girls be inside? Could the SEALs risk going into a dark space if there were enemies inside while the SEALs were backlit by daylight outside the cave? If they shoot anything that moves, would it be a bad guy or a kidnapped girl? Normally, they would set an explosive charge at the entrance, but they could not risk it with so many girls from the school everywhere. Another consideration was what if the caves had been booby-trapped?

Lieutenant Cosgrove was down among the bodies, turning men over so they were face up. He was searching for Aljibal. The chief was ministering to the three wounded men. Some of the girls were coming out of their places where they had hidden during the attack.

One of the SEALs was organizing the girls to identify the dead men by name. As each dead person was identified, their name was printed on a 3x5 card, which was placed under their chin, and a photo was taken of their face and the card. Among the dead was Jubal el-Madoush, Aljibal's main deputy leader.

It was just beginning to dawn on the girls that they had been rescued from the Haqqani Network. Some of the girls were smiling for the first time in many weeks.

Another SEAL who spoke Pashto was questioning groups of girls about where the Haqqani's laptop computers and telephones were to be found.

One man was found alive in a cave. He was badly mauled with two rounds to his chest. He probably would not live more than another hour. This reduced the number of escapees to eight. That was the good news. The bad news was that al'Asad Aljibal was still on the loose.

There was a lot of work to be done before the girls could be set completely free. One of the SEAL operators was making a list of all the girls who were still alive at the camp. He was also trying to get a list of those who had been killed by the Haqqani mujahideen.

It was 1000 when Pogo and Koala informed Lieutenant Cosgrove that they were heading back to camp to retrieve their truck and the rest of their gear, and then they would set out in pursuit of Aljibal.

"Go get the bastard," Cosgrove said. "We will continue to hunt for him in this area, but my gut tells me he is headed for the Tribal Area of Pakistan, where he will be safe from us."

"He won't be safe from us no matter where he hides," Koala said.

Pogo said, "We have one unfinished piece of business. That crucified girl on the road needs to be properly buried."

"My operators will take care of her after we clean up here. She will receive proper care and respect. It takes a lot to make my men sick with revulsion, but Aljibal succeeded. We'll do the right thing by her."

"Thank you, Lieutenant. We have to get moving. "We would appreciate it if you didn't mention us in your after-action reports."

"You were never here. You two are the most unique team I have ever seen. Good luck. Get that bastard."

With that, Pogo and Koala turned and hiked away to continue their hunt for Aljibal.

50

STUART KEATON

Assistant Secretary of State for Near Eastern Affairs
Islamabad, Pakistan
Sunday, September 2

Keaton was unaware that the Haqqani Network was under attack in Afghanistan as he prepared for his confrontation with Pakistani President Harraf. He had a thumb drive with all the pertinent information encoded. He suggested that Dave Cooper not accompany him for this confrontation, as Cooper would have to deal with Harraf in the future. It would be better that Keaton be seen as the heavy.

The appointment with Harraf was set for 1:00 p.m. Keaton appeared at the Presidential Palace at 12:50 p.m. By the time he had worked through the security people and the receptionists and had gotten to the door of Harraf's office, it was 1:02.

"Good afternoon, Mr. President," Keaton said as he entered the office.

"Good afternoon to you, Mr. Secretary," the president responded. Harraf turned to an aide who was in his office. "You may leave now." President Harraf was seated behind an antique wooden desk that was supposedly once reserved for Queen Victoria during a royal visit to the Indian Raj. A visit that never actually transpired.

Harraf motioned Keaton to an upholstered chair in front of his desk.

Keaton did not sit and got right to the point. "I am here as a special envoy from the President of the United States of America on a most serious matter. We have evidence that Field Marshal Bouradin is complicit in the murder of the United States Secretary of State and forty-seven other Americans while they were here on official duties. This was a direct attack on the United States government facilitated by the military forces of Pakistan. The president is ready to ask Congress for a declaration of war. The Congress is demanding that the president take action to punish those responsible for this cowardly attack on an unarmed United States government airplane. I will show you the proof that my government has, and then we will speak of what needs to be done."

Harraf had already heard what was on the cockpit voice recorder. He'd already read the article in *The People's Voice Daily* and seen the video taken by the German tourist many times. He knew that the air traffic controller and the colonel who had transmitted Bouradin's order had all disappeared. What more could Keaton show him? "I will be happy to look at your evidence, Mr. Keaton."

"Is your computer connected to your TV?" Keaton asked.

"Yes. I have an extra computer here that is not password-protected. I believe this computer will fulfill Ambassador Cooper's request."

"Then let us begin." Keaton inserted the thumb drive in the USB port of the computer. When it was linked, he ran the only program on the thumb drive. "This first video is of satellite images taken a month ago when there was an alleged terrorist attack on the airport at the same moment Secretary Hadley's plane was taking off."

The video, with the July 29 date and timing notated at the top left corner, showed the rendezvous of the Haqqani attackers with the Pakistani officer next to runway 10R. Then it leaped ahead to the failed attack on the plane with two rockets and the pickup racing down the dirt road.

Keaton explained, "There are no perimeter patrols before or after the attack. Yet, normal perimeter patrols are conducted every 8 to 10 minutes, 24 hours a day. The military officer the attackers spoke to was obviously in charge of the perimeter patrols and caused them to miss their scheduled rounds. This attack failed, and we were not even aware it had been meant for Secretary Hadley.

"Now let us look at the satellite images from August 24th."

The images on the computer repeated the rendezvous between Aljibal and the Pakistani officer. Then the images fast-forwarded to the plane repeatedly taxiing and waiting, finally arriving at the end of runway 10R and being told to wait yet again. The air controller's voice said he had his orders. Then the video showed the actual attack on the plane and the destruction and loss of life.

"Again, note the absence of the perimeter sentries," Keaton points out. "The complicity of the Pakistani military in this terrorist attack is clear, and it repeats twice in the same locations and circumstances."

President Harraf was unable to muster any excuses when faced with the satellite images.

Keaton continued, "As we are sitting here looking at these images, the *Stennis* carrier group and the *Kennedy* carrier group are off the Pakistani coast in the Arabian Sea. American Navy fighter-bombers are flying over Karachi, Pakistan's most important city. The *Reagan* carrier group and a Marine Expeditionary Force are scheduled to arrive tomorrow. Nuclear missile submarines are poised to send their payloads toward Pakistan. Islamabad is a mere 400 km from Bagram Air Force Base in Afghanistan, where there are hundreds of U.S. Air Force planes that can level this city. Seventy American warships and many hundreds of American aircraft are ready to bring death and destruction to Pakistan because of the orders given by Field Marshal Bouradin to cooperate with a terrorist attack on our Secretary of State.

"Did Pakistan expect us not to realize what its people have done? Did you think that the American people would let this slide by?"

President Harraf realized that despite its own nuclear weapons, Pakistan would soon look like Iraq and Afghanistan with total destruction and death everywhere in his country. "What can we do to make amends to the American government?" he asked.

"Our first demand is that you, as Commander-in-Chief of the military, fire Field Marshal Bouradin and strip him of all his military commands immediately. Bouradin is to be taken into custody and tried for complicity to commit murder.

"Our second demand is that Bouradin is to be forever barred from holding any government office or employment of any type at any level, high or low, for the rest of his life.

"Our third demand is that Pakistan must fully cooperate with the United States in the hunt for the Haqqani Network terrorists.

"Fourth, should Bouradin ever attempt a coup d'état of the Pakistani government, the United States will eliminate him as the common criminal he is.

"Fifth, should Bouradin ever leave the territory of Pakistan, we will arrest and try him in the United States for the murder of Secretary Hadley and forty-seven other Americans. We still have the death penalty for federal crimes.

"The decision is yours. If you want to bring war, famine, and destruction to your country, do nothing. If you want to avoid the wrath of the American people, get rid of Field Marshal Hakim Mouhammed Bouradin.

"You have 24 hours to act to avoid total annihilation. If the United States is not happy with your actions by 2 p.m. tomorrow, we will set our military forces loose against your country. If you refuse to meet our demands, we will hold you personally complicit as an accessory in the death of Secretary Hadley and will arrest you and put you on trial when we find you.

"You may keep the satellite data I have brought today. If our demands are not met by tomorrow, you should know that the images on that computer will be broadcast to all Americans, and there will be no saving Pakistan or your life or that of Field Marshal Bouradin's after that. Your fate and the fate of Pakistan will be sealed."

"You leave us no options," Harraf said.

"There is an option. If you meet our demands and arrest Bouradin, President Decker will invite you to Washington for a state visit, complete with all the pomp and honors that such a function entails. You will be the savior of Pakistan and a hero to all your people."

Keaton rose from his chair. "You can reach me at the American Embassy until tomorrow at 2 p.m. After that, the embassy will be evacuated and closed, and I will be unavailable.

"I will leave you now, Mr. President. You know what must be done. Goodbye." Keaton turned and left the president sitting behind his Queen Victoria desk.

51

PRESIDENT MAHMOUD HARRAF

Islamabad, Pakistan
Sunday, September 2

"Summon the head of my personal security detail," Harraf ordered his secretary. Within a minute, Suleman Kahn knocked and entered the president's office.

"How can I serve you, Your Excellency?"

"I have an unpleasant duty to perform. But first, I want you to see something." Harraf ran the computer program that was on the thumb drive for Kahn. When it was done, Kahn sat very silent.

Harraf said, "This video was given to me by the Americans. They are threatening to declare war on Pakistan unless we arrest Field Marshal Bouradin. They have nuclear submarines in the Arabian Sea. There are two supercarriers off the coast of Karachi, with a third one scheduled to arrive tomorrow, and a Marine invasion force is also due to arrive tomorrow. We can fight them if we wish, but they will beat us, and the country will be destroyed as they have destroyed Iraq and Afghanistan. The worst thing about this is that I believe Bouradin is guilty of aiding the terrorists and of complicity in the plot."

"How can we save Pakistan?" Khan asked.

"Before 2 p.m. tomorrow, we must arrest the field marshal. After 2 p.m., the Americans will launch their attacks on Karachi and Islamabad."

"What do you want of me?"

"I will summon the field marshal here. I want you to have 10 heavily armed men with handcuffs and leg irons ready outside my office. When I give the signal with my buzzer, I want the ten men to enter with guns drawn, overpower Bouradin, and arrest him for conspiracy to commit murder. I want you in charge of the arresting detail."

"I will do it. I would like a copy of that video so I can show it to my team. They must be made to believe they are doing this to save Pakistan from destruction. They are patriots, and they will do what must be done to save the nation."

"You can take the thumb drive. The program has already been downloaded to the computer's hard drive. The Americans will make this public tomorrow. If we have already arrested Bouradin, then they will be satisfied. If we do not arrest Bouradin, then death will descend upon us from the air and the sea. Our two major cities will be leveled. Our people will die for a senseless, childish gesture committed by people who have no moral limits."

Suleman Kahn first transferred the logo showing the thumb drive to the trash folder, making it safe to remove the drive itself. Then he took the thumb drive from the computer. "I will show the men and explain the importance of what we must do. Only those who understand will be here to arrest the field marshal."

"Do not delay. Hours can be critical," Harraf urged.

"I will not delay. You will have your men to get your man."

As soon as Kahn left his office, Harraf buzzed his secretary. "I need to speak to Field Marshal Bouradin immediately."

A moment later, the intercom buzzed. "Field Marshal Bouradin on line one," the secretary announced.

"Field Marshal, we need to have an immediate strategy conference in my office. The Americans are threatening us. Can you be here within the hour?"

"I am aware of the Americans, and I am taking steps to counter them."

"We cannot afford a war against the Americans. We need a political solution that presents a united front of the military and civilian Pakistan. That will be best done by a joint statement from both of us. Come here and let us prepare for the confrontation." Harraf hoped he hid his true intentions well enough.

"All right. I will be there in about 40 minutes," Bouradin conceded.

After he hung up on the field marshal, Harraf called Kahn. "Field Marshal Bouradin will be here in about 40 minutes. We must be ready by then."

"We will be ready," Kahn assured. "My men are watching the videos now." Harraf broke the connection and began nervously pacing his office. Will Bouradin step into the trap he had laid?

Forty minutes later, Bouradin had not arrived. He did not arrive until almost an hour had elapsed. By then, Harraf was really nervous, thinking that Bouradin had suspected a trap.

Bouradin came bustling into the president's office with two colonels in his wake. Harraf said to the colonels, "I need to speak privately with Field Marshal Bouradin. Please step outside."

After the colonels were gone, Harraf said, "I want you to watch this video. It was given to me by Secretary Keaton today."

Bouradin snapped, "I don't have time for video games. I am too busy!"

"You had better watch this video now." Harraf pressed play.

Bouradin saw the attackers meeting with the military officer at runway 10R. Then the video fast-forwarded to the attack itself and the overlaid voices from the cockpit voice recorder. He had already heard what was on the voice recorder, but when it was presented in synchronization with the satellite images, it was much more powerful.

When the video was done, Harraf said, "The newspaper reporter who spoke to the air controller wrote that the order to delay Secretary Hadley's plane came from your office. Which means the order came from you. You set up the murder of Secretary Hadley and the forty-seven other Americans on that plane."

Bouradin was shaken by the accusation. "I did not know there was to be an attack on the plane! I ordered the delay as an insult to the proud Americans. I wanted revenge for the way he spoke to us. That Aljibal would choose that moment to attack the plane was a mere coincidence. I never had any inkling that there would be such an attack."

"The Americans believe you did. They are demanding your resignation, or they will attack Pakistan by 2 p.m. tomorrow. The Constitution of Pakistan states that I am the Commander-in-Chief of the military. Therefore, in that capacity, I am relieving you of all your duties in the armed forces of Pakistan, effective immediately."

Bouradin bristled, "You cannot do that! I will have you arrested, and you will never be heard from again."

Harraf pressed the button of the buzzer at his desk.

A side door of his office opened, and Suleman Khan stepped in, followed by ten men with pistols drawn. Khan announced, "Hakim Mouhammed Bouradin, you are under arrest for treason." To his men, he said, "Handcuff him and put him in leg irons."

Bouradin called out to his two colonels by their first names, "Help, Kamal, Ahmad, I need help!"

The two colonels burst into the office. They were met with ten pistols pointed at them.

Harraf said, "Arrest these two as well. Their loyalty is not to Pakistan, but to Bouradin."

In moments, all three men were handcuffed and wearing leg irons.

Khan said, "I have a van outside in the courtyard."

Harraf held up a hand. "There are two prison cells in the basement. Take him there instead. Before we take him out of here, remove every symbol of rank from his clothing. In fact, remove his tunic and cap. And throw that stupid baton in the garbage."

Bouradin's uniform jacket was unbuttoned, but it could not be removed because his hands were handcuffed behind his back. Harraf produced a large pair of scissors. "Cut the sleeves up the length and across the front of the jacket. Then you can throw that away too with all his fake medals."

Bouradin snarled, "You will pay for this. I will have my revenge."

"Yes, the way you had your revenge on Secretary Hadley, which led our nation to the brink of disaster. Can you see what your childish revenge has brought upon all of us? You are done. Finished. You have shown yourself to be a traitor to Pakistan."

To Khan, Harraf said, "Get this filth out of my office." Motioning toward the colonels, "Get those two to Directorate S as a gift from me."

After Bouradin and the two colonels were removed, Harraf turned to Khan. "Inform the press that I will be making an urgent statement to the nation in an hour. Set up a computer and TV in the news conference room. I will have an important display for the press."

Suleman Khan responded, "Yes, Mr. President."

"Suleman, I don't want that man ever to leave that cell alive. He can commit suicide in his jail cell. No one may stop him or step in to save him. In fact, if he is afraid to do it himself, we should assist him. Hanging is the punishment for treason."

"I understand what you want, Mr. President. It shall be done."

"Let me know when he is gone to Allah."

"Yes, sir. I shall."

Thirty-five minutes later, Suleman Khan returned to the president's office.

"He has gone to sit beside Allah," and Khan smiled. "My men had to assist him, but it is done. We took the handcuffs off afterwards."

"Good, now the Americans will not destroy Pakistan. Today, we have both saved the nation."

Harraf continued, "In the news conference for the press in another half hour I will be showing them what the Americans have shown us. I will tie it all in with the newspaper article and the suicide of Bouradin. I hope it works to mollify the Americans."

"Who will be the new field marshal?" Khan asked.

Harraf had the answer ready, "No one. I will not allow such a concentration of power in one man ever again. There will be a system similar to the Americans', with a rotating head of the military establishment every two years. No man may control the military who is stronger than the civilian authority above him. I will send a draft of such a law to Parliament today. Maybe those prattling fools in Parliament will pass it, maybe they won't. But I want it on the record what the country needs. I should announce that proposal at the news conference as well."

After Khan left Harraf's office, Harraf instructed his secretary, "Call Secretary Keaton at the U.S. Embassy."

Three minutes later, Stuart Keaton was on the phone.

"Hello, Secretary Keaton. I have news. Field Marshal Bouradin resigned and was arrested for treason. I have a reliable report that he committed suicide in his prison cell."

"Thank you, Mr. President. I will inform President Decker, and the order to stand down the U.S. forces will be given."

"Bouradin admitted to me he ordered the delay of Secretary Hadley's takeoff from the airport. He claimed not to have had any prior knowledge that Aljibal would attack the plane. I did not believe him."

"Nor do I. Nor does the president. The American people shall see the evidence, and they shall also be informed that the responsible party has been arrested and that he committed suicide while in custody."

"That will be good," Harraf said.

"There is another piece of news," Keaton added. "President Decker has informed me that at dawn this morning, Navy SEALs attacked the camp of the Haqqani Network and killed almost all the men there. The schoolgirls have been rescued. American military doctors will be sent in to care for them."

"That is good. It is a fitting end to a terrible situation caused by terrible men. I will be giving a news conference soon to show Pakistan what you have shown me. I want my people to understand that we still stand with America."

"Goodbye, Mr. President. You saved your country today."

Harraf paused for a heartbeat. "I wonder what history will say about today? Goodbye, Mr. Secretary." Then he hung up the phone.

52

JACK & LAURA

The Eastern Hills of Afghanistan
Sunday, September 2

Pogo and Koala left the Haqqani Network camp to track down al'Asad Aljibal. From the count of the dead and wounded, they surmised Aljibal escaped with seven of his men. Including Aljibal, that meant there were eight men capable of killing people and causing more trouble in Afghanistan.

They hiked back to the SEALs' camp. When they arrived, they worked together to remove the camouflage netting covering the truck. All their gear had been hidden under a dark blanket. Except for Jack's M40A5 sniper rifle and twenty rounds of ammo, everything else they had was still on the truck floor in the locked cab with the balance of the rifle ammo and sniper scope. A dark blanket and a car door lock were the flimsy limit of their available anti-theft security.

As they drove away from the SEALs camp, they discussed the morning's operations. Jack was still upset that he did not shoot Aljibal. "I don't know how that piece of shit escaped. The guy behind him jumped up at the alarm and caught Aljibal's bullet in his back."

Laura guessed, "There had to be another exit from the caves that we didn't know about. Somehow, he got out with his seven other men. The only stuff they had with them was what they carried on their backs.

They have nothing but their rifles and a few rounds of ammunition. It's possible that in the rush to escape, some of them left their rifles where they were praying."

"I'm sure you're right. He will need to resupply his men with weapons and ammo. They have no food, probably no blankets or camp equipment. They certainly have no money. The SEALs found his cache of dollars, afghanis, euros, and rupees in his cave. A total of almost $80,000 worth of currency. His laptop was there too. They'll turn that over to Naval Intelligence, which will share it with the CIA."

"If you were Aljibal and had nothing but the clothes on your back, where would you go?"

"I'd head for Pakistan. The border is really close. Our friends in the Paki Intelligence will give him anything he needs once he links up with them. The Tribal Area is as lawless as the Wild West. The government forces seldom venture in there because of the high casualties they take from the mujahideen. Any local population is sympathetic to jihad and will support the terrorists. Except they see the terrorists as holy warriors fighting for Allah with the promise of Paradise for the faithful."

"I'm always amazed that 1.6 billion Muslims have bought into the idea that this life is to be endured in misery because there will be Paradise with Allah and the Prophet in the afterlife. These people don't hesitate to spread death wherever they go and almost welcome death for themselves."

"Well, it is our job to make sure their wish comes true. If they want death for themselves, then I want to help them get there."

"Will we get good guys points if we help them meet Allah?"

"Hey, I'm a Marine. It is our duty to arrange a meeting with Allah as soon as possible. I would like to send them to Allah in large groups."

"Let me help you. Your goals are too big for one man working alone. You need a faithful partner to help when the going gets rough and the bullets are flying."

"OK, you get the job. But I warn you, there will probably be sexual advances from the boss."

"Who said you would be the boss? Women rule the world; men just haven't realized it yet. Eve led Adam around by his putz, and that hasn't changed since the Garden of Eden. You are a second-rate member of this partnership because you have the putz, and I have the place you want to store your putz."

"Wow! A putz in a pussy. That is very alliterative. I wonder if we can market a board game called 'Put the Putz in the Pussy.' The title is very catchy. And I can just imagine the game's action. Everyone will be a winner in the end."

"It's something you can work on after we kill Aljibal. Until then, keep your imagination working on the problem of finding him."

"I'd rather have my imagination working on me, potentially placing my precocious pulsing putz in your profoundly pretty pussy. It's like a hobby to keep me off the streets and out of trouble."

"That was too much alliteration for me. I am giving you a dementedly dangerous derangement demerit."

As they drove along, the banter continued, but each one had eyes alert for any danger that might lie ahead. They were lovers and best friends, but always warriors.

53

DOCTORS STURDIVANT AND DENT

CDR Peter Sturdivant, M.D. & LCDR Anita Dent, M.D.
Camp of the Haqqani Network
Eastern Hills of Afghanistan
Sunday, September 2

Duty at Bagram can be boring days of nothing to do, followed by unremitting hectic activity until you look forward to the boredom of nothing to do. Such was the fate of Commander Peter "Sturdy" Sturdivant, M.D., and Lieutenant Commander Adrian Dent, M.D., two Navy doctors who were summoned to fly by helicopter from Bagram to the camp of the Haqqani Network.

The attacking SEALs had secured the camp area. The liberated schoolgirls were milling about. SEALs were compiling a list of the survivors' names. A list of the dead and the escaped terrorists was also made. Histories of who among the girls had perished or been abused and by whom were being recorded. Individual girls were telling their stories. All were hesitant to tell of the rapes they had endured, ashamed of what had befallen them at the hands of the terrorists.

Lieutenant Commander Dent, being a woman, was having more success than Commander Sturdivant. Finally, Sturdivant said to Dent,

"I think we'll get more done if you get the histories and do the GYN exams, and I'll treat the injuries and bruises. The girls just won't talk to me about anything that has to do with sexual assault."

"It has to do with their Islamic culture. They don't know yet that you can be trusted."

Sturdivant said, "I will distribute the HCG pregnancy test strips to the girls. I will write their names on the ends of the strips in the best way I can spell their names. They will have to dip the strips in their urine themselves. I will record the test results."

Dent said, "Every test that is negative will require retesting in 3 weeks. If any of them just became pregnant, it won't show on the test strips for at least two weeks after the last assault."

"These kids have been through enough! And now they might find out they are pregnant with babies they probably won't want. This is no way to grow up or live. I only hope things will be better for them in the future."

"The problem is Islamic men. They think women are their chattels to be exploited and to serve them. These girls won't ever get a break unless they get away from Islamic society. Enough chatter. Let's get to work."

When the day's work was done, both doctors were exhausted. Nine of the girls, the youngest was 13, and the oldest was 15, tested positive for pregnancy. All nine of the girls were devastated. Five of the girls suspected they might be pregnant because their breasts were tender and a bit painful. But they had received so many blows and beatings at the hands of their husbands that they weren't sure what caused the tenderness. None of the girls wanted the children that resulted from being raped. It would be a dishonor that would follow them all their lives.

Commander Sturdivant got on the radio with his superiors at the base hospital in Bagram. If the girls were willing, a D&E abortion could be performed at the base hospital.

Arrangements were being made to transfer the girls to Jordan, Egypt, or Morocco for political asylum. These countries were relatively liberal in their treatment of women compared to other Islamic nations. Remaining in Afghanistan would subject them to a lifetime of stigma because of their captivity.

Five of the girls were originally residents of Sinjara. They were not homeless orphans. These five had to be handled more carefully. If their families did not want them back, then they were to be granted asylum. If their families wanted them returned to Sinjara, the doctors wanted to be assured that the girls would be treated as victims of a terrible crime instead of being stigmatized as prostitutes because they were rape victims. Fortunately, none of the five tested positive for pregnancy.

Lieutenant Commander Adrian Dent watched the girls move about the courtyard like a slow tide, bare forearms catching the light where cloth had been shed. "Sturdy, they'd be better off taking asylum," she said, voice low. "Going back to Sinjara will be a death of sorts—socially. In this place, a woman who's not a virgin is marked. Her family may never see her the same, and the village won't either. Even if they accept her, the kindness won't last."

Commander Sturdivant's hand closed in a fist. "You're probably right. Going home is a lose-lose. The people who should protect them become their judge."

Dent turned, eyes sweeping the milling girls. "Have you noticed most of them have lost their burqas?" he asked. "They treat them like shackles."

Sturdivant's laugh was short, brittle. "The burqa's a symbol of second-class status. I can't imagine why it persists."

"Because the wrong gender controls it," Dent said. A bitter laugh escaped them both.

Lieutenant Cosgrove appeared. "Sirs, Bagram is sending four buses to take the girls back to the base. There will be a few female airmen on each bus. You can go back with them, or I can request a bird for you."

Commander Sturdivant said, "I think we should go back by helicopter. There is a great deal of prep work that has to be done at the base before these girls arrive. So, dial up the bird, please." He paused, "I hope we will meet you guys again. You did a great job here today. Not one of your guys suffered as much as a sprained ankle, and you wound up with a small mountain of dead bad guys. Well done, Lieutenant."

"Thank you, Sir. I will pass the compliment on to the men. If you will excuse me, I see something that needs my attention." Cosgrove turned and left.

Lieutenant Commander Sturdivant said, "These guys are amazing. I'm glad they are ours."

Dent agreed. "I would never want them mad at me."

54

PRESIDENT SAMUEL DECKER

The White House
Washington, D.C.
Monday, September 3 (Labor Day)

Summer green filled the trees of the White House Rose Garden, their leaves touched here and there with the first hint of autumn yellow. A flawless lawn stretched beneath them like a lush carpet, without a weed or bare patch. Above, azure sky arced to the west, streaked with a few wispy clouds. Sunlight warmed the air—a pleasant 81 degrees.

The D.C. Chamber of Commerce could not have ordered up more perfect weather to celebrate Labor Day. Distinguished guests, including the Secretary of Labor, the Vice President, and many members of the capital elite, were present. The D.C. press corps was arrayed in rows on folding chairs behind the distinguished guests, awaiting the president's arrival. TV camera crews were making last-minute adjustments for video and sound.

After a few moments, an aide announced, "Ladies and gentlemen, the President of the United States, Samuel Decker."

Sam Decker stepped up to a lectern adorned with the circular Seal of the President of the United States and a bank of microphones.

President Decker was wearing a smartly tailored gray summer-weight suit, a light blue dress shirt, and a striped tie in red, white, and blue.

President Decker, speaking from his prepared notes, delivered his Labor Day message, extolling the virtues and the can-do spirit of American factory workers and farmers who built America into the envy of the world through the skills of their hands and the sweat of their brows. Polite applause greeted the speech when he was done with his notes.

Then the president added, "I have one more important announcement, which I received less than 15 minutes ago. Due to the position of the International Date Line, it is still September 2 in Afghanistan. On September 2, which is today over there, Navy SEALs operating in Afghanistan attacked the camp of the Haqqani Network in the wild hill country near the town of Orgun. Orgun is located in southeastern Afghanistan, very close to the Pakistan border. As you all know, it was the Haqqani Network, led by al'Asad Aljibal, that was responsible for the murders of forty-eight Americans in a terrorist attack at the Islamabad Airport on August 25th. In this attack, our late Secretary of State, Archer M. Hadley, perished. Of the forty-two Haqqani Network fighters at the camp, thirty-one were killed, three were severely wounded and captured, and eight escaped. Among those who escaped was their leader, al'Asad Aljibal.

"The attacking force of SEALs did not suffer any casualties during today's attack. They are currently gathering whatever intelligence can be gleaned from the Haqqani Network dead and wounded.

"Liberated by the SEALs in this attack were approximately 120 schoolgirls from the Pashto School who were kidnapped by the men of the Haqqani Network. These girls, between the ages of 10 and 15, are being attended by Navy medical personnel and will be evacuated to a place of safety at a major American military base. From the base, when they are ready to travel, they will be directed to sanctuary and resettlement in friendly Muslim nations, as determined to be appropriate in each individual case.

"In the raid on the Pashto School, Dr. Clara Wilson and Dr. Henry Wilson, the school's founders, were also kidnapped. They were later brutally executed on live television after a kangaroo court trial conducted by al'Asad Aljibal. For this mockery of justice alone, al'Asad Aljibal deserves to be hunted down and to receive the ultimate punishment.

"Elements of the SEALs and other Special Forces are continuing the hunt for the remaining eight Haqqani Network terrorists, with particular emphasis on their leader al'Asad Aljibal. We will not cease our efforts until these terrorists have been captured or killed. Unfortunately, I have very few other details to share with you at this moment. The Navy Department Public Affairs Office at the Pentagon will release additional information as it becomes available.

"Recent evidence collected via satellite images has shown that some Pakistani military elements cooperated with the Haqqani Network in the attack on Secretary Hadley's plane. This evidence will be shared with the American public and the world later today with recordings and satellite images. These guilty military elements have been arrested by the civilian authorities of Pakistan. Among those arrested and relieved of command was Field Marshal Hakim Mouhammed Bouradin, the highest-ranking officer of the Pakistani military establishment. Hakim Bouradin committed suicide by hanging himself in his cell. Whatever connections he might have revealed to interrogators died with him.

"Were it not for the skills and dedication of our analysts at the National Security Agency, the connivance of certain sympathetic military personnel in the Pakistani Army might never have been discovered. The NSA staff analysts also helped us locate the Haqqani Network camp, which resulted in this morning's successful attack on the terrorists.

"I say to terrorists and enemies of whatever stripe: You can run, but you cannot hide; America will make you pay for your crimes.

"A special thank you and a hearty well done goes out to the Navy SEALs and to the men and women of the National Security Agency. This is a perfect example of effective American teamwork bringing punishment to the evil elements of the world.

"Thank you all for being here on this beautiful day, and I am happy that we were able to share this good news with you today. That is all I have to report."

Every reporter had a dozen questions to ask the president. He fielded the questions without giving any information other than what he initially announced. He refused to identify the SEAL unit that conducted the raid or reveal any of the names of those who took part in any of the NSA efforts to track down and attack the Haqqani Network. After another thirty minutes of questioning, the president announced that he had another commitment and left the Rose Garden.

The excitement of the president's announcement caused the interruption of regular programming on TV and radio and was announced at public sporting events to loud cheers. Even a golf tournament, where gentlemanly decorum and civilized order are always maintained, was momentarily disrupted by the spread of the news and spontaneous cheers from the crowds.

News programs minutely reviewed and analyzed the satellite images released by the NSA and the Pentagon. The cockpit voice recorder evidence, overlaid on the satellite images, was the most damning. The video shot by the German tourist was rerun over and over. Footage of the destroyed airplane, the charred bodies lined up on the runway, and the remains returned to Dover AFB with Keaton walking among the rows of flag-draped caskets was shown again. Fervor for a retaliatory strike against Pakistan was momentarily high. When the news of Bouradin's suicide and the arrest of other military men was included, there was a noticeable tamping down of the fervor.

In the end, it was agreed that the American government had acted properly and that the Pakistani government was making the right moves to punish those responsible for aiding Aljibal. The combination of the Navy SEALs attack, NSA analysis, liberation of the schoolgirls, Pakistani military arrests, and statements by various government officials served to cool rising tempers.

That Monday night, as Americans lay themselves down to rest, a feeling of pride and satisfaction seemed to suffuse their sleep. America had won one for the good guys.

55

JACK AND LAURA

Eastern Hills of Afghanistan
Tuesday, September 4

Where the hell had those bastards gone? Jack and Laura tore down the dirt tracks, dust boiling up behind the truck. Somewhere out here, Aljibal and his killers were on the run.

Jack fired off a quick text to Stevens, copying Watson.

> **No sign yet. If Aljibal's smart, he'll slip into Pakistan. Any chatter?**
>
> Pogo

Laura leaned closer. "Remind them that he bolted fast. No food, no rifles. Somebody has to be missing supplies."

Jack thumbed it in, then hit send. Then the waiting started. Every minute felt like an hour.

Twenty minutes later, his phone buzzed. One line from Stevens:

> **Nothing. No sightings. No raids. We're watching.**

Jack cursed under his breath. The trail was still ice cold. Within a few minutes, a message from Herb Watson was received.

NSA intercepted two Pakistani police radio reports from a farming community 50 km SW of Miram Shah in the Tribal Area. This is near where their camp was located in Afghan. 1. There was a report of a stolen pickup truck. The driver and female passenger were both killed. Assume whoever did this also took the driver's weapon(s). 2. Later in the day, a farmer reported theft of a farm animal and food to local police who radioed report to HQ. Report claims a band of several men stole a goat and twenty kilos of flour plus some vegetables. The farmer reports the theft but claims he never saw the thieves. This might be our targets. If you cross the border, be very careful. We are not supposed to be there without permission from Pak military. If we ask and they get to him first they will warn him so we are not going to ask. Better he should think he is safe from us. Go get him. Good luck.

Watson

"Well, that looks like Herb is telling us to go get Aljibal in Pakistan. So, let's do it."

Laura laughed, "I always wanted to tour Pakistan. I guess now is the time to do it."

Jack grinned. "It isn't a very scenic place. It looks a lot like Afghanistan. No five-star hotels or great restaurants."

"I am deeply disappointed. I guess when you've seen one 'stan' country you've seen them all." Laura ejected the magazine from her M-16 to make sure it was fully loaded. She was satisfied that it was, so she inserted it back into her rifle. Laura looked at Jack, "Well, let's get going before he steals another goat for dinner. The goats of Pakistan are counting on us to keep them safe."

56

JACK AND LAURA

The Tribal Area of Pakistan
Wednesday, September 5

Laura suggested they go back to the Haqqani camp and follow the dirt track that led into the Pakistani Tribal Area. Aljibal wouldn't be there, but it would be a place to start following him.

Three days after the SEALs attacked, the camp was totally devoid of people. The schoolgirls had been relocated to Bagram Air Force Base. The SEALs were preparing for other assignments. The dead and wounded were all removed to Bagram to be examined for any forensic evidence that might aid the chase. All the cell phones, Aljibal's laptop, and anything in writing would all be analyzed for clues as to who assisted the mujahideen and where their allies could be found. With skill and luck, other terrorists would be located and neutralized. But at this moment in time, the camp was dead quiet.

Laura drove the pickup truck down the dirt path. She realized they didn't have four-wheel drive on this truck, and that they could easily get stuck. If they got stranded, they would have to abandon the truck and become pack mules with their gear. Maybe she should have insisted on a 4x4 when they were back at Bagram. Too late now.

They were making slow progress on the dirt road when they spotted a cloth lying by the side of the path. Jack called, "Stop the truck." He exited the truck and examined the cloth carefully to make sure it was not booby-trapped. Satisfied, he picked it up. By now, Laura was out of the truck, too. The cloth was stiff and crusted with dried blood.

"It looks like one of them is wounded and was bleeding badly," Laura said.

"Wounded, but he is still with their group. At least he was when he dropped this, and he didn't stop to pick it up. He must be able to walk with the others, or they would have killed him if he slowed them down too much."

Laura was checking her map and GPS coordinates. "I think we are in Pakistan right here."

"How far are we from a shopping mall?"

"By my best guess, I'd say 1,500 miles. That's how far it is to Tel Aviv."

"Bummer."

"What do you need?"

"A price sticker," Jack answered. "When we get Aljibal, I want to put a zero-price sticker on his forehead. Then, I would like to put a bullet through the zero like a bullseye. But if I can't find a zero-price sticker, I'll have to think of something else."

"Enough daydreaming. Get back in the truck and let's get going."

"Yes, Boss," said Jack as he returned to the passenger's seat.

Laura continued driving until the dirt track met a larger, more heavily traveled dirt road. She then increased speed to 50 km/hr (35 mph). Any faster, and the unevenness of the road would have shaken their teeth loose. Although this was a more heavily traveled road, they met no one going in either direction.

After an hour of driving on the larger dirt road, they saw an isolated farm a kilometer down the road.

"I'll bet this farmer is missing a goat and a few kilos of flour," Jack guessed. "Let's stop and talk to him."

"Good idea. But first, you have to get in the driver's seat. If you want him to talk to us, I had better wear a burqa."

Laura pulled over, got out, donned her burqa, and then got back in the passenger seat. Jack got behind the wheel and drove to the farmer's driveway, a rutted dirt track, worse than the road.

The farmer was working with a hoe in one of his fields. Jack left his rifle in the cab with Laura. He left the truck and began walking toward the field. The farmer stopped working and stood up straight when he saw Jack approaching.

"*As-Salamu Alaykum* (Peace be with you)," Jack said.

"*As-Salamu Alaykum*," the farmer replied.

Multiple Islamic greetings of two strangers meeting for the first time were exchanged in Urdu. The name of Allah was invoked and praised many times, *Subhan Allah* (Glory to God).

After the formalities were done, Jack asked, "I am looking for a group of men who may have come through here a few days ago. Is it possible that you saw them?"

"Yes, I saw them. I spit on the memory of seeing them," said the farmer.

"How long ago did you see them?" Jack asked.

"On Itwaar (Sunday), four days ago. They are thieves." The farmer spat on the ground near Jack's boot.

"What was taken from you by these men?"

"My milk goat was taken, they stole twenty kilos of flour, and two baskets of fresh vegetables, may Allah damn all of them to Hell."

"How many were there?" Jack asked.

"There were eight. Four of them had guns. I could not resist them, or they would have killed me. One of them had his arm in a sling. The leader was an evil man."

"You are fortunate that they did not steal your truck."

"But they did steal a truck. My cousin is on jihad in Syria, and he left his truck with me. If he ever returns, he will think I sold his truck and kept the money. Those spawn of the Devil stole my cousin's Toyota pickup truck."

"Why did you not report that to the police when you reported the theft of your goat?"

"Because my cousin stole the truck." Suddenly, the farmer realized he might have said too much to a complete stranger. "Are you from the police?"

"No, I am not," Jack answered. "I do not care where your cousin got his truck from. It is of no concern to me. What was the value of your goat?"

"That was a milk goat they took. It was worth 1500 rupees."

Jack did a quick calculation in his head. At 140 Pakistani rupees to the dollar, the farmer valued his goat at roughly 11 U.S. dollars. "For giving me this information that you have told me, I would like to pay you for the loss of your goat. I do not have any rupees, but would you accept 10 euros? I could make it 15 euros to cover the cost of the flour and the vegetables as well. At least you could buy another goat at the market."

"Ah, you are most kind to a poor farmer. I accept your offer. Allah must have sent you to me. What about my cousin's truck? What shall I tell him when he returns from jihad?"

"Tell your cousin that I do not deal in stolen goods. The truck is his problem—if he ever returns from jihad."

Jack extracted 15 euros from his pocket by feeling the different sizes of the bills. "This is a gift for telling me the truth. May Allah bless you." Jack gave the farmer the money and stepped back two paces.

"May Allah smile upon you and all your sons," the farmer said.

Jack returned the blessing and turned to leave. Then he added as if it were an afterthought, "Did they say where they were going when they left with your goat?"

"No. They said nothing. But they drove down the road in the same direction as you are going. I hope you catch them. They owe you 15 euros."

"If I catch them, I will make them pay," Jack said. And then he smiled when he realized the deeper meaning of what he had said.

57

JACK AND LAURA

The Hills of the Tribal Area, Pakistan
Thursday, September 6

Jack's phone vibrated. One second later, Laura's phone vibrated. The caller ID showed Herb Watson's phone number. They opened their identical messages.

> Report of attack on a village 125 km south of your current position. Only food and a pickup truck taken. Two civilians killed while resisting the thefts. Appears that A has reversed direction and is heading deeper into Tribal Area. NSA reports a Pakistani military truck waiting at coordinates shown below. Suspect a resupply linkup with ISI personnel. Caution advised.
>
> Watson

"We are already south of their northernmost flight from us. They have come back south and have passed us by. We could get to the position of that ISI truck in less than an hour," Laura said as she checked their own position relative to the position of the Pakistani military truck on her map.

"Let's go," Jack said. "Keep checking the GPS. I don't want to get too close with our truck. I want to take out Aljibal first before we finish off the rest of his crew of killers."

"There are two tracks roughly parallel to each other. He didn't pass us, so he must be on the other road. There is a place ahead where we can go cross-country to get to the other road. The contour lines say it is a very low hill. Let's risk it even though we don't have an all-wheel 4x4."

"OK. Sing out when we are close to the spot to turn off."

Twelve minutes later, Laura said, "We're coming up on the turnoff. Let's hope there aren't too many bushes in the way."

Thirty seconds later, Laura motioned left, and Jack turned off the road. They were able to avoid most of the bushes, but ran over two of them. As they got further up the hill, the low crest was covered with evergreen trees.

Jack headed south a bit, looking for a wide spot to get the truck through. He found a space that required some zigzagging to get through. He was halfway through the trees when a bullet smashed into the windshield. The second bullet hitting the weakened windshield had the effect of knocking all the windshield glass out of the frame. Tiny nuggets of broken glass were everywhere.

The two cab doors flew open as Jack and Laura hurled themselves out of the truck. Both were lying prone on the ground, rifles ready, looking for the shooter.

"I see motion down there by the other road. The guy was firing uphill, so I'll bet we have a bullet hole in the roof," Jack said. Then, without exposing himself, he reached up into the cab through the open door and retrieved his M40A5 sniper rifle with the scope. "Laura, crawl 10 meters to the right in case he has an RPG down there. I'll go 10 meters left. I think this guy is a lookout."

After he traversed the 10-12 meters, Jack sighted down the hill to where he thought he had seen the movement. Another bullet smashed into their truck. This time, it hit the front grille, and the radiator leaked coolant fluid.

The muzzle flash gave the shooter's position away. There was no incoming return fire from up on the hill. The shooter was confident that he had two easy targets near the truck. Jack was waiting for him to show himself to shoot again.

The shooter rose up from behind a rock to aim. He was just a second too slow. Jack fired one shot that hit him in the head. The shooter was dead before his body hit the ground.

Jack motioned Laura forward, then rose up in a crouching run and headed down the hill to the other side of the road. Laura was doing the same thing 25 meters away. Jack found cover under a thick bush. He texted Laura: They will come out to see what the shooting was about. They will advance to the truck. We will be behind them. Let's ambush them from down here.

Laura read the message and responded: OK.

Minutes later, a flicker of motion stirred in the rocks. Bushes shivered—not from wind, but from men who had no idea how loud their stealth really was.

Jack and Laura tracked their positions.

Two of them slipped across the road and started up the hill. "Careful," their leader hissed. "That truck could be booby-trapped."

The men approached the truck. Examined it carefully for tripwires. When they were satisfied, they began to loot the truck of anything valuable.

The two men retreated from the truck once they had gathered all the food.

Jack realized that the man 20 feet away from him was a Pakistani soldier. He did a count of the tangos left of the axis of the truck. He saw six. He sent a text to Laura: I have six tangos on the left axis of truck.

She replied: I have 7. Do you have A?

Jack responded: not sure.

Jack summed up his situation. There were seven men left in Aljibal's group. That meant there were six Pakistani soldiers with the supply truck. Jack texted Laura: Go for the ones nearest you at 0922 exactly.

Jack's digital clock on his phone blinked from 9:21 to 9:22. He fired three-shot bursts at the three men nearest to his position. All were hits. Laura's weapon was firing at the same time.

All the men on the hillside took cover on the ground.

Jack immediately rolled to another bush for cover. Answering fire peppered the bush he was initially lying under. Jack spotted two muzzle flashes and laid two three-round bursts into where he thought the two shooters were located.

One man cried out in pain. The other man's weapon went silent.

Laura was shooting. The sounds made by an M-16 firing are distinctly different from the clacking of the AK-47 Kalashnikovs.

Silence descended on the hillside. Jack did a cartridge count in his head. He had started with thirty-one rounds. One round in the chamber, thirty rounds in the magazine. He had fired fifteen rounds. That meant he still had sixteen rounds left. He was pretty sure he had hit five enemies. Laura probably had a similar situation.

Jack shouted in Urdu, "You are surrounded. Throw down your weapons and surrender." Then he repeated the command in Arabic.

A voice in the bushes called out, "Do what he says. Surrender."

Two Pakistani soldiers near Laura raised their hands above their heads. "We surrender."

One man near Jack stood with his hands raised.

It was Aljibal.

Two other men were crying out in pain while they lay on the ground.

In Arabic, Jack ordered, "Drop your pistols and knives" Then he repeated it in Urdu for the Pakistanis.

One Pakistani soldier drew his pistol and dropped it to the ground. The second soldier drew his and started to raise the weapon toward Jack's voice. A three-round burst from Laura caught him in the chest. Jack fired at the same instant. Jack's three-round burst hit him in the neck and head. He fell to the ground without firing a shot.

Aljibal yelled, "Don't shoot. We surrender."

Jack ordered, "Put your hands on top of your head. Move to the road. Lie face down in the center. No talking. Do not make any sudden moves, or you will die."

The two men slowly walked to the road with their hands clasped on their heads. They lay down in the center, a few feet from each other.

The Pakistani soldier was speaking softly to Aljibal. Laura put one round in his butt. He lay there, writhing and screaming in pain.

Aljibal lay face down, as still as a corpse.

Jack went to the three wounded men and fired one round into each man's heart. He did not want to risk their pulling some heroic last-ditch fight when he was busy with Aljibal. All of the bad guys were dead except Aljibal and the soldier with a bullet in his ass. The Lion of the Mountains was really a toothless kitten.

Jack returned to the road. Laura was standing over Aljibal and the soldier.

Jack said to the soldier, "Can you stand?"

Slowly, painfully, the soldier stood.

"Take off your shirt, pants, and boots."

"I cannot do that in front of a woman," he protested.

"Do it or die," Jack said.

The soldier did what Jack ordered. With difficulty, he was soon down to his undershirt, his undershorts with blood in the back, and his socks.

"Who do you work for?" Jack demanded.

"ISI," the soldier answered.

"Where in ISI?" Jack persisted.

"Directorate S," whispered the soldier.

"They will punish you for your failure today. Now start walking," Jack ordered. He indicated he wanted the soldier to walk north. "Get out of here before I change my mind." The soldier started walking. In minutes, he was almost lost to sight, limping and hopping because of rough stones and pebbles in the roadway.

Jack turned his attention to Aljibal.

"Where are your trucks?" Jack demanded.

"We were down the road around the first bend," Aljibal answered. His hands were still clasped on top of his head.

"Roll over onto your back," Jack ordered.

Laura stepped into his line of sight.

"Why is there a woman carrying a gun?" Aljibal asked.

"Because it was me and her who killed all your men today. Just the two of us. You were beaten by a woman. A Jewish woman. You fierce Arabs are no match for a Jewish woman. You have been shamed and defeated by a superior woman. She is a warrior. You are a coward."

"This cannot be," Aljibal muttered. "A woman…."

"Do you remember Inaya, the schoolgirl you shot in the face?"

Aljibal said, "Yes. She was a loud-mouthed whore. She deserved to die because she defied me in front of my men."

"Do you remember Naila, the schoolgirl you shot because she was crying and screaming at you after you killed Inaya?"

"I will not tolerate a woman yelling at me, even a child."

Jack drew his M9 pistol. "Those girls you killed were my nieces, part of my family." Jack fired once into Aljibal's right knee. "That is for Inaya."

Aljibal clutched at his knee with both hands and screamed in pain.

When he finally stopped screaming, Jack fired a round into Aljibal's left knee. "That is for Naila."

Aljibal screamed again with one hand on each knee, his hands covered in his own blood. He was crying like a baby.

"Do you remember the Wilsons that you had beheaded in front of the world on live television?"

"They had a trial," Aljibal blubbered.

"This is your trial. I am your judge and your jury. The next bullet is for Clara Wilson. And the one after that is for Henry Wilson. They were my friends." Jack shot Aljibal in the right shoulder, and then he shot him in the left shoulder.

"Do you remember the plane you blew up with forty-eight Americans on it?"

Aljibal was unable to answer.

So, Jack answered for him. "Of course, you do. How could anyone forget such a magnificent triumph? You told the world all about it. These next bullets are for the forty-eight Americans you killed." Jack shot him twice in the lower abdomen.

"Do you remember all those schoolgirls you caused to be raped by your men? What a great leader you are that you gave those girls to your men. This is for the girls you had raped." Jack shot him in the testicles.

Aljibal was unable to move, but he was still conscious. He lay slackly on the road.

"Do you remember that little girl you tied to a tree by her wrists and ankles? This is for that little girl." Jack put a bullet into each ankle.

Aljibal's hands were now lying limply by his sides. Jack shot him once in each wrist. The close range tore the skin and shattered the bones. His left hand hung at a strange angle, held to the arm by strips of skin. Only the impacts from the bullets brought any movement to Aljibal.

Blood was pumping out of multiple wounds all over the body of al'Asad Aljibal.

Laura looked at him with disgust. "I think he is in shock right now."

"Good. I want him to linger and suffer. He is an evil man. He must suffer as much as his victims suffered. The slower he dies, the better I will feel. He is a disease on the human race."

"Let's take a photo of his head and upper body for proof that we got him." Laura took out her phone and snapped the photos. Aljibal's eyes were closed, and his facial muscles were obviously slack. He appeared to be dead in the photos. Laura carefully avoided the holes Jack had made in Aljibal's body.

Insects began to collect on Aljibal's wounds. Three vultures circled overhead. Soon, the three vultures were joined by five more birds. All eight were quite a sight. Within ten minutes, there had to be at least twenty-five of the birds circling overhead, large and dark in the sky. Nature's sanitation department.

Laura said, "We ought to get all our stuff from our truck, including the things those two liberated from us. Then we should hike down the road, get one of their pickups, and get out of here. The birds and jackals will clean up the mess we left."

"I'm not satisfied yet. His body must be defiled even more."

"Enough, Jack! If he isn't dead now, he will be in an hour. Don't become like an Arab with a never-satisfied lust for revenge. He is finished. His Haqqani Network is finished. Let's go."

"You are right. You usually are." Jack paused, took a deep breath. "OK. Let's go."

They gathered everything they could find that was theirs. Loaded themselves up and started walking down the road to get a truck.

Laura laughed. "If one of those trucks is a Toyota, the one from the guy on jihad in Syria, that is the one I would like to take. We'll be turning it in at Bagram. The idea of the Americans using his truck appeals to me."

"Whatever makes you happy is OK with me," Jack said. He was emotionally drained. Killing Aljibal was not enough to sate the anger he felt toward that evil man. There was no way to make him suffer enough for the pain he had caused while he was alive. There was justice today, just not enough to balance the scales.

58

POGO AND KOALA

The Hills of The Tribal Area, Pakistan
Thursday, September 6

A military 6x6 truck was standing in the roadway, facing north. Two pickups were facing south, nose to nose with the military truck. As they approached, they could see the name Toyota on the tailgate of the nearest pickup. The other truck was a Hyundai.

"We'll take the Toyota," Laura decided. "The price of fighting in jihad for ISIS is the loss of your pickup truck to the Americans."

Jack's composure had returned almost to normal by the time they arrived at the trucks. "We had better send Herb a message with the photos, so he knows we are still alive and Aljibal is not."

"Sounds like something we should do before we leave here," Laura agreed. "The photos are on my phone, so I'll send the message."

Tribal Area of Pak. Mission accomplished. Aljibal and all seven of his men are dead. Also killed 5 ISI, Directorate S, soldiers. One wounded man survived and set free. Directorate S men met up with Haqqani men to resupply them. Will destroy all supplies and their trucks. Photo of Aljibal attached. Extraction to initial in-country location in progress. Please express our appreciation to NSA geeks.

Pogo & Koala

She hit the send button. Copies of the message were sent to Stevens and to Mossad headquarters.

Afterwards, Laura said, "I want to siphon gasoline or diesel from the tanks of these two trucks and burn them."

Jack rooted around inside the body of the 6x6 truck. He called out, "This one has two M60 machine guns with a few thousand rounds of ammunition and sixteen jerry cans of fuel in the cargo bed. After we repatriate the M60s and ammo, we can use the fuel in the jerry cans to burn the trucks. Then the fuel tanks can explode and really destroy these trucks."

"I like your thinking, but let's keep some fuel for our truck and burn the balance. The machine guns and ammo will fit nicely in the pickup."

Jack drove the Toyota around to the rear of the military truck. First, they loaded the M60s and the ammunition boxes into the pickup. There were 12 AK-47s with fifty ammo magazines. They loaded those in the pickup, too.

There were a few cartons of fig-based energy bars, and Jack decided to leave those in the truck. Then they filled the Toyota's gas tank. Four additional cans of gasoline went into the back of the Toyota. Jack looked at the machine guns and jerry cans. "Damn, this stuff is all American G.I. equipment. We gave it to them as a gift, and now they are giving it to our enemies to use against us. Pakistan is some ally."

"Stop complaining and start sloshing fuel on everything. I want to get moving with as much daylight as possible."

"And I want to go back and kick Aljibal in the head. He hasn't suffered nearly as much as the people he hurt."

Laura looked strangely at Jack. "Are you sure you aren't an Arab? If he isn't dead yet, the vultures will finish him. Being eaten by vultures while you are still alive sounds like a fitting end for him."

"I hope they start on his eyes so he won't be able to see, but he still can feel the pain as they pick at his guts."

"That hillside will become a feeding frenzy of birds, jackals, and bugs in no time. They won't care if he is dead or alive as long as he isn't moving," Laura said.

"Well, I care. I have to drive back and put a bullet in his head. I have to be certain he is dead."

"If that is what you need, we will do it," Laura conceded. "Do you have a match?"

"There is the gizmo we use to start our cooking fires in my backpack. I'll get it, and you can do the honors."

"Good, but first we must get this truck away from the ones we are destroying. You move the Toyota to the north, and then we can go back and shoot Aljibal if he is still alive."

Jack drove the pickup around the stopped trucks again and waited for Laura.

A minute later, there was a loud *whoomp* as the gasoline went up in a wall of heat and flames.

Laura came running up to the truck. "Do I still have eyebrows? I might have burned them off."

Jack held her face in both of his hands. "You still have eyebrows, and you are still beautiful." He tenderly kissed her lips.

She put her arms around him and kissed him back. "I love you, Jack."

"I love you, Laura."

They both got in the truck. Laura drove. They went back to the scene of the battle. Black smoke from the burning trucks filled the sky behind them. A sudden explosion caused them both to start.

"I think that was the gas tank on the Hyundai," Laura said. Before they reached the battle site, there was another explosion followed by lots of noise of metal parts falling out of the sky and hitting the trucks. "That is both of them."

As they turned the bend in the road, they could see the vultures in the roadway. Four birds were on Aljibal. Two were tearing at his head. One had torn open his abdomen. The fourth one was strutting around looking for a spot to start his lunch. At least thirty more vultures were just about to land, but scattered at their approach.

"Luncheon interruptus," Jack joked.

Laura stopped the truck. Jack got out. The vultures had eaten Aljibal's face. His eyes, ears, and nose were gone. His neck was torn open. What had remained of both hands was missing. Jack was satisfied. Aljibal was dead.

He got back in the truck without saying anything.

Laura put the truck in gear. Silently, they began the journey back to Bagram and the first leg home.

59

POGO AND KOALA

Bagram Air Force Base
Afghanistan
Friday, September 7

Jack and Laura arrived at Bagram after driving nonstop from the Tribal Areas in Pakistan. While one of them drove, the other napped.

The only real difficulty they encountered was when they tried to bring the two M60s onto the base in a pickup truck. They had to get Kevin Waters to vouch for them at the gate. Quietly, they told him how they acquired the M60s. Waters laughed hard and long. The guard looked at him strangely. Finally, on Water's authority and signature, Pogo and Koala were allowed to enter the base.

Once they arrived in Spooksville, they were assigned a desk in a small office and instructed to complete their action report. They did the report in as much detail as they could remember, prompting each other on details that might have been omitted. When they were done, they signed the report with their code names. The report was then whisked away for transmission to CIA HQ in Langley.

They went back to visit Kevin Waters. After greetings and basic courtesies, Jack asked, "How soon can you get us out of here?"

Waters responded, "What? You don't love autumn in Afghanistan? You want to leave this Paradise? Are you both crazy?"

Laura chimed in, "Well it had occurred to me that I had an appointment with a hairdresser back in Maryland, and you know how fussy those guys can get and how hard it is to even get an appointment, so I thought we should get back there so I don't have to cancel, cause then he'll never give me another appointment and my hair will look a mess forever."

Kevin gave a thoughtful look. "That is an urgent need. I'll see if I can arrange a flight to Germany for you tonight. You'll have to make onward arrangements in Ramstein. Will that be soon enough?"

"Sounds good, Kevin. Thank you," Jack said.

"I read your report. Did Aljibal really die from his wounds, or was he assisted in his desire to meet Allah?"

Jack answered, "He died from his wounds. It was a somewhat slow process, but eventually he died. We were so busy we couldn't even give him first-aid. He died, we snapped his photo, and left him for the vultures and jackals. By now, I doubt that there is much of him left."

"It's better that the vultures get him than they have one of those mob scene funerals where the shit heel is hailed as a hero, and they carry his open casket through the streets shouting, 'Death to America'. Every time I see one of those, I expect the crowd to drop the casket and spill the shit heel's body into the gutter."

Koala and Pogo both laughed.

Waters picked up his phone. "Let me see what I can arrange for tonight." He dialed a base number and said, "Hi Jeanne, this is your favorite spook."

Waters listened for a moment while Jeanne did her thing on the phone. "I have two people I need to get back stateside tonight. Have we got any open space for them?"

Waters held on while Jeanne checked some lists on her computer. She told him what was available.

"We'll take the C5A at 2125. Where should my passengers pick it up?"

He got further instructions.

"They are traveling as Pogo and Koala." He listened some more. "Yeah, they are cute. But I don't think I would mess with them." Waters thanked Jeanne, hung up the phone, and began writing out the instructions on how Pogo and Koala should connect with their plane.

Jack and Laura stood. Kevin Waters stood. They all shook hands.

Waters said, "I am glad you both made it back in one piece. After-action death reports are a bitch."

Koala said, "We would hate to foul up your day by doing something so inconsiderate as dying. It is in our nature to make life as easy as possible for our handlers."

Waters handed the page of instructions to Koala. "Don't miss this flight. The other available flights are on aircraft that aren't as reliable or smooth."

Pogo said, "We'll be on it. You can count on it."

Waters walked them to the door of his office. "You guys did well on this operation. It would not have succeeded without your brains and skills."

"Thanks, Kevin. There is a lot of satisfaction in getting a job done. It is also nice to know that other people think you did well, too." Pogo turned to Koala. "I need her; she needs me. I really think I need her much more than she needs me."

Koala said, "I keep him around as a pet. He's useful at bringing in the newspaper and getting my slippers. Thanks again, Kevin. We'd better get going before our heads are too big to fit through the door."

60

PRESIDENT SAMUEL DECKER

The White House
Washington, D.C.
Friday, September 7

At a special Friday news conference with the White House press corps, President Decker was enjoying himself with a little back-and-forth banter with a few friendly reporters. Having a sympathetic press corps makes the hassle of politics a little bit easier. The press won't lie for you, but they might sometimes give you the benefit of the doubt and not heap crap on your head when they can.

An intern approached the president from the side and handed him a sheet of paper.

"Excuse me, folks," said the president to the press corps. He read the page he had just been handed and broke into a broad smile.

"Ladies and gentlemen, I have an important announcement. United States special operatives have tracked down and killed al'Asad Aljibal, the man who headed the Haqqani Network terrorist organization. All our people have returned safely with only one minor injury. All the men accompanying Aljibal have suffered the same fate as he: they are all dead. It took a few days to track him down and eliminate him. But he is gone.

"Aljibal was responsible for many murders, most notably, he destroyed Secretary Archer's plane and killed everyone on board. He was also responsible for the raid on and kidnapping of the schoolgirls at the Pashto School. Following that raid, he held a kangaroo court and executed Drs. Clara and Henry Wilson, a gifted and dedicated pair of Americans who founded and ran the Pashto School to educate orphans of the Afghan War. Al'Asad Aljibal caused hundreds of deaths through both his personal attacks and the attacks of his Haqqani Network killers. The world is a safer place without him."

One reporter raised a hand. The president nodded toward him.

"You referred to those who brought down Aljibal as 'special operatives'. The SEALs refer to their team members as 'operatives.' Does this mean that the SEALs were the ones who eliminated Aljibal?"

"I cannot answer that question since I do not know who actually did the operation on Aljibal. It was an American operation. If I have not been informed, it is because the military wants to keep that information secret. Therefore, I must answer your question with a 'no comment.' I would suggest that a follow-up be done with the Naval Public Information Office. I have a note here that a postmortem photo of Aljibal will be released by the Navy this evening in time for the five o'clock news."

A hubbub broke out among the reporters. Another reporter got the president's attention, and he recognized her. "Was the CIA involved in this takedown of Aljibal?"

"The simple answer is I don't know. I would expect that any agency with information regarding Aljibal's whereabouts or strengths and weaknesses would share it with our men and women in the field. That goes for the CIA, the NSA, our various military intelligence arms, and the State Department. In short, this was an all-out effort by all agencies working together to achieve the desired result. Please understand that we must protect our personnel in the field. Theirs is dangerous work. Bad people would quickly try to affect what our field people do by taking actions against their families here at home. When we say 'no comment,' we are not trying to hide anything from you. We are trying to protect those who are out there protecting us."

More questions followed, most of which were met by a 'no comment' answer. Despite the president's explanation, the press was relentless in their questions. Eventually, the press conference ended.

With all of the president's 'no comments,' the press became completely convinced that Aljibal had been killed by the SEALs.

That was what they would report on the next newscasts and in tomorrow's newspapers. Whether it was true or not, it was what they wanted to believe. Every society needs its heroes. SEALs were like supermen, and they fought on our side, so why not make them the American superhero? Besides, it was probably true anyway.

Inside the White House, the president called Arnold Greensman, head of the CIA. "Arnold, congratulations on bagging Aljibal. I just heard the news. Give me the details, please."

"Mr. President, those two agents I didn't want to send over, but you strongly suggested I do, were the two who got him. The woman, Koala, was instrumental in detecting an anomaly that helped locate the Haqqani Network camp. They worked well with the SEALs, which means they are really tough. They got involved in two fights before Aljibal and won both of them. The score was 3-0 and 5-0. Our guys were the winners. Bad guys were the losers.

"Then, when one of Aljibal's men spoiled the SEALs' surprise attack on the Haqqani camp, they set off alone to track down Aljibal and his men. Aljibal went to the Pakistani Tribal Area to hide out and regroup. Pogo and Koala followed. They caught Pakistan's Directorate S resupplying Aljibal's group. In the ensuing fight, they killed all of Aljibal's men and Aljibal himself. They also killed five of the six Pakistani soldiers who were sent out on the resupply detail. The score was 13-0. They purposely allowed one soldier, who was shot in the butt, to escape, but first they stripped him down to his underwear and socks before letting him go. Aljibal died from his wounds. They photographed him and left him where he died.

"When they examined the military truck being used by the Directorate S people, they found two American M60 machine guns and thousands of rounds of ammunition for the guns, some Russian AK-47s, and many fuel cans where the cans themselves were U.S. military aid. All that matériel was intended for Aljibal's group. Subsequent satellite photos showed they effectively destroyed the Pakistani vehicles when they left."

"The Pakistanis are not our friends. We always knew it. This just seals the deal in spades. When will Pogo and Koala get home?"

"They will arrive stateside tonight at Andrews. We'll do a full debrief tomorrow at Langley."

"What a story. Too bad we'll never be able to tell it to the public. It is like having two James Bonds on one team."

"I must admit, Mr. President, that I really felt it was wrong to send them, but I bowed to your pressure. They did the job when none of my other teams could get results, and they are returning in one piece, except she has a minor wound on her leg. My personal take on these two is that they are more than just working partners. That is another reason not to send them out together. But I cannot argue with the results. They rescued the Keatons, and now they bagged Aljibal and helped to rescue all those school girls."

"To tell the truth, I had second thoughts about pushing them on you. I'm happy that it all worked out."

"Yes, it did, Mr. President."

"The entire national security team worked and played well together. I will need a list of which people need to be praised."

"I'll get in touch with the Navy and NSA. I'll get the list together for you."

"Thank you, Arnold. Goodbye."

"Goodbye, Mr. President."

After he hung up, the president told his secretary, "Get me Stu Keaton on the phone. He is in Pakistan at the moment."

Five minutes later, his secretary was on the intercom. "Mr. President, we are patched through to Ambassador Cooper's secure phone in an embassy limo. Mr. Keaton is there as well, and he is on the line."

"Hello, Stu. Have you heard the news yet?"

"About Aljibal? Yes, I did. Who actually got him?"

"It was those two you talked me into making Greensman send—Pogo and Koala."

"Are they both OK?"

"Oh yes. Koala got a small wound, but she was able to carry on to the end. They chased him into the Tribal Area. Not only did they kill Aljibal, but they killed all of his men who escaped with him. Directorate S was resupplying Aljibal with equipment that we had given them as military aid. Machine guns, ammo, and fuel in American military containers. There were six men from Directorate S present. They caught those guys, too. Five of them are dead, one of them is wounded in the butt, but they set him free in just his underwear and socks. He must have been quite a sight when he checked in."

"Let me get this straight, Mr. President. Directorate S was resupplying Aljibal with weapons, ammo, and fuel, some of it American military aid?"

"From what I have heard, they were supplying U.S. machine guns and ammo, plus fuel in U.S. military containers. They also had AK-47s and ammo."

"That is very interesting news indeed. At this moment, Dave Cooper and I are on our way to meet with Vice Field Marshal Embali, who wishes to protest our violation of the Tribal Areas because of an alleged ambush on Pakistani military personnel by two CIA agents."

"The Pakistanis are not loyal friends. It's time we cut them loose. If they won't cooperate in an honest manner, then we will have to force cooperation down their throats. Some of them favor the democracies. Others are closet Islamic supporters. Let the bastards know we know what they are doing. I think Harraf is a good man. If he isn't good, at least he is realistic. Make sure he knows about this. He already dumped Bouradin. This Vice Marshal has to be a bad guy like Bouradin or Bouradin would never have promoted him to the job."

"Dave Cooper knows him. Dave thinks Embali is a five-headed snake."

"Do what you think is best, Stu. They are burning bridges, not us. I don't see any long-range benefit for America if Pakistan is playing both sides of the conflict and playing us for fools with our generosity."

"We'll see how it goes tonight, Mr. President. We'll call you when it is over."

"Thanks, Stu, and thank you, too, Dave."

After he hung up the phone, the president summoned his chief of staff.

As soon as he stepped into the office, President Decker asked, "When is the period of mourning over for Archer Hadley?"

"Tomorrow. On September 8th."

"On September 9th, I want to be ready to send Stuart Keaton's name to the Senate for confirmation as the next Secretary of State."

"That'll ruffle a few feathers in Foggy Bottom."

"I don't care. He is the man I want. Ensure there will be no opposition. If there is any inkling of a negative vote, I want to know it long before the Senate casts any votes for or against Stu Keaton."

"Got it, Mr. President. Is there anything else?"

"Not at the moment. Thank you."

When the chief of staff left the Oval Office, the president sat there thinking about the pluses and minuses of Pakistan. The many minuses kept outweighing the few pluses. Where the hell is King Solomon when I need him most?

61

STUART KEATON

Assistant Secretary of State for Near Eastern Affairs
Islamabad, Pakistan
Friday, September 7

Vice Field Marshal Kadin Embali was almost a living carbon copy of the late Field Marshal Hakim Bouradin. They had identical Saddam Hussein mustaches, identical paratrooper boots polished to a mirror finish, identical braids on their right arms, an almost identical field of campaign ribbons, and similar batons. The only actual difference was that Embali's baton was mahogany with silver ends, while Bouradin's had been ebony with silver ends. They probably practiced their attitudes together when Bouradin was alive.

Embali arrived 10 minutes late for the appointment. Tonight, he was wearing severely tailored camouflage BDUs. A combat uniform with all that colorful crap on it looked ridiculous.

Keaton and Cooper fully expected Embali to be late for the meeting, and Embali did not disappoint.

He swept into the room with a two-star general and two colonels as his aides and said, "Gentlemen, we have a most serious violation of Pakistan's territorial integrity. Not only that, but the United States has murdered five Pakistani soldiers in cold blood and grievously wounded a sixth soldier. How do you propose to rectify this situation?"

Dave Cooper spoke slowly and distinctly. "How many soldiers are involved in this event you are referring to?"

"Six. Five dead and one wounded," snapped the Vice Field Marshal as if he were talking to a child.

"And where did this event happen?"

"In the Tribal Area," snarled one of the colonels.

"You sent six soldiers into the Tribal Area by themselves? Don't you usually send only company-strength units into the Tribal Area?"

"This was a unit of six men. And your agents ambushed them, killing five and wounding one who managed to escape."

"Goodness me!" Cooper said. "What were these men doing all alone in the Tribal Area?"

The vice field marshal decided that this meeting was not going the way he had intended. He was looking for an American apology, not an interrogation of why his men were there. "Your forces were in the Tribal Area, where they did not belong. That is a gross violation of the territorial integrity of Pakistan. I want to know what you are going to do to make amends to the government of Pakistan?"

Keaton spoke for the first time. "How about we withdraw all military aid from Pakistan for the foreseeable future? And the next time Pakistan has a natural or humanitarian crisis, we will stay home instead of rushing to your assistance."

"Your people killed five of our soldiers," accused the Vice Field Marshal.

"That part you got right," Keaton said. "We killed five. We could have killed six, but we let one go so you would know who killed the other five. They were killed by one man and one woman. The woman was a better soldier than any of your Pakistani men."

"And what do you propose to do to compensate Pakistan for your foul attack by these two outlaws?"

"Nothing."

"Nothing? Nothing? Five men are dead, and you will do nothing?"

"Exactly correct," said Keaton. "Now I will tell you why your six soldiers were in the Tribal Area by themselves. They went there in response to an appeal from al'Asad Aljibal for weapons, ammunition, fuel, and other supplies. The men were part of Directorate S of your ISI. The military supplies you were bringing them were machine guns and ammunition supplied to Pakistan by the United States as military aid in the fight against terrorists. The fuel your men from Directorate S were bringing was in metal containers supplied by the United States for the use of the Pakistan Army. Pakistan did not pay one lousy rupee for these gifts of military equipment from the United States. And then you have the temerity to take our equipment and deliver it to world-condemned criminal terrorists so they can use it against us and against innocent civilians. Your position is the height of hypocrisy. Instead of arresting Aljibal, you were assisting him in continuing his attacks against legitimate governments and innocent people. That is why we will do nothing."

"But you sent your agents into Pakistani territory without our permission! That is a violation of the territorial integrity of Pakistan."

Keaton stood up and looked down at the vice field marshal. "Mr. Embali, you and Pakistan have no integrity of any kind. You can take your territorial integrity and shove it so far up your ass that it comes out your mouth. A man who aids murderers is a common criminal. You have aided one of the world's most notorious mass murderers with weapons and supplies. You are nothing more than a common criminal in a fancy suit—which, by the way, looks totally ridiculous on you. We are finished here."

"No one speaks to me that way!"

"Well, I just did. And what I said represents the position of the United States of America. Come and get your revenge against us if you dare. You are a tinpot rooster strutting around in your fancy ribbons and silly boots. And you can shove your pretentious baton right up next to your territorial integrity. Goodbye."

Keaton and Cooper walked out of the meeting room together.

The two-star general in the room actually snickered.

Embali whirled upon him and struck him across the face with his baton. The general's hand flew to the place where he had been struck. Then he drew his pistol and shot Vice Field Marshal Kadin Embali in the heart, right through his campaign ribbons. The other two colonels stood frozen in shock, so he shot them as well.

Two privates who were standing guard outside the meeting room rushed in, their rifles at the ready. The general looked at them and shouted, "Atten-hut!"

Both privates snapped to attention, rifles at their sides.

The general then said, "Get a detail together and clean up this mess." He then holstered his pistol, still with wisps of smoke coming from the barrel, and walked out of the room.

62

POGO AND KOALA

CIA Headquarters
Langley, VA
Saturday, September 8

The campus of the CIA headquarters is a contrast of serene green spaces outside and intense activity inside. Jack and Laura arrived at the office of Herbert Watson III at exactly 0800 as ordered. Watson had been in the office since 0600, handling routine paperwork and was awaiting their arrival.

Today, Jack Miller, code-named Pogo, was going to be debriefed by an expert at the debriefing task. The agent conducting the debriefing would be familiar with what transpired in the field and would seek inconsistencies in the story told by the field agent.

Laura Halevi, code-named Koala, would not be debriefed. Laura was a Mossad agent on loan to the CIA. The CIA had no formal authority over Laura and would not even attempt to exercise any. All Laura would do was submit a second field action report for the record. If any action were ever required against her, Mossad would have to do it. However, her field action report would be minutely compared to Jack Miller's debriefing to ascertain what really happened in Afghanistan and Pakistan.

Laura was given a small conference room to write her report. Her instructions were that she should write her report exclusively from her experience and point of view.

Jack was led away to an interrogation room where he would face another, much older agent, experienced at debriefings.

Jack sat at a small table, relaxed and confident.

The debriefer, MacNiel Flinders, sat opposite him. A pile of papers representing every daily check-in and after-action report from Jack and Laura's time on this operation was in front of him.

Both Jack and Mac had done this sort of debriefing many times. Both men knew that every word said in this room was being recorded for later transcription to a written record.

MacNiel Flinders got the ball rolling. "Good morning, Pogo. Would you like some coffee or water before we start?"

"A bottle of water would be nice. I will probably talk myself dry several times before we are done today. Dates of the actions may be fuzzy sometimes because of the time differences between Virginia and the Middle East."

Mac turned and removed a twenty-ounce bottle of spring water from a small fridge behind him on the floor. He placed it in front of Jack.

"Pogo, what was your assignment on this operation?"

"Primary assignment was to locate and kill al'Asad Aljibal. The secondary assignment was to neutralize the Haqqani Network by whatever means were effective. The third assignment was to liberate the schoolgirls kidnapped from the Pashto School by Aljibal and the Haqqani Network."

"How do you think you did?"

"I believe I, with my partner Koala, accomplished all three assignments."

"Where did you go in-country?"

"We landed at Bagram. We intended to link up with a SEAL platoon that was tasked with finding the men who had kidnapped the schoolgirls."

"You had a special relationship with two of the girls at the Pashto School, did you not?"

"Yes, Inaya and Naila, two sisters, were at the school because I had brought them there to get them out of a war zone. I thought it was a much safer place for them to be. I even made financial contributions to the school because I believed in the school's mission."

"What happened to the two girls?"

"According to witnesses who were there, during the raid by Aljibal and his men, they were both killed. Aljibal announced that the girls were to be forced into marriage with his men. Any surplus women were to be sold into slavery in Saudi Arabia. Inaya spoke out against the practice of selling people as if they were livestock. Aljibal shot her in the face and then emptied the rest of a Makarov magazine into her head while she lay on the ground. Naila was present when this happened and cursed Aljibal for what he had done. She was overcome with grief and screaming. Aljibal took a rifle from one of his men and shot Naila to silence her."

"What was your reaction when you found out about what happened at the school?"

"I felt responsible for the girls. They were like my nieces. We wrote each other letters, and I cared about what happened in their intellectual and physical development. I even planned to put them through college in the USA when they grew old enough and had sufficient academic preparation. When I read about what had happened to them, I promised myself that Aljibal would die by my hands."

"And did he?"

"I don't know who fired the shots that killed him. I expect that it was me. I hope it was me. Aljibal died from wounds he sustained in a firefight between Koala and me on one side and a combined Haqqani/Pakistani military force of fourteen men on the other side. He was shot in the lower abdomen and groin area. When we discovered him on the ground, I did not render any first-aid or try to alleviate his suffering. I did not treat his wounds. I wanted him to suffer maximum pain. He could not move much. I relieved him of his weapons and left him to die. When Koala thought he was dead, she photographed his corpse. Koala and I became involved in other activities relating to the Pakistani military efforts to resupply the Haqqani forces. I wanted to make sure Aljibal was dead. When we returned to Aljibal later, the vultures had gotten at him and eaten most of his face and torn a gaping hole in his throat. I was satisfied that he was dead. At the time, a thought crossed my mind that Aljibal's body could be toxic to the vultures."

Mac smiled at Jack's comment. "OK. Let's take it by the numbers from day one. Let me have everything you remember."

Jack began recounting the story of the operation, starting from when he read the newspaper at the airport. Two hours later, he was all talked out. He ended with his and Laura's return to the United States from Bagram via Ramstein. He really tried to be complete, with the exceptions of Keaton's intercession with the president and of how Aljibal met his final end.

MacNiel Flinders asked an occasional question to clarify a point or two, but mainly he let Jack tell the story in his own words, in his own way.

When Jack was done, both Mac and Jack sat silent for a few moments.

Mac broke the silence first. "That is a hell of a story. What is really scary about it is that I believe everything happened exactly as you said it did. I might add that I am really proud that you and Laura are on the side of the angels. I would hate to have you two fighting against America."

"That will never happen," Jack said. "I truly believe that America represents the good guys of the world. Freedom is always threatened by bad guys who want to tell everyone else how to live their lives."

Jack continued, "Fate acts in strange ways. But in the end, it acts best through the barrel of a gun held by a good man."

ABOUT THE AUTHOR

Murray Eskenazi was born in New York City and raised in the Bronx, where he attended Bronx High School of Science. He went on to Columbia College, where he majored in mathematics with a minor in mechanical engineering, and later earned his MBA in marketing and business law from New York University's Graduate School of Business Administration.

At Columbia, Murray swam competitively under legendary coach Ed Kennedy (although he never scored a point in any swimming meet). He joined Psi Upsilon Fraternity, a lifelong commitment that has led to him serving as president of Psi U's Columbia alumni association and as a member of Psi U's International Executive Council. For his decades of service, he was honored as a Life Member of the Executive Council and as a Distinguished Alumnus.

Murray married Doris Sims. Together they raised two daughters, Lynn and Nancy, and took great pride in their three grandsons, Jake, Noah, and Michael. The couple lived in East Rockaway, NY, for 53 years, during which Murray devoted over four decades to local government, serving as both a volunteer and elected official, including as Trustee and Deputy Mayor. He also enjoyed his work with the East Rockaway Fire Department, where he helped design and purchase firefighting equipment. Sadly, Doris passed away in 2022.

Murray's business career has been as varied as it has been successful—from engineering with International Trucks, managing and designing clothing factories and warehouses, to running his own company for 30 years, providing medical and paramedical services to the life insurance industry.

Now retired in Delray Beach, Florida, Murray spends his time writing, inventing games (he created *Super Scrabble* and holds three U.S. patents), and enjoying life. He is a longtime member of MENSA. Murray believes laughter is the elixir of life.

www.ingramcontent.com/pod-product-compliance
Lightning Source LLC
Chambersburg PA
CBHW042031120726
47911CB00026B/563